Sins the of Their Fathers

a Pride & Prejudice
variation

TIFFANY THOMAS

ISBN 978-1-956548-02-0

ACKNOWLEDGMENTS

A tremendous thank you to my husband for believing in me and for encouraging me to continue writing.

I am also grateful for my sister, Rebecca, who was willing to be a sounding board and beta reader. Her advice and insights have proven invaluable.

This book is dedicated to you, my readers.
This book wouldn't exist without you.

Table of Contents

Prologue

Five-year-old William Collins shrank farther back into the cupboard, burrowing himself under the soiled linens that had yet to be washed.

"Where's my supper, woman?" his father's loud voice demanded.

Her gentle murmur was met with the sound of a fist hitting flesh, causing William to put his hands over his ears. He had learned from experience that it would not drown out all the sounds, but it would help block out his mother's sobs.

After what seemed an eternity later, the door to his cupboard opened. His tear-filled eyes met his mother's, one of which was already swollen and purple. His eyes widened at the sight.

"Come out, love," she said with an overly bright smile and tremulous voice. "I bet you're hungry." William's stomach growled at the words, and her smile faded slightly. "I've got a bit of bread left for you."

William crawled out and put his arms around her, hiding his face in her apron. "Where's Father?" he asked in a shaking voice.

Her smile faded further as she answered, "He's had his supper and has gone to bed."

Loud snores from the bedroom echoed the truth to her words. William looked at the door fearfully, then back at his mother.

"Not to worry," Mrs. Samantha Collins said comfortingly. "I don't believe he'll be waking before morn. He had a hard day at work, your father. You must be sure to thank him in the morning for all he does

1

to put food on our table and a roof over our heads."

William nodded in agreement; he'd been told to do that every day since he'd begun to speak. His father was rapidly mollified by words of praise and gratitude, although, even then, sometimes they were not enough to pacify his rage.

William quietly crept over to the table, looking at the small crust of bread left on his father's plate. At his mother's urging, he picked it up and ate half of it. He then extended a chubby fist to his mother, who shook her head in denial.

"You're such a thoughtful boy, but I'm not hungry tonight." The growl of her stomach gave lie to her words, but she pretended not to hear it.

William reluctantly finished the bread, then helped his mother by carrying his father's plate over to be washed with the empty pot of stew that had contained the first portion of dinner. His mother thanked him again and told him to wash up and change for bed.

William went to the corner of the kitchen, where a thin pad lay on the floor along with a ragged blanket that served as his bed. He put on his nightshirt, and his mother winced at the sight of his ribs jutting out from his skin. She smoothed down the worn cotton, then tucked him into bed, humming softly as she did so.

"Mama, could you tell me a story?" he asked.

"What would you like to hear tonight?" she asked, smiling fondly.

"The one about the pastor from when you were a little girl," he responded, bouncing up and down.

She laughed and said, "Aren't you tired of that yet?"

He shook his head vehemently, and she laughed again. "Very well," she said, smoothing his hair. "Once upon a time, there was a good pastor. He was the vicar in the town where I grew up. Do you know why he was a good pastor?"

"Because he helped the people!" he said excitedly.

"That's right, my darling. This pastor was very good because he followed the scriptures where it says to love one another. He was kind to everyone he met, and he never raised his voice."

"Not even when the boys threw rocks at his pigs?" he asked eagerly.

"Not even then," she said reassuringly.

Mrs. Collins continued, telling William wonderful tales about how the pastor saved one person after another who was in need. William's eyes shined with excitement as he envisioned the noble man who cared for everyone, no matter their station in life. When the story concluded, William looked at his mother and said, "When I grow up, I want to be a pastor. Then I will be able to help you!"

She smiled at him. "I would be very proud of you if you were to become a pastor who was kind and helpful. But to be a pastor, you must learn your letters and work hard."

William looked down sorrowfully. "Father says reading is a waste of time."

She shook her head. "He only says that because reading is so difficult for him. He mixes up the letters in the words, and his father was quite harsh on him for it. He had to pretend he didn't care for so long that now he believes it."

"He still will not allow me to learn."

"Don't worry, love." She smiled at him. "I won't let him find out."

He smiled back, then let out a big yawn. She laughed and kissed him on the forehead. "It's time to go to sleep, now, love."

William obediently closed his eyes and listened to her humming until he finally drifted off to sleep.

Staffordshire, 1796

"Get up, boy!"

The angry voice, accompanied by a kick to his ribs, startled William Collins awake. At ten years old, he still slept on the same worn-out mat in the corner of the same kitchen where his mother once hummed him to sleep.

William sat up blearily, rubbing his eyes, only to feel his father's meaty hand strike his head. "Do you think you're better than me, to be sleeping in? Expect me to wait on you, do you, boy?"

"N-no, sir," William stammered, but his father's rage continued.

"I told your mother that learning your letters would be the ruin of you! And it has—I've never seen such a proud and disdainful boy."

"No, Father!" William exclaimed as his father reached his hand back to strike again. "I would never dare to dream of thinking myself better than you! You are by far the greatest man in the county. I know it was my own weaknesses that caused me to sleep in. I was only up so late helping Mother that—"

"Now you dare to presume that you are better than I am? All because you helped your mother during the night while I slept? Such insolence!"

"Of course not, Father! Please, I know you deserve your sleep because you work so tirelessly during the day to provide for us. I only mentioned it to show how much I understand that you are worthy of uninterrupted sleep. I would not dare to…"

"Enough!" cried the elder Mr. Collins.

William flinched, but his father lowered his hands. William sighed in relief; his words had indeed had the calming effect he'd hoped.

"Hurry up, boy. I need to stop by the tavern on my way to work, and I can't do it on an empty stomach."

William's heart sank at the knowledge that his father would be imbibing before the start of a work shift, but he dutifully arose and went about preparing breakfast. He took the single remaining egg out of the basket and quickly fried it. Glancing at his father and seeing him otherwise occupied, he scraped a small amount of egg off and dumped it into the pot of gruel cooking over the fire. He then cut the mold off the last of the bread and placed the egg on it, carrying it to his father.

Mr. Collins frowned at his plate. "Is this all, boy?" he asked gruffly.

"It—it was a small egg, sir, and the only one left," William answered quietly. He silently said a prayer of forgiveness for the white lie.

His father grumbled but ate quickly, then gave his son a stern look. "You take care of your mother, y'hear? And I don't want to hear nothin' about you spendin' all day long readin' instead of finding ways to earn money for more food."

William quickly acquiesced in the humblest way possible, which meant his father left without a final strike. Once he could no longer hear the footfalls down the path, he turned back to the gruel and stirred in the egg. After it finished cooking, he carried it into his mother's room.

"Mama?" he asked quietly, knocking on the door.

"Come in," she whispered before breaking into a coughing fit.

William entered the darkened room and crossed to her bed. After sitting on the small chair next to her, he placed the bowl on her lap.

"I put some egg in the gruel for you today," he told her as he spooned a few bites of breakfast into her mouth.

"You mustn't have done that," she said in a rasping voice. "Your father needs his strength to keep his job."

"*You* need your strength," he insisted, "or you will never get well. That is what Dr. Marshall told me."

"Now where did you come by the funds to call the doctor for me?" she asked in alarm.

"I—I didn't," he said, lowering his head in shame. "I was not able to keep them from Father to save enough. I met the doctor in town and asked him what I could do to help someone who was sick. He told me a sick person needs rest and lots of good food and water."

His mother raised her eyebrows in surprise. "That was very kind of him. But you should not have importuned him, William."

"But Mama—"

A coughing fit interrupted his protests. William quickly grabbed the chamber pot as his mother's body rejected the food he'd fed her. The blood mixed in with her stomach contents made William's heart clench.

"Mama, you're bleeding," he whispered. "You must allow me to fetch the doctor."

She shook her head in protest. "You know we haven't the money to pay him, and your father would be furious if he found out."

She broke again into such a coughing fit that William ceased arguing, not wanting to upset her. Once she regained her breath, he took the chamber pot out the door and dumped the contents at the back of the yard. His eyes filled with tears as he rinsed the bloodstains, but he willed them back, determined that she not see his weakness.

William entered the kitchen and began to clean up the dishes from breakfast. Looking at the clock, he sighed in sorrow to see that he would once again have to miss lessons at the local church. The vicar there, a kind man, often gave free lessons to the poorer children in the neighborhood who could not afford a tutor or schooling. Although generous, the vicar was also somewhat stern about students being prompt.

Once everything had been straightened, William took the chamber pot back to his mother's room. He knocked on the door lightly, calling for her. When she did not answer, he entered quietly. She appeared to be sleeping, so he placed the pot next to the bed and gently shut the door.

William spent the remainder of the day going from house to house, offering to do the odd chore for a spare egg or loaf of bread. Unfortunately, there was little work to be found for a small boy of only ten years old. One woman took pity on him and asked him to sweep the path in front of her house in exchange for a bit of stale bread, which he accepted gratefully.

As the afternoon sun grew strong, William returned home, hopeful that the bread could be softened with some broth he'd made the day before. He entered the house and prepared the simple lunch, then knocked on his mother's door. When she again did not answer, he turned the knob and silently entered.

She was in the same position she'd been in earlier that morning when he returned the pot, which lay untouched by the bed. William approached her with soft steps and called her gently. "Mama?"

When she did not move, William placed his hand on the sleeve of her faded nightdress, repeating himself. "Mama?"

Again, she did not move. Alarmed, the young boy grabbed her hand. "Mama!" he cried out when felt the ice-cold skin.

Grabbing her by the shoulders, he began shouting over and over. "Mama! Mama!"

Her head wobbled unsteadily as he shook her, desperate for her to wake up. After several minutes, the boy collapsed onto the bed, curling himself into her. "Mama, oh, Mama, please wake up. Please wake up," he sobbed into her.

How long he lay like that, he did not know. The hours passed as day turned into evening, the young boy crying hopelessly on the only person in the world who'd loved him. Not even the slam of the front door and his father's heavy steps could pull him from her side.

"What's this? No supper! Boy, get in here!" Mr. Collins bellowed in anger.

When there was no response, the burly man stormed into his wife's room. He took one look at his dead wife on the bed and his frail son curled up against her. His face turned white, then purple.

"You killed her!" the man screamed in rage. He ripped the boy from the bed and beat him savagely with his fists. "You've killed her! I'll kill you for this!"

The boy screamed in fear and agony as the blows hit his tiny body. He collapsed to the floor, where his father then kicked him. William crawled out of the room in an attempt to escape, but his father followed behind him, kicking and punching. The boy collapsed onto the floor in front of the table and lost consciousness.

The beating continued until the father could no longer move, the alcohol he had drunk before and after his work tiring his body more quickly than it should. He stumbled out the front door, muttering to himself.

William finally regained consciousness some hours later. Unable to move from the pain, he lay on the cold floor. The evening hours passed, and finally around midnight, there was a knock on the door.

"Hello?" a sharp voice called from the outside. "Is anyone home? This is Constable Baker."

William lifted his head but was unable to do anything but groan in anguish.

The door opened, and the local constable entered. "Hello? I apologize for the intrusion, but I really must speak with Mrs. Collins immediately."

William let out another groan, attempting to respond.

"Good God!" the man exclaimed.

William heard the constable kneel next to him. William attempted to open his eyes, but they were swollen closed. His mouth opened, but no sound came out.

"Oh, thank the Lord, you're alive," Constable Baker said in relief. "I don't see how, however. You stay here, boy. I don't want to leave you, but I must fetch the doctor immediately."

William tried to protest but could not speak. Footsteps ran out the door, and he began to shake fearfully. *What will Father say when he finds out the doctor has been called for?* he thought in terror. The trembling caused waves of agonizing pain throughout his body, but he could not stop himself.

After what seemed to be an eternity, he heard footfalls running up to the house. "This way, Doctor!" cried the constable. "The boy is here on the floor."

William heard the doctor's swift intake of breath. "Good Lord," he muttered. "I've never seen such viciousness against someone so young."

"Good thing his father's dead," responded the constable. "His death will probably save this poor boy's life."

William startled at this, causing fresh waves of pain. *Father's dead?* he thought in bewilderment. *He can't be! He was just here!*

"Easy there, boy," the doctor said gently. "Try not to move. I need to make sure nothing's broken."

The doctor's hands moved efficiently over the boy, testing his arms and legs, pressing on his stomach and back. Jolts like lightning shot through William's ribs as the doctor felt around.

"He's got a few broken ribs and some sizeable bruising and swelling. An arm and a leg are broken, too, by the looks of it. His stomach is soft, however, so I do not believe he is bleeding on the inside," the doctor informed the constable.

"So he will live?" the constable inquired.

"Yes, but it will be a slow, painful recovery."

"Where is his mother?" the constable demanded in frustration. "Why did she not put a stop to this?"

William heard the sound of footsteps walk away and a door open. "Doctor!" shouted the constable. "There's another patient!"

The doctor patted William gently and whispered, "It's all right, boy. I will return shortly."

William could hear the low murmur of voices as the doctor joined the constable in his mother's bedroom. He knew what they were talking about, but he didn't want to hear it. Unable to move his arms to cover his ears, he was helpless to avoid the conversation.

"Looks like she's dead, too, Constable."

"Was it the husband's fault as well, Doctor?"

"No, I believe she died of consumption. The poor boy asked me just yesterday how he could take care of someone who was ill. Had I known she was the sickly, however, I would never have given him hope of recovery. Perhaps if I had known sooner, something could have been done."

William felt tears streaming down his eyes. *Father was right. It's my fault Mama's dead. I should have asked the doctor sooner. I've killed her.*

The two men quickly joined William, and the doctor patted him reassuringly. "It's all right, lad. It will all be all right. I know it hurts. We are going to take you to my home until you have recovered."

"Do you mean to raise him, then?" the constable asked in surprise.

"Certainly not," the doctor said somewhat primly. "I could not expose my daughters to him. Goodness knows the type of man he will grow into with his father as an example."

"I will make some inquiries to see if he has any other family," the constable replied, "but I don't know if it will do any good. They weren't from here, so there's no family nearby."

"There appeared to be a letter on the table by the bed," the doctor remarked. "Perhaps it will have some details."

The constable went quickly to the bedroom and returned with the letter. "Well, this is lucky. This seems to be from the boy's father's cousin. He writes to say that his wife has given birth to another child."

"Then he shall go to them," the doctor said firmly. "As soon as he can travel."

"How long will that take?"

"Perhaps a week, but only if he is lucky and an infection does not set in. He can stay in our spare room, but once he can move about on his own, he will need to leave."

"I will write to this Mr. Bennet of Longbourn at once," the constable said. "I will inform him of the death of Mr. and Mrs. Collins and tell him the boy will be sent by post."

"How did the father die?" the doctor asked. "You did not call for me before coming here to inform the mother, so I imagine he was not ill like his wife? Although with the amount of damage to the boy, the father could not have been."

"No," said the constable grimly, "he was certainly not sick, unless you call drunkenness an illness. He came into the pub in a terrible fury and insulted a man who was in his cups. The man stabbed him in the gut with a knife, then fled. I was about to pursue the man, but after seeing how badly this boy's been beaten, I say good riddance to Mr. Collins."

"Good riddance indeed," the doctor replied with fervor. "Let us hope the sins of his father do not follow this boy."

The constable nodded in agreement, then lifted William Collins into his arms. The young man let out a whimper of pain and lapsed into unconsciousness again. The doctor followed them out, gave a lingering look at the miserable house he left, and closed the door firmly behind him

Chapter 1

Derbyshire, 1796

"How *could* you?"

Fitzwilliam Darcy's eyes flew open as he heard his mother's distressed voice coming from the corridor outside his bedroom. At twelve years old, he would be attending Eton shortly, so his father had moved him from the nursery to his own bedroom in preparation for departure.

The fact that his mother was about to give birth to a second child also played a part in the decision, as Fitzwilliam had little desire to share the nursery with a crying infant. He was happy that one of his mother's many pregnancies had been able to last as long as it had, but he knew from one of the boys in the village that a new baby brother or sister often woke up at night frequently, crying loudly to be fed.

The rooms in the family wing of Pemberley often allowed voices to carry, so Fitzwilliam could hear his mother's sobs clearly through the wall between their rooms. He sat up in bed, ready to go to her aid. *Where is Father? Is he not aware that someone is causing my mother distress?*

The sound of George Darcy's voice halted Fitzwilliam's movements. "It was so long ago, Anne," he said pleadingly.

"Not when I just found out the truth, it's not!" she cried in anger.

Is Father the one causing her distress? Darcy wondered. His parents were not a love match, but they were always very fond and affectionate towards one another. He could not remember the last time they spoke to one another in anger.

"How long has the lovely Mrs. Wickham been your mistress, George? Before she was married, when she was my lady's maid? That's how long ago the affair had to have happened in order for her son to be yours."

Fitzwilliam's mouth fell open in surprise. *Georgie is my father's son, not his godson?*

He knew it was not gentlemanly, but he could not help himself. He crept out of bed and walked quietly across the room towards the door so he could hear better. Knowing his parents would be furious if they caught him eavesdropping, he remained silent as he pressed his ear against the wall.

"*Never*, Anne! I swear it to you!" George exclaimed vehemently. "That woman has *never* been my mistress."

"Then how could she claim tonight at dinner that Fitzwilliam will be gaining *another* sibling? You did not deny it, did you?"

"Anne, will you please calm down and just *listen* to me, for God's sake!"

"I'll thank you not to invoke the name of our Lord while you defend your adultery," she snapped.

"Then for our son's sake, Anne. Please, I beg of you, listen to me," George said in a broken voice. "I promise you, it's not what you think at all. Please, Anne."

Fitzwilliam held his breath as he awaited his mother's response.

"Very well, George," she said coldly. "I will hear what you have to say."

George sighed in relief as did Fitzwilliam.

"Do you remember when Fitzwilliam was born? How you almost died?" George asked his wife.

She gave a short laugh. "How could I forget? *I* was the one giving birth, remember?"

Ignoring her sarcasm, George continued, "When the doctor told me the baby was fine but your bleeding would not stop and you would most likely die, I lost my mind."

"And apparently, your honor," Anne snapped. "You sought to replace me with my own maid!"

"*No, Anne. Never.* I went to my study, trying to distract myself. The doctor refused to allow me to see you or the baby, and I was desperate to forget his words. I filled a glass with brandy. Again and again, I drained it until the man's foul words of your demise ceased to exist."

Anne gave a snort of indignation. "I daresay my memory ceased to exist as well."

"It wasn't like that," George protested. "I don't remember anything after that. All I know is when I awoke, I found Mrs. Wickham—Molly Jones, as she was called then—in the study with me. My clothes were undone, and she was disheveled. She claimed I had forced myself on her and threatened to tell you, but I begged her not to do so. In your fragile state, it could only cause harm."

"So instead you installed her right next to Pemberley?"

"I could not very well terminate her employment without giving cause, and there was also the very real threat that she would tell you. When she came to me a few months later, however, to tell me that she was pregnant with my child, I could not do nothing. She demanded a large settlement. I was tempted to give it to her, but Wickham convinced me I should not."

"You told *Wickham*, but you didn't tell *me*?"

"Anne, you were still very ill! You had not left your bed since giving birth to our son. I could not burden you with this information!" George's voice rose as he spoke, but then he softened his tone and continued. "Wickham could tell there was something bothering me, and being the good friend and steward he is, he questioned me until I had told him everything. He said I should not pay her off but that he would marry her and raise the child as his own."

There was silence for a few moments. "Why would he do that?" Anne asked suspiciously.

"I asked him the same thing. He told me that he had been quite taken with Molly and that the two of them had been sharing a bed for the past six months."

"*What?*" gasped Anne in shock.

"I was just as surprised then as you are now. Wickham assured me that he had no knowledge of her infidelity towards him, but given the circumstances, he could not be sure if the child was even mine. There was a much greater likelihood of the boy being his. Since he was fond of her and had first compromised her, he said he would be the one to take the responsibility. He even offered to find employment elsewhere."

"Then why are they still here?" Anne asked in frustration.

"Because he is my friend, and he is the best steward Pemberley could ask for. And," he hesitated, "the child *could* have been mine."

"But it is unlikely?" Anne asked.

"Extremely unlikely," George confirmed, "especially as I have no recollection of any congress on my part."

"You think she lied?" Anne asked in a surprised voice.

"I think her to be very opportunistic," he said firmly. "I also know I would never betray vows I made to you before God. I take them seriously."

"I know you do," Anne said in a quiet voice.

"I would have denied it immediately, but I simply have no memory of that night. There is no way to be certain. If there is even the slightest chance that young George Wickham is my son, then I have an obligation as a gentleman to provide for him. A man should never, ever avoid meeting his obligations and caring for that which is his responsibility."

"Your sense of duty has always been one of your greatest strengths," his wife replied.

There were several minutes of silence, then Anne asked, "Why did you not tell me this before? Why did I have to hear it from her?"

George let out a sigh of frustration. "I meant to tell you. Once

15

your health had recovered, I did not want to upset your joy over our son. Then you were increasing, and I did not want to endanger your health. When you lost that babe, I thought you would never smile again. How could I have told you?"

"I never thought I would smile again, either," Anne admitted. "Those were dark times."

"And they continued with each subsequent loss. Each time you recovered, I would tell myself that it was the time to confess, but I could not bear to be the reason you were no longer smiling. With each pregnancy and loss, the cycle began again."

"Would you have ever told me?" she wondered.

"Only if it would not endanger your health or the health of a babe," George answered.

Another several minutes passed in silence before Anne finally said, "I think I understand. That doesn't remove the hurt or pain of betrayal, but I understand the position you were in. In fact," she continued, "the more I think on it, the more my anger is directed towards Molly Wickham. How could she have betrayed me this way? Even though she was my lady's maid, I truly thought we were friends. At least, as much as we could be as mistress and servant."

"I don't know, my dear," George said sadly. "I, too, thought she was loyal to you. Until she demanded a large payment and Wickham confided in me about their relationship, I thought I had forced myself on her while deep in my cups. How I hated myself for the longest time. I would not blame you for hating me now."

"I don't hate you," Anne said softly. "I wish things had been different, but I do not hate you."

"You will not ask me to send them away?" George asked.

After a pause, she replied, "No, I will not. It would be unfair to our son to have his friend taken away so cruelly. It would also be unfair to Mr. Wickham and little George. No, they should remain."

"Thank you, Anne. I know this is not easy for you. I promise, I will never give you any cause to doubt me again."

16

Fitzwilliam sighed in relief as his parents' voices continued in calm tones on the other side of the wall on the other side of the wall where his parents sat embracing one another. *Could Georgie really be my brother?* he wondered as he crept back into bed.

Several minutes later, Fitzwilliam came to the conclusion that there was no way to know for sure. Young George Wickham took after his mother in appearance; very few features could be compared to the father. He looked neither like George Darcy nor old Mr. Wickham.

I wonder if Georgie knows. Either way, that experience had taught Fitzwilliam a very important lesson: one should always be in control of one's behavior. *I will never take a drink of alcohol,* he vowed to himself as he fell asleep. *I will not make the same mistake my father did.*

Hertfordshire, 1796

Mr. Bennet set down the letter he was reading with a frown. As he contemplated the news, he heard a shriek of laughter come from the hallway outside his study. A moment later, the door burst open and four-year-old Elizabeth flew into the room.

"Papa, Papa, you will never guess what happened!" she shrieked, a broad grin on her face. Shortly behind Elizabeth was seven-year-old Jane, who followed her younger sister at a more sedate pace. "Lizzy," Jane admonished, "a young lady does not run nor does she shout."

Elizabeth gave her sister an unrepentant grin and responded, "But I had to tell Papa the news right away!"

Mr. Bennet chuckled and patted his eldest daughter fondly on the head, saying, "It's quite all right, Jane. What did you wish to tell me, child?"

"Kitty said my name!" Elizabeth cried in delight, clapping her hands.

"That is quite an accomplishment for a two-year-old," Mr. Bennet responded solemnly, a slight twitch of his lips being the only hint of the inner amusement he felt.

"And I can read!" Elizabeth cried with delight. "Jane taught me! I can read 'see Jane run' from my little book!"

Jane nodded solemnly at her father. "She asked me what I was doing, and I showed her the words and told them what they were."

"Excellent work, Jane," her father praised. Jane gave a shy smile in return, which faded slightly as he continued by asking, "Where is your mother?"

"She is in bed," Jane said with some concern. "She said she was feeling unwell today."

Mr. Bennet frowned in concern. "She is still in her room? It is past lunch! Have you girls had anything to eat?"

Jane hesitated to answer, but Elizabeth declared, "No, and Mary is crying that she is hungry."

"We cannot allow a three-year-old girl to be hungry!" Mr. Bennet declared. "Else she will remain three years old forever!"

Elizabeth giggled in delight while Jane gave a small smile.

"Come, girls," Mr. Bennet said. "Let us find Mrs. Hill."

"She is with Mama," Elizabeth said. "I tried to tell Mama that we were hungry, but she was being sick in the chamber pot," she added, wrinkling her nose.

Mr. Bennet's frown of concern deepened. "Let us all go together, then," he said.

The three climbed the staircase, and Mr. Bennet could indeed hear Mary's cries from the nursery. He knocked once on the door to his wife's chambers, then entered without waiting for a reply. Looking around the room, he saw his wife in bed, with Mrs. Hill mopping her brow with a damp cloth.

"Mrs. Hill," he said sternly, "please find the children's nurse and discover why on earth they have not yet had their lunch."

Mrs. Hill looked up at him in alarm. "I was on my way to tell you, sir, that the nurse left sometime during the night."

"Excuse me?" Mr. Bennet asked in astonishment. "Do you mean to tell me that the nurse has disappeared without any word of explanation? Without requesting a reference or even collecting her quarterly pay?"

Mrs. Hill grimaced and said, "It may have something to do with the fact that I caught her drinking the mistress's sherry when she was supposed to be tending the children yesterday."

Mr. Bennet's eyes widened in surprise. "Why on earth would she do that?"

Biting her lip, Mrs. Hill looked from her complaining mistress to her master. "May I speak freely, sir?" she asked quietly.

"Please do," Mr. Bennet responded, "as I would prefer the truth."

"The children are too difficult to manage for just one nurse who is underpaid for the number of charges she tends," Mrs. Hill blurted out. "The girls are all very good girls, but Miss Elizabeth is so lively and Miss Kitty so fragile with her cough that it is impossible for just one girl to tend them all."

"I see," Mr. Bennet replied gravely. Seeing Mrs. Hill open her mouth again then close it with hesitation, he asked, "Is there more?"

Mrs. Hill looked again at her mistress, who had fallen asleep and was oblivious to the entire conversation. "It isn't my place, sir, but I believe the nurse had the impression that there would be yet another child to care for in a six-month."

Mr. Bennet's eyebrows rose. "Ah," he finally said after opening and closing his mouth a few times. "And would this impression be an accurate one?"

Mrs. Hill nodded mutely at him, pressing her lips together tightly.

"Well," he said after several moments, "that certainly changes things."

Mr. Bennet looked around the room, taking in his sleeping wife, the tired housekeeper, and his hungry daughters. Letting out a tremendous sigh, he said resignedly, "Mrs. Hill, I will take over caring for Mrs. Bennet for the next few hours. Would you please help the girls get lunch? After they are settled, please rejoin me here so we can discuss the situation more thoroughly."

Mrs. Hill nodded in relief at someone taking charge and ushered the girls from the room. Alone with his wife, Mr. Bennet sat on the end of her bed, contemplating the position in which he now found himself. The weight of the day's unexpected information weighed heavily on him.

When the housekeeper returned, Mr. Bennet awoke his wife. "Mrs. Bennet," he said gently, "I believe we have some things we need to discuss."

Mrs. Bennet blinked at her husband dazedly, then began to cry. "Oh, Thomas, I don't think I can do this again. Not so soon."

Mr. Bennet tenderly put his arm around his wife as she cried on his chest. Each pregnancy had been like this: frequent tears and strong emotions. It had been that way ever since the early birth and subsequent death of their son six years prior. The babe, born sometime in between Jane and Elizabeth, had come into the world too early and was unable to take more than a few breaths before he died.

"I know, my dear," he said softly, stroking her hair. "I have some news that I think you will want to hear."

Mrs. Bennet sniffed loudly and looked up at him. "What news?" she asked, wiping tears from her face with the handkerchief Mrs. Hill had placed in her hand.

"I have received word that my cousin, Mr. Collins, has passed away," he said solemnly.

Mrs. Bennet gasped. "That awful man is dead? Why, that is wonderful news!" she exclaimed. "What a fine thing for our girls, especially Jane!"

Mr. Bennet shook his head at her. "No, my dear, the entail is carried on through his son, Mr. William Collins."

Mrs. Bennet slumped back into her pillows, disappointed. "What will become of us if this child is not a boy?" she whispered.

Mr. Bennet patted her arm and said, "With the death of my cousin and his wife, their son and the heir of Longbourn is now an orphan. I received the letter today informing me of their passing, as well as the fact that they will be sending the boy by post to our home, seeing as he has no other family left."

"The boy? How old is he?" Mrs. Bennet asked.

"I believe he is only about ten years of age," Mr. Bennet said.

"Oh, the poor child!" cried Mrs. Bennet. "To be all alone in the world! Why, of course he should come here! Who else should care for your heir if not the current owners of his future estate?"

Mr. Bennet smiled at his wife. "I thought you might feel that way. If he stays with us and is raised as our own son, then perhaps when he inherits the estate, he will look on you and our daughters with compassion. Provided this child is a girl."

"What if it is a boy, though, Thomas?" Mrs. Bennet asked. "What will the lad do then?"

"He will still be part of our family," Mr. Bennet said firmly. "He would not inherit the estate, but we could help him find a profession that would best suit him."

At this news, Mrs. Hill cleared her throat and looked at Mr. Bennet pointedly. "Another child, sir? Who shall tend all these children with the nurse gone?"

"The nurse is gone?" exclaimed Mrs. Bennet in alarm. "Who is caring for my babies?"

"Not to worry, my dear," Mr. Bennet said. "I will take care of it. With the heir of Longbourn residing here at the estate, we should be able to afford two nurses to take care of all the children together. In a few years, the young man will go to Eton for his schooling. I only hope his character does not take too much after his father's. The late Mr. Collins was an illiterate, miserly man, which was the cause of the separation between our two lines."

"What if he does? Will our girls be safe?" Mrs. Bennet whispered with concern.

"Then we shall keep them separate until he goes to school and have him remain there over the holidays," he replied calmly.

"I must admit, it would be wonderful if the heir of Longbourn were on good terms with us. It would do much to ease my mind about our children's futures."

"As it would mine, Mrs. Bennet."

The couple rested contemplatively for a minute, each pondering the possible futures in front of them. Much would depend on young Master Collins and whether he had inherited his father's viciousness.

"Well then," said Mr. Bennet, patting his wife's hand fondly, "I had best send our letter and the carriage to fetch the young man. It is my understanding he was somewhat injured at the time of his father's death, although the letter did not share all the details. I would hate for him to travel by post, all alone with injuries, at his young age."

With that statement, Mr. Bennet returned to his study to compose the letter that would change his family forever.

Chapter 2

William Collins winced as the carriage hit another rut in the road. It was not particularly well sprung, and his injured ribs protested the jostling movements that had begun two days before when Mr. Bennet's carriage came to collect him from Staffordshire.

His journey to his cousin's home had been delayed for several days, a situation that was entirely beyond his control. While residing at the doctor's home, he developed a severe fever that turned into pneumonia. The doctor declared that it was a result of the same infection that had taken his mother's life, combined with his father's mistreatment.

After William had recovered sufficiently, he was moved to the parsonage to recuperate enough to make the journey.

The week that William spent in the vicar's house was like a dream. He felt as though the pastor from his mother's stories had come to life. Although William spent most of his time in his bed, allowing his bones to heal, the elderly gentleman spent a few minutes each night with him. Mr. Lyman, as he was known, read the Bible aloud to the young man.

Although the vicar was all that was kind, William's days and nights were still filled with the memories of horrors he had endured the first decade of his life. He was much too afraid to engage in conversation with the man of the cloth, let alone ask him questions, although Mr. Lyman did all he could to encourage him.

At last, when William was finally able to sit up in bed, it was time for him to depart. The poor boy, still in terrible pain from his injuries, fought back tears. He wanted to beg the vicar to allow him to stay, but he knew it would not be possible.

Mr. Lyman, sensing the boy's fear, embraced the lad and said, "Not to worry, my boy. As the apostle Paul said to the Romans, all things work together for good to them that love God."

William nodded bravely into the man's waistcoat, then turned and boarded the carriage, using an old set of crutches the doctor had scrounged up to support his broken leg. He looked out the window for as long as he could still see the parsonage that had been the only safe home he'd ever known, then turned to face forward in the seat.

The journey was a long one for William. He had the Bible the parson had generously gifted him to read along the way, but that could only distract a boy of ten years for so long. Between the long duration of the travel and the painful jostling of the carriage, William did not think the journey would ever end.

He was not sure if he wanted the journey to end, however. Mr. Bennet, his father's cousin, was an unknown. *What if he is just as cruel as Father? Will he drink too much and lose his temper? Will he allow me to attend school?*

All these questions filled William's mind, and the horrors from his father's house were still fresh in his memory. By the time the carriage arrived at Longbourn, William was almost senseless with pain, fear, and exhaustion. He had been too injured to be moved into inns along the way, and the apothecary in Staffordshire had not wanted to send laudanum with a young boy and an unknown coachman. The coachman, after seeing William's injuries, determined it would be best to travel as swiftly as possible, stopping only a few hours each night to sleep inside the carriage.

It is little wonder, then, that William had such a violent reaction to meeting Mr. Bennet. When the carriage arrived and the door was opened, the coachman lifted William down and set him unsteadily on the ground.

William looked up at Mr. Bennet, who extended a hand in welcome. William took one look at the man who so closely resembled his father and collapsed to the ground. "I'm sorry, Father, I'm sorry!" he sobbed over and over. "I didn't mean to kill Mama, and I wasn't the one who fetched the doctor. Please don't hurt me!"

Mr. Bennet stood there in shock, his hand still outstretched, as he stared blankly at the boy sobbing at his feet. Mrs. Bennet, who had come to the door to welcome the boy, began to cry as well. She lifted her skirts and ran towards him, even though she was six months pregnant. She collapsed to the ground beside him and pulled him into her arms.

"There, there, sweetheart, it will be all right. I will not allow anyone to hurt you here. You're safe."

Mrs. Bennet's actions shook her husband from his stupor. He looked at his wife rocking the traumatized child, and he shook his head in dismay. *What hell has this child escaped from?* he wondered. For once in his life, he was glad a man was dead.

The three remained in that state for several minutes until Mr. Bennet saw Jane and Elizabeth standing at the front door, peering out at the scene before them. With a fresh sense of just how blessed he was with his family, he turned to Mrs. Bennet and said, "My dear, I believe the young man should be taken indoors. I would carry him, but..." His voice trailed off as he thought of how violently William had reacted upon seeing him for the first time. "I had not remembered how much my cousin and I resembled one another. As boys, we were often mistaken for brothers, but that was many years ago."

Mrs. Bennet nodded in understanding and replied, "We can have Hill come carry the young man. I daresay a hot bath and fresh clothes will do him a world of good."

With those words, Mr. Bennet entered the house and called for Mrs. Hill. He passed on Mrs. Bennet's instructions, and the good woman turned and immediately began issuing orders to her husband

and the maids. Then Mr. Bennet took his daughters by the hand and returned them to the nursery, where the newly installed nurse, Alice, looked at him in dismay. She was changing Kitty's nappy and had to send Jane to fetch Elizabeth, who had run off when the carriage arrived.

"No to worry," Mr. Bennet reassured the young woman, "I know my little Lizzy can be a handful! The second nurse I hired should arrive in the next fortnight, and I have begun searching for a governess as well. Until then, we shall all have to have patience with one another."

The nurse gave him a grateful smile and bobbed a curtsy while finishing the pins for the fresh nappy. "That is very good of you, sir," she said. "Will young Master Collins join us shortly?"

Mr. Bennet frowned and said, "The lad seems to be a bit overwrought between the journey and his parents' death. Mrs. Bennet will take charge of him for the time being until we can help him adjust to his new circumstances."

Nodding in understanding, the nurse set a freshly diapered Kitty on the floor next to her sister Mary, who was holding a book upside down and leafing through the pages, looking at the pictures. The nurse sat with the two girls and began to read the story to all four girls. Mr. Bennet looked at the scene fondly, then left to go check on Mrs. Bennet and William.

He found the two of them in an empty bedroom of the family wing. William was just emerging from the bath, and Mr. Bennet bit back a gasp of horror. The boy's body was completely covered in bruises from head to toe. His ribs were black and blue, and the bones were clearly protruding from his thin frame.

Mrs. Bennet heard the gasp and looked at her husband, eyes glittering with tears. She gave him a small shake of her head, and he gave a slight shake of his head before he pasted a smile on his face and entered the room. William's eyes widened with terror as he looked at Mr. Bennet.

"William," Mrs. Bennet said gently, "this is your father's cousin and my husband, Mr. Bennet."

Mr. Bennet crouched next to the boy, who was now covered in a warm dressing gown, and looked him in the eye on his level. "Hello, William," he said softly, "I am so very glad to meet you. I hope you will like it here. I want you to know that in this home, you are safe. No one will ever hurt you here."

The boy looked at Mr. Bennet, uncomprehending. "But what if I want to read?" he whispered fearfully.

Mr. Bennet sat back in surprise. "Then, my boy, I shall read with you."

William's eyes filled with tears. To everyone's surprise, he threw his arms around Mr. Bennet and began to sob. Mr. Bennet's eyes closed in pained heartache, then he wrapped his arms gently around the boy's thin frame. "There, there, my boy," he said soothingly. "I've got you now. I won't allow anyone to mistreat you ever again."

A few months later

"William?"

William Collins shrank back at the sound of his name. Even though Mr. Bennet had used a soft and gentle tone, the boy still flinched whenever someone spoke to him. The fact that Mr. Bennet so resembled William's father in both appearance and voice made the situation even more difficult.

William had been living at Longbourn for a little over a month. His wounds had mostly healed physically, but emotionally was another story. William hardly spoke. When he did, his words were subservient and obsequious. Nothing Mr. or Mrs. Bennet did had made much of an impact.

It was the week before Christmas, and Mrs. Bennet's lying-in was approaching quickly. With four daughters, a traumatized boy, and a pregnant wife, Mr. Bennet had given little thought to the approaching holiday.

"Yes, sir?" William's soft, timid voice cut through Mr. Bennet's distraction.

"Would you like to read with me in the study today?"

William's eyes widened in surprise. Until this point, he had remained in the nursery with the girls. He would often sit in the corner, reading over the children's books that were placed in there for the nurse to read to the children.

Alice, was a miracle worker. She was a kind, cheerful girl who genuinely cared for the children, and she seemed to possess an infinite supply of energy. The second nurse, Edith, was a quiet girl who would do well with the youngest children.

Mr. Bennet was in the process of hiring a governess to teach Jane and help with Elizabeth. This would ease the burden Alice and Edith currently had with caring for five children and another on the way. Alice insisted it was not necessary, but Mr. Bennet refused to drive another set of nurses away due to his negligence.

William's eyes darted around the nursery desperately. The last thing he wanted to do was be alone with the man who looked so much like his father.

When nothing came to mind, William hung his head and nodded miserably. In truth, going to the study was the last thing he wanted to do, but he was too terrified to say no. In the past, any refusal led to a beating.

Mr. Bennet led the way to the study, William following behind with trembling hands and shaking legs. He had never been in the study before, and the unknown was more terrifying than anything else he had experienced at Longbourn. What would happen when Mr. Bennet had William away from Mrs. Bennet and the other children? After all, his father had seemed like a good man in front of other people.

Once inside the study, Mr. Bennet said, "Well, son, what would you like to read?"

William forced himself to lift his gaze from the floor, and his eyes widened in amazement. He had never seen so many books before in his entire life! An entire wall of the room was made up of bookshelves, and each shelf was completely filled with books of all sizes.

William had never seen such a magnificent room. He turned in awe towards Mr. Bennet and saw the man looking at him kindly with a twinkle in his eyes. "William, every single book in this room is yours. You may take any book at any time to read."

William nodded solemnly.

For the next several weeks, William could be found in the book room with Mr. Bennet any time he was not eating or sleeping. At first, the boy could hardly focus on the words—he was much too frightened that he would make a mistake that would bring about punishment.

On the third day, however, William turned a page. Suddenly, in the silence, there was a loud ripping sound as the page half tore out of the book. William stared in horror at the damaged page in his hand. His eyes flew up to rest on Mr. Bennet, who looked over with a slight frown. William dropped the book, ducked under his chair, and put his hands over his head as he sobbed, "I'm sorry. I'm so sorry. I'm so sorry."

Mr. Bennet's face softened, but William was too engulfed in his terror to notice. The older gentleman lifted himself out of his chair and came over to sit next to the boy. The slight grunt he made as he lowered himself to the floor caused the boy to look up. When William noticed how close Mr. Bennet was, he tried to scramble backwards. Mr. Bennet reached out and pulled the hysterical boy into his lap.

"Shh, William, it's all right," Mr. Bennet said in a quiet voice.

He held William in a hug and rocked him while murmuring soothing words. Eventually the sobs turned into quiet sniffs. Once the boy had calmed down, Mr. Bennet set him back gently in the chair. Picking up the book, he smoothed the pages and handed it back to William.

"Now, my boy, a torn page is nothing to worry about. Oh, we want to be careful with books, but I have torn more pages than years you have been alive."

William looked at Mr. Bennet in disbelief. "But I've ruined it. You must be so angry with me. I know I need to be punished."

"Not in my house," Mr. Bennet replied firmly. "Now, if you were being careless and throwing my books, then the worst that would happen would be that I would ban you from my book room. But why would I punish you for what was clearly an accident?"

"But the book is ruined!"

"Not entirely. Tomorrow, I will take you to the bookstore. There is a way to replace a page in the binding if it is needed. Sometimes it is less expensive to purchase a new book. Or, if it is a small tear, we can simply leave it how it is and be more careful next time we read it."

True to his word, Mr. Bennet took William into Meryton the next day. It was resolved that the book could be repaired, and a price was agreed upon.

On the way back from Meryton, William looked at Mr. Bennet and said, "Sir, what if I do something that makes you so angry with me you need to punish me?"

Mr. Bennet knelt down and looked William directly in the eye. "I have never struck a person in my life, William. Not once. There is no excuse for a man to hit a child. I promise you now that I will never strike you in anger or as a way to punish. I would much rather have you learn from your mistake, to grow and improve. Fear and pain will only teach you what not to do; not how to correct your mistake."

William nodded but still looked doubtful.

Mr. Bennet sighed and changed tactics. "You wish to take orders, correct?"

William nodded again. "I would like to serve God."

"What is the greatest gift that God has given us?"

"His Son died for our sins."

"Exactly, my boy," Mr. Bennet said approvingly. "And the reason He died for our sins is because we are not perfect. When Christ was on the earth, He taught that those of us who were without sin were the only ones who could cast the first stone. Now, I am not without sin. Therefore, I have no justification in beating and chastising you. I am here to help you learn and grow. That is what a parent does."

William's eyes filled with hope and understanding. He threw his arms around Mr. Bennet, just as he did that first day in Longbourn. "Thank you, sir."

Mr. Bennet wobbled slightly as he fought to regain his balance in his crouch. "I think we can leave behind this 'sir' business. Would you like to call me Papa as the girls do?"

William froze and tensed.

"No, I imagine that is what you called your father. Very well, then. How about Father Bennet? Because William, I am going to care for you as I would my own child. Even though you were not born from my wife, you are my son."

William nodded into Mr. Bennet's shoulder. The two remained there until Mr. Bennet's feet had fallen asleep from kneeling so long. He released William, and the two walked hand in hand the rest of the way home.

Derbyshire, 1797

Fitzwilliam Darcy sighed blissfully as he sank onto the bed in his chambers at Pemberley. He had just arrived home for holiday after his first year at Eton, and the luxurious mattress on his estate was like sleeping on clouds compared to the one in his dormitory room.

A knock sounded on the door, and he rolled over on the bed to look at the door. "Enter," he called.

The door banged open, and in burst twelve-year-old George Wickham. The two friends had not seen one another since the previous year. Fitzwilliam had returned home for the holidays, but George had been away visiting his mother's family. His mother had passed away the month before the celebration of their Lord's birth.

"You're finally back!" George exclaimed. "I am so glad you are here!"

The boys met in the center of the room and clasped hands. "I'm so sorry about your mother, Georgie," Fitzwilliam said.

George shrugged in indifference, but Fitzwilliam could see the pain in his eyes. "Not like I saw much of her when she was alive," Mrs. Wickham's son said bitterly.

"At least you have your father," Fitzwilliam offered in consolation, but he watched his friend's face carefully.

Wickham's face tightened. "Ah, yes, my father. He can't wait until I go to Eton with you, I bet. Then he doesn't have to worry about all the trouble I cause him."

"You don't mean that," Fitzwilliam said softly. "I know your father loves you."

Again, Wickham's face twisted with an indecipherable look, but it was quickly replaced with his typical devil-may-care expression. "No matter, Will. Not when you're here! We're going to have the best summer ever!"

"I may not have much free time," Fitzwilliam warned his friend. "Father wants me to start learning estate business with him now that I'm in school."

George's face fell, and he turned away. "Bet you think you're too good for the likes of me, now that you've been to school and been fawned over as the heir to a great estate. What good do you have for the son of a steward?"

Fitzwilliam's eyes widened at the bitterness he heard in his friend's voice. "George, you know we will always be friends." When George refused to look at him, he continued, "You're...you're like a brother to me."

George whirled on Fitzwilliam, fury written across his face. "That's because I *am* your brother!" he screamed in rage.

Fitzwilliam gasped in surprise at the tears in George's eyes. "You know?" the eldest Darcy boy asked incredulously.

The question stopped George in his tracks. "*You* know?" he asked in surprise.

Fitzwilliam hesitated. How much should he reveal to his friend? It was clear George was not fond of his mother, who never had time or a kind word for him. "When did you find out?" Fitzwilliam asked.

"The day my mother died. She told me that I was supposed to be living here, but when I was born, your father forced her to marry my fath—Mr. Wickham instead. That way he didn't have to pay me a portion of the inheritance that was my right by birth."

Fitzwilliam shook his head in dismay. He spent the next hour relating all he had overheard the year before. He hesitated sharing the woman's duplicity with George, but it was clear that only the complete truth could clear up the confusion the spiteful woman had caused on her deathbed.

"Do you think it's true?" George asked his friend. "What your father said about him not remembering anything, I mean."

"I do," Fitzwilliam said with confidence.

"How do you know he wasn't lying to make your mother feel better?" George challenged.

"Because it makes the most sense. It explains why he never drinks spirits, and why you are settled near here instead of being far away. If he truly wanted you gone and out of the way, he would have sent you and your mother away with Mr. Wickham when he had the chance."

George nodded slowly. "I think you're right. Do you think we're brothers?"

"It doesn't matter," Fitzwilliam said firmly. "You are my best friend, blood or not. The only way that would change is if we started hating each other."

"Why would we hate each other?" George asked in surprise.

"I dunno," Fitzwilliam said, "maybe if you became resentful that

I'm my—I mean, maybe our—father's heir."

George was silent for a few minutes, then he said slowly, "I think I was angry the last few months. I mean, you get to live in the big house and have servants. You won't ever have to work or answer to anyone, and you'll have so much money. If your father is also mine, shouldn't I have some of that?"

Fitzwilliam nodded in agreement. "You're right, you should, but there's no way of knowing for sure. But don't worry, George. I'll take care of you."

"You will?" George asked in surprise.

"Yes," Fitzwilliam said firmly. "Whether or not you're my brother, you're also my best friend. I wouldn't leave you to fend for yourself. You just tell me what you want to do. If you want to be a rector, I will give you a living. If you want to be in the army, I will purchase you a commission."

"But what if I don't want to do anything?" George asked.

Fitzwilliam couldn't quite tell if George was serious or not. "You have to do *something*, George!"

"But you're inheriting Pemberley. You won't have to work for a living. You can sit back, drink port, and go to parties," George said somewhat petulantly.

"But being the heir and master of an estate isn't nothing. You see how hard my father works with yours. There are some days during planting and the harvest that I go for days without seeing my father because he leaves with the sun and comes home long after dark. Plus, my father no longer drinks any spirits. You know that."

"That *is* true," George admitted reluctantly. "From what I hear in Lambton, your father spends a lot more time on his estate helping his tenants than any other master."

"And I heard stories at school about other fathers. Some don't even ever go to their estates but stay in London all year round, drinking and carousing. They don't even go home for planting or harvest."

"How does the steward know what to do, then?" George asked in disbelief.

Fitzwilliam shrugged. "A lot of them either have really good stewards or they are heavily in debt because the estates do not prosper. Tenants have left the lands because the houses are in poor repair or the rents are raised too high. Some estates even have stewards who pocket the money for themselves."

George shook his head in dismay. "I always knew your father worked hard, but I thought it was just because he wanted to. I didn't know estates could just... fail, I guess."

"My father has always told me that being the master of Pemberley is a great responsibility. There are many people whose lives depend on us being honorable and doing our duty," Fitzwilliam informed his friend. "To be honest, it kind of scares me."

"It *scares* you?" George exclaimed in amazement.

Blushing slightly, Fitzwilliam said, "What if I fail? What if I make poor decisions? What if the tenants don't trust me when I take over for my father? There is so much to know and do, and my father makes it look so easy. The more he shows me, the more I realize how inadequate I am for the task."

George sat silently for a minute in contemplation, then said firmly, "You won't fail, Fitzwilliam."

"How do you know?"

"Because you try hard. And I know if you try hard at something, you can't fail at it." When this failed to reassure his friend, George added, "And I will help you!"

"You will?" Fitzwilliam said, startled.

"Yes," George stated emphatically. "I will be your steward. We will learn together this summer from *both* of our fathers."

Fitzwilliam didn't miss the subtle emphasis George placed on the plurality of the last word. "You're not... you're not still angry with my... our... my father?"

George shook his head. "What does it matter which man is my father? There's no way to know, and Mr. Wickham is the man who raised me and loved me as his own, even though he didn't know. Mr. Darcy is my godfather, and he has always treated me just as kindly as he treats you. He's even sending me to school with you! I know I was angry, but now I don't feel that way anymore. I want to be like you. I want to work hard and make Pemberley a great estate, and I can do that no matter if I am your friend or your brother or... or whatever!"

Fitzwilliam smiled at his friend in gratitude. "Thank you, George. Whether blood or not, you have always been as good as a brother to me."

George gave his trademark smirk and said, "And the best friend you'll ever have! Now come on, I smelled fresh biscuits on my way up here! I bet if we ask nicely enough, Cook will let us have some."

Chapter 3

Longbourn, 1798

"Come on, William!"

William Collins looked up from his book at Elizabeth and smiled. "Where are we going?"

"Mr. Hill says the new kittens in the barn have opened their eyes! Come and see!"

William's grin widened, and he closed his book eagerly. After fetching his shoes and jacket, he took Elizabeth's hand. Together, they walked down to the barn, Elizabeth skipping and singing as she went.

As William listened to her rambling, made-up song, a feeling of contentment and peace swept over him. It had been two years since he had come to Longbourn, and he had never been happier. The Bennets had embraced him as one of their own. The love he had yearned for as a child filled every nook and cranny of his battered soul.

The pains from his biological father had faded over the months until they were naught but a distant memory. His mother's love, however, felt stronger than ever, amplified by the tender hugs and kind words of his new family.

William's thoughts were interrupted as Elizabeth let out a wild shriek of joy and ran toward the barn.

"Elizabeth, be careful!" he cried, his heart leaping into his throat.

He sprinted after her and caught her in his arms. She squirmed against him, fighting to escape his hold.

"I want to see the kittens!" she wailed.

"Elizabeth, you know better than to just run into the barn! What if a horse had been removed from its stall? You could have been injured!"

She went still in his arms. "Oh, I forgot," she said quietly.

"You frightened me." William's heart was still pounding, and his hands shook slightly.

"Sorry, William." Elizabeth hung her head.

"I forgive you. Let's go see the kittens, shall we?"

Elizabeth's down-turned face lit up in a smile. She took his hand, and the two entered the large doors to the barn.

"Good morning, Master William, Miss Elizabeth."

It took a moment for William's eyes to adjust to the dimmer light of the barn. He blinked several times before he could finally see the stable master, Neils, leading the newest purchase into its stall.

The skittish horse bucked a few times on seeing the new arrivals, but Neils maneuvered it with a firm hand into place before latching the stall tightly closed.

"See, Elizabeth?" William said.

The girl nodded solemnly. "He could have stepped on me."

"Or kicked you or trampled you under his feet," William added.

Elizabeth gazed at the large horse for several long moments. "I will be more careful."

William smiled at her, and Neils nodded approvingly.

"Would you like to see the kittens now?" William asked Elizabeth.

She nodded eagerly. "Yes!" she whisper-shouted.

Neils and William chuckled, and Neils led them over to where the kittens were bedded with their mother. William watched Elizabeth tenderly lift a kitten and cuddle it to her chest. "Oh, William, have you ever seen anything more wonderful?"

Looking at his adopted sister, William had to admit that he had not.

Longbourn, 1800

Eight-year-old Elizabeth growled in frustration and banged her hands on the pianoforte. The instrument made a loud groan of protest.

"I don't think that's quite what Mozart had in mind when he wrote that movement," a wry voice said.

Elizabeth turned her head and glared at her fourteen-year-old adopted brother. "I doubt Mozart had children's small hands in mind when he was composing."

William chuckled at this witty retort. "You will grow eventually, Elizabeth."

"I don't want to grow up!" she cried, throwing her hands into the air and stamping her small foot. "I want to run and play and climb trees."

"I know," he said soothingly. "Unfortunately, God did not create us to always stay children. You still have time to do those things, but you also need to learn how to be an accomplished lady."

Elizabeth stuck out her bottom lip in a pout. "It's so unfair. Gentlemen get to hunt and fish and do sports, even as adults. Ladies do nothing but play piano and sew."

"Oh, there is much more to being a lady than that," William said. "You run the household, manage the servants, ensure the tenants' needs are being met, care for children, and much more. A lady has a tremendous influence on her family and those under her care. The difference between a kind lady and one who is uninformed, or even cruel, is tremendous."

Elizabeth looked at him. "And how will learning to play the pianoforte help in those matters?"

"Because you will learn discipline, patience, and fortitude. There will often be circumstances or tasks that are unavoidable throughout your entire life. How you handle them will make all the difference in your happiness. You may not be able to control your circumstances, but you can control how you respond."

Elizabeth nodded slowly. "I think I understand."

William gave her a tender smile and kissed her on the top of the head. "This isn't easy for adults, let alone a child. But I think you're on the right path."

She nodded, then turned her attention back to the sheet music. William listened as she slowly played each note, taking time to press the correct keys. When she finished the line, she turned back to him with a wide smile. "I did it!" she cried.

"Excellent work," he said, clapping his hands.

"I had best let Mary have her turn now," Elizabeth said. "I will work on it again tomorrow."

William chuckled as Elizabeth dashed from the room, hollering for Mary.

"Well, one thing at a time," he told himself.

London, June 1802

Fitzwilliam Darcy looked in frustration at the broken pocket watch in his hand. He had commissioned the item as a birthday gift for his father the last time he was in London. The outside was engraved with a simple drawing of Pemberley, and he had paid quite a sum for the unique etchings.

Now, on his return to London, he had retrieved the watch an hour before from the shop. It had been wrapped and boxed for him, and it wasn't until he returned home and opened the parcel that he was able to see the item up close.

While the heft and feel of the watch appeared genuine, Fitzwilliam was concerned by the coloring. He went to a window and held it up to the sunlight, frowning. On closer inspection, the tint just seemed darker than other watches he had seen his father use.

He wound the watch and opened the clasp, listening to the ticking noise. He shook it gently and was dismayed to hear a small rattle. His fingers tightened slightly, snapping the watch closed.

Fitzwilliam watched in shock as a crack formed in the front of the watch. Peering more closely, he saw smaller grooves begin to spread and flecks of paint fall to the ground. He scratched at the surface with his fingernail, and more paint fell away to reveal dull, cheap tin underneath.

Furious, Fitzwilliam strode toward the front door, determined to go back to the shop immediately. At eighteen years old, he was proud of finally being considered a man. Having been fooled by a tradesman into parting with almost a quarter's allowance for a cheap item smarted his pride.

The well-trained servants made no comments about Master Fitzwilliam's odd behavior. They quietly retrieved the carriage that they'd just finished storing, their stoic faces betraying none of their frustration at having to undo all the work they had just done.

Tears filled Fitzwilliam's eyes as he rode through the city back towards the shop. He told himself it was the sting of the wind and the smog of the city that caused him to cry. Frustration and emotion had nothing to do with it.

After what seemed to be an eternity, the carriage came to a stop outside the shop. Darcy furiously descended, but he only took two steps before the wind was knocked out of him by a thump to the stomach.

"Oomph," he groaned, doubling over slightly.

Fitzwilliam looked down to see a ragged boy no more than eight years of age lying on the ground, moaning.

"Are you all right, lad?" He knelt next to the boy, who groaned and lay still.

"Oy, Jeremy! What happened, mate?" Another boy around the same age approached and knelt near his friend.

Fitzwilliam turned his attention to the newcomer. "Do you know him?"

"It's Jeremy. What did you do my friend?" the young man spit venomously.

"Nothing!" Fitzwilliam said, shocked. "He ran into me after I got out of the carriage."

"You probably weren't watching where you were going. Just like you toffs, not noticing a poor boy under your foot. Now Jeremy might die!"

Fitzwilliam rolled his eyes slightly at the dramatics. "Now, now, I'm certain your friend won't die. And I wasn't the one running through the streets!"

Jeremy let out another groan and began to sit up. "What happened?" he asked, rubbing his head.

Fitzwilliam turned back to the boy on the ground.

"This gent knocked you down!" the friend declared.

"I did no such thing!" Fitzwilliam protested.

He looked around at the crowd that was starting to gather, surprised to see so many poorly dressed people in the neighborhood.

"Do you lads need help?" a disheveled man asked.

"Should we call for the constable?" a woman in a ratted skirt added.

"No need for that!" Fitzwilliam insisted. He knew once a constable game, the gossip would be unstoppable. "The boy is quite all right. He may have a sore head, but that is all. See look, he's up and moving!"

Indeed, Jeremy had risen to his feet. His friend gave Darcy a glare. "That sore head may end up costing him his work, and then where will his family be?"

Darcy sighed and said, "I quite understand. Here…"

He began to search in his pockets for a coin, but he froze when Jeremy said, "Never you mind! I don't want nothin' from the likes of you."

The boys spat on the ground and ran off as Fitzwilliam watched with his mouth slightly open. He looked around, and the ragged crowd that had gathered had suddenly disappeared, leaving only a few members of a higher class looking on with interest.

Fitzwilliam shook his head in confusion, then went into the shop.

"Back again, sir?" the shop owner asked with mock surprise.

"Yes, I am afraid there has been an issue with the watch I purchased. It is clearly of inferior quality."

"I say, that's quite an accusation to make," the man said in a hard voice. "Let us take a look at it."

Fitzwilliam reached into his pocket to pull out the watch, but it was empty. He put his hand in another pocket, thinking he simply misremembered, but that pocket was empty as well.

"Well?" the owner asked with a small grin.

"It must have fallen out in the carriage," Darcy said. "I will return."

"Very well," the man let out a long-suffering sigh.

Fitzwilliam left the shop and boarded his carriage. A quick glance around did not reveal the missing watch, so he began to inspect more thoroughly. He lifted cushions, checking in each nook and cranny.

"Perhaps I dropped it at home," he said to himself after several minutes of searching.

Resigned, he rapped his cane on the roof and told the driver to head home. As they started off, he glanced out the window towards the shop. To his surprise, Jeremy and his friend were standing at the door. Jeremy smirked towards the carriage, and the boys entered the shop.

Something clicked in Fitzwilliam's brain.

"Those bastards!"

They were all in on it: the shopkeeper, the boys, and the out-of-place crowd.

Fitzwilliam fumed the entire ride back to his home. Upon his arrival, he was told that his father wanted to speak with him. He entered his father's study and sat heavily down in a chair.

Mr. Darcy looked up in surprise. "Well, now, what's got you so upset, son?"

Fitzwilliam clamped his lips tight and scowled at the floor. Embarrassment and anger warred for dominance in his chest as he fought to gain control.

His father waited, staring at him. After several long minutes, the entire story came spilling out.

Listening quietly, his father waited until Fitzwilliam lapsed back into silence. "What do you intend to do about it?"

"I was going to send a message to the constable," Fitzwilliam began.

Mr. Darcy shook his head. "I'm afraid you have no proof, my boy. The watch is missing, so you cannot prove that it was of inferior quality. The boys did not get caught in the act of thievery, either. All a report would do is make you a laughingstock."

Fitzwilliam hung his head in shame.

"It's an expensive lesson to learn," his father said gently. "You aren't the first, and you won't be the last. Those of higher society sometimes have to learn the hard way that all too often, you are seen for your wealth, not yourself. To those who are beneath you in social status and finances, you are not a person but a resource from which they can pull money."

"But the Wickhams aren't like that!" protested Fitzwilliam. "Neither are the tenants of Pemberley."

"Ah, but persons of integrity are rare, regrettably. I work diligently to ensure that Pemberley is surrounded by those who are willing to work together to help their fellow man. It is not always easy."

"Surely a man's station does not affect his character," Fitzwilliam insisted.

"But a man's experiences often shape how he views the world," replied his father. "Unfortunately, many of the lower classes experience poverty and hardship. That builds anger and resentment towards those who seem to have an easy life. Conversely, many of our class mistreat those below them, which only furthers the envy."

"So what do we do?"

"Nothing, I'm afraid. We have to protect ourselves from those who would take advantage. Whether it's a matchmaking mother out to increase her daughter's standing or a shopkeeper wanting to barter for more than an object is worth, there will always be people who want to take what they have not earned. You must guard yourself, son, especially in your dealings with those below you in status and wealth."

Fitzwilliam nodded. An expensive lesson, indeed, but one he vowed he would not need to learn again.

Derbyshire, two months later

Fitzwilliam's leg bounced nervously, adding to the swaying of the carriage. His father laughed and reached out, gently putting pressure on his son's knee.

"You'll turn us over if you keep doing that, son."

George snickered, and Mr. Wickham covered his mouth to hide a smile. Fitzwilliam's face turned red, and he gripped his knees tightly.

"Excited to see Alice Cummings, eh?" George teased.

"Shut up," hissed Fitzwilliam, his face turning even more red.

The group of men was on their way to an assembly in Lambton. With Fitzwilliam about to begin his first year of university, the two fathers had determined it was best to have the young men come out into society. Fitzwilliam was only convinced to attend when George was also given permission to accompany him.

"Ah, is your eye on Miss Cummings, Fitzwilliam? She's a pretty girl," Mr. Wickham responded.

Fitzwilliam felt as though his face would catch fire. "I suppose," he murmured.

George snickered again, and Fitzwilliam gave his friend a dirty look. Since returning to Derbyshire after his disastrous London trip, he had encountered sixteen-year-old Alice Cummings each time he went into Lambton. The pretty girl had asked him questions about himself, not once mocking him when he stumbled over his words.

Her looks alone had made her the subject of many a bedtime fantasy, but the way she attentively listened to him speak about school, Pemberley, and books made her even more compelling.

Fitzwilliam felt as though he had found the one with whom he could truly be himself. Unlike the sisters of his school friends, she seemed to be interested in him for him. The fact that she was from Derbyshire and her father was friends with his own made him think he could marry her in a few years when he was finished with Oxford.

Tonight would be their first time at an assembly together, and she had promised to save him a dance. He planned on asking her for the final dance as well to give their mutual acquaintances the signal that he was interested in her. It was the only way he could ensure that she would not be snatched up while he was away at school. While he was confident in her regard for him—indeed, her smiles and attentiveness made it clear—he knew a girl had little say in whom her father arranged for her.

At last, they arrived at the assembly. As soon as the door was opened, Fitzwilliam bounded down from the carriage ahead of his father and the Wickhams. He was barely able to politely greet the master of ceremonies in his haste to search out Miss Cummings.

Finally, he spied her. His heart swelled, and he eagerly made his way across the floor towards her. Her eyes lit up when she saw him approach, and she gave him a smile.

"Mr. Darcy," she said, curtsying.

"Miss Cummings," he replied with a bow. "May I have the honor of a dance?"

She graced him with another smile, and his heart fairly stopped in his chest. "Of course, sir."

She handed him his card, and to his delight, he saw that her first dance was open. He wrote his name down on the first line and, after a brief hesitation, put his name down for the last as well.

He passed the card back, and her eyes widened when she saw his name both times. She gave him a wide grin instead of the socially acceptable demure smile. "I look forward to dancing with you, Mr. Darcy."

Fitzwilliam bowed in reply, then returned to his father's side. Mr. Darcy looked at his son with a touch of concern. "I know you are eager to dance with her, but you mustn't make your attentions so obvious."

He looked at his father with surprise. "But I am quite sincere in my regard for her."

Mr. Darcy's frown deepened slightly. "Son, I am sure she is a lovely girl, but she is quite an unsuitable match. While technically the daughter of a gentleman, her father's estate is quite small. Furthermore, her mother was the daughter of a steward."

Fitzwilliam narrowed his eyes at his father. "Mr. Wickham is a steward, and he is one of your closest friends! George is *my* closest friend, yet his status is the same as Miss Cummings! In fact, she is above him!"

"There is quite a difference between friendship and marriage," Mr. Darcy said firmly. "A friendship will not endanger your children's futures. Marriage to a woman of lower birth with no dowry will not help Pemberley prosper. What do you know of her abilities to run a large household? To manage servants and take care of tenants?"

"I don't know," retorted Fitzwilliam sullenly. "But she listens to me. She is interested in the books that I read, and she asks me questions about myself. I like her."

Mr. Darcy's gaze softened. "I understand, son. I am not forbidding you from speaking or dancing with her, or even marrying her. However, you must be certain that her positive qualities outweigh all the negatives she brings to the match."

There was no time to respond, as the musicians had finished warming up and the dancing was about to commence. Fitzwilliam gave his father a quick nod of acknowledgment, then hurried to find Miss Cummings.

The dance was everything he imagined it would be. She asked him questions and listened attentively to answers. Her beautiful face became flushed with the exertion, and her shapely form bounced along with her. She was everything he could ever want.

After the musicians played the final notes of the song, he escorted her to her mother and offered to fetch them both drinks. He quickly made his way to the punch table, collected three glasses, and then made his way through the crowd back towards the two women.

"What an utter bore he is," he heard her say as he came up from behind her.

He froze, unsure of what she meant. Could she be speaking about him?

"Mother, I don't think I can stand to hear one more word about his ridiculous books or estate matters. Why on earth should I care?"

"Alice, silence," whispered her mother sharply. "You know we are depending on you to make a good match to save your father from his debts. Bore he may be, but Fitzwilliam Darcy stands to inherit one of the largest and most prosperous estates in the kingdom."

"But how can I bear to spend a lifetime with such a dull man?" whined Miss Cummings.

"You put up with his company and warm his bed until you provide an heir and a spare. Then you can amuse yourself however—and with whomever—you wish. Until then, keep a smile on your face and be attentive," Mrs. Cummings hissed.

Fitzwilliam could not move. He felt as though his heart had shattered into a thousand pieces. Suddenly, he felt a large hand on his shoulder.

"I'm sorry, son," said Mr. Darcy softly. "But it is better you found out now than after you had committed yourself."

Fitzwilliam nodded mutely. At that moment, Miss Cummings turned around and spied him. "Oh, thank you, Mr. Darcy! I declare, I was quite parched."

Still unable to speak, Fitzwilliam numbly handed the drinks over.

Miss Cummings smiled at him, her head bowed coyly. Only now could he see the hint of avarice in her eyes and the coldness of her smile.

"I'm afraid I have received an urgent note from Pemberley," Mr. Darcy smoothly interjected. "My son and I must return home immediately."

A hint of anger flashed across the girl's face, but it quickly melted into an understanding mien. "Of course, sir," she said.

Turning to Fitzwilliam, she added, "I shall miss our last dance together. I promise I will sit it out. No other partner could compare."

This falsehood shook Fitzwilliam out of his shock. Angry heat soared through his body, and he gave her an icy stare. "It is of no matter, madam," he said coolly. "You may do as you wish."

She blinked at him, then looked at her mother uncertainly. Mrs. Cummings's face went white with shock, then changed to understanding and resignation.

Fitzwilliam gave a short, stiff bow, then turned his back on the ladies and departed.

The Darcy carriage was silent as they made their way back to the estate. Each mile hardened Fitzwilliam's heart until it felt like stone. Between the tradesman and Miss Cummings, Fitzwilliam vowed to never allow himself to be so ill-used again.

Chapter 4

Cambridge, 1803

"Look, there it is!" shouted an excited George Wickham.

Fitzwilliam Darcy smiled at his friend's enthusiasm at seeing the stately buildings of Cambridge come into view from the carriage window. The younger man was about to begin his first year of studies at old Mr. Darcy's alma mater while the elder was returning for his second year of study.

"Now, don't forget, Darcy," he continued, "you must call me *Wickham* from now on. I am to be George no longer."

Darcy laughed and said, "Yes, *Wickham*, I am familiar with the forms of address a man receives when he reaches his majority. I have been here a full year, after all."

Wickham gave his friend a rakish grin and replied, "I just wanted to make sure you would not embarrass me in front of everyone. First impressions and all that."

Darcy let out a bark of laughter. "I think it is rather the reverse—hopefully *your* antics will not reflect poorly on *my* reputation!"

The two friends smiled at one another, then Wickham said, "I wish we could share a room, Darcy. Then I would have at least one friend whom I could trust."

Darcy looked at his friend in bewilderment and said, "What in heaven's name do you mean? You are one of the most gregarious people of my acquaintance. I cannot imagine you having difficulty finding friends!"

"In Lambton, yes, because I was on equal standing with those in the village. Here, however, I am merely the son of a steward. Mr. Darcy is my godfather, yes, but I am hardly of the same social circle as you," answered Wickham soberly.

Darcy stared at his friend. "You know that has never meant a thing to me," he replied emphatically.

"But it matters to *them*," retorted Wickham, "and since I will be living with them, how they think of me will make a difference in how pleasant my time at school will be."

Fitzwilliam frowned in response. He knew Wickham was correct. The previous year had shown him that rank and societal position mattered even at school, where boys were treated with respect or with rancor based on their parents' status.

"I'm sorry, Wickham," he said softly. "I wish there were something I could do to change the situation. All I can say is that I will not allow you to be mistreated when I am around."

"Thanks, Darcy," Wickham said gratefully. Then his face tightened, and he straightened his shoulders. "I will, however, need to stand on my own two feet. I cannot expect you to protect me all the time."

The boys fell into silence as the carriage reached the front building of the school. The previous years had brought them closer together as they weathered the deaths of their mothers and their entrance into adulthood. Now, with university looming, Darcy could not help but feel everything was about to change.

Three months later

Darcy crossed the manicured lawn, heading towards his dormitory. The shadows from the sinking sun stretched across the grass as his long stride carried him quickly towards his bed. He had been studying with classmates to prepare for an upcoming exam, and it was almost past the time for curfew.

His footsteps paused as he heard singing coming from the distance. *Drunk idiots*, he thought in disgust as he spied a group of five or six boys stumbling towards him. As they approached, he squinted and looked more closely at a familiar figure.

"Wickham?" he exclaimed in dismay.

"Darcy!" Wickham's voice echoed loudly across the empty campus. "I haven't seen you in ages! Come meet my new friends!"

Darcy looked more closely at the boys with his friend. "Stanton?" he asked in surprise.

"Hello, Darcy old boy!" said the young viscount. "You know our new friend Wickham? Jolly good sort, even for the son of a steward."

Wickham beamed with delight, but Darcy frowned. "I'm surprised to see you spending time with him," he said slowly. "You typically do not care to associate with those below your station."

The grin on Wickham's face disappeared and was replaced by a scowl. "You saying I'm not good enough, Darcy?"

Alarmed, Darcy said, "Now, Wickham, that isn't what I meant at all. You know that."

Wickham scowled further. "Then what *did* you mean?"

Great, he's belligerent when he's drunk, thought Darcy wryly. "I have known Lord Stanton for some time now, and he has always been quite vocal about only associating with peers and their children, that is all."

"Well, I was about to have some fun with Wickham here down at the pub, maybe dump him in the horse trough," explained Stanton, clumsily clapping his hand on Wickham's shoulder, who stumbled to the side. "But then he offered to buy us all a round of drinks. How could I say no to that? Besides, it would be ungentlemanly to dunk him afterwards!"

Stanton laughed uproariously at this, and the remaining lads joined in with him. Several patted Wickham on the back, who teetered off-balance under the pressure.

"I see," Darcy said. "In that case, might I suggest we all head off to bed before curfew so you can sleep off the drink?"

"Excellent idea!" Stanton said. "Come along, lads."

The young men all staggered off towards their different dormitory buildings. Fitzwilliam watched them in concern until they were all safely inside. Then he turned back towards his own building, resolving to speak with Wickham the following day.

Unfortunately, it took nearly a fortnight before Darcy was able to catch Wickham alone. Each time he had found his friend, the young man was surrounded by some of the more prominent members of society. One afternoon, however, he spied Wickham walking alone towards the gate that led off the campus.

"Wickham!" Darcy called, hurrying to catch up to his friend.

Wickham spun around, eyes flashing slightly with panic. The tension in his face eased as he saw who had called his name. "Darcy!"

"How are you doing, Wickham? I've barely seen you since we arrived, and it's already almost time for us to go home for Christmas."

"Er, about that, Darcy. I've been meaning to tell you—truly, I have—but I won't be going to Pemberley for Christmas. Stanton invited me to join him in London."

Darcy looked at his friend in surprise. "Why would he do that?"

"Maybe because he enjoys my company?" retorted Wickham sarcastically. "Really, Darcy, I don't know why you are always so surprised that someone other than yourself wants to be friends with me."

"Wickham, that isn't what I meant!"

The conversation was interrupted when Lord Stanton himself approached the two friends. "Darcy!" he exclaimed congenially, "I hope you don't mind that I'm borrowing your friend for Christmas. I'm sure your father won't mind the loss, though, eh?"

Darcy's brow furrowed. "I'm sure my father will miss Wickham's company," he said cautiously, "but I imagine Mr. Wickham might feel the loss more keenly."

Wickham shot Darcy a look of alarm, then said, "Well, I daresay my father will miss my company, but it's not to be helped. Stanton insists on my attendance."

"Ah, yes," Stanton said drolly, "for who else will buy my drinks and lose badly at poker to me?"

Darcy's eyebrows shot up, for he was quite familiar with Wickham's ability to count cards. He'd lost a fair amount of pocket money before he learned not to play against his friend.

"Well, then, that's settled," Wickham said hastily. "Come, Stanton, I believe you owe me a chance to win back what I lost last night!"

"With your luck? I doubt it! But you can console yourself with the charms of the barmaid again. I'm sure she wouldn't mind!" Stanton laughed uproariously and clapped Wickham on the back.

Darcy watched in concern as the two friends walked away, feeling as though a stone had settled deep in his stomach. He dreaded telling his father and Wickham about the situation in which his friend had found himself.

As circumstances would have it, Darcy never did get the opportunity to tell either man about his concerns. The snow fell heavily the next day, and the roads towards Derbyshire became impassable. Darcy spent a lonely Christmas holiday in an inn halfway to his home with other stranded travelers. By the time the roads had cleared enough for travel, it was time for him to return for the new semester. He considered writing his concerns in a letter, but he did not think he would be able to properly convey the worries he had over his friend.

Wickham's second half of the school year continued much like the first. Darcy hardly saw his friend, but the few glimpses he caught of the man did nothing to alleviate his concerns. Wickham avoided Darcy's gaze and conversation, but Darcy could not help but notice the fine cut of newly tailored clothing, carefully styled hair, and a devil-may-care attitude.

How can he afford these things? Darcy frequently asked himself. *Perhaps his skill in poker has improved?*

The worry over his childhood friend gnawed at his stomach every time he wrote home, but he held back answering the questions his father asked. He only responded that he rarely had occasion to see his friend, to which his father always replied with a chastisement to put his books away and look out for his friend. "Your relationship with a man you have known since infancy should supersede your desire to improve your education," stated Mr. Darcy in his most recent letter.

Darcy had crumbled the missive and thrown it across the room in frustration. *How can he think that I do not care about Wickham? Does he think me cold and heartless?*

In an effort to distract himself, Darcy dug deeper into his studies. He found solace in the logic of Latin and mathematics, and he spent his anger with boxing and foils. The passion he felt deep inside was used to fuel his debates, and soon Darcy was well known across campus as being a sharp debater, a keen intellect, and a master with both fists and blades.

Finally, the end of the term arrived. Darcy's high marks paled in comparison to the relief he felt at being able to present Wickham to their fathers. Arrangements were made for the carriage to take them home, and Darcy's rooms were packed quickly.

The evening before the journey, Darcy sent a note to Wickham to meet him the next morning at the carriage. Shortly after sending it off with a servant, a knock was heard at his door.

"Enter," Darcy called from his bed, where he was reading a history of the Roman Empire.

Instead of Wickham, whom he was expecting, a young boy from the local village entered.

"Beggin' yer pardon, sir," the boy said, "but me pa sent me to ask 'bout the payment for yer bill at the tavern."

"I beg your pardon?" Darcy sat up and fixed a stern look on the lad, who swallowed nervously. "I do not believe I have ever visited that establishment."

"N-no sir," the boy gulped and stepped backwards, "but yer brother has."

Darcy's frown deepened. "I have no brother," he said in an icy voice.

Now the boy looked confused. "Y-yer Mr. Darcy, right?"

"Yes, I am."

"Yer brother said that ye'd pay fer all his debts, sir. Fer the drinks and the company."

Suspicion welled up inside of Darcy. *No, he wouldn't.* Forcing himself to say the words, he asked, "What is my brother's name?"

The boy looked at him confused. "They called him 'Wickham,' and I reckoned it was on account of 'is bein' younger than you. A middle name, p'rhaps."

Darcy closed his eyes and sat back, understanding pouring over him. "I see."

Opening his eyes, he went across the room and opened his valise. Pulling out a handful of notes, he asked, "How much does Wickham owe?"

The boy gave a number that caused Darcy's eyes to widen in surprise, then narrow in anger. He counted out the money and handed it to the lad. "Now listen closely," he said sternly. "That man is *not* my brother. Tell your father that no Darcy will ever pay that man's account in the future."

The boy swallowed hard and took another step back. He turned to leave, then paused. "But what about th' others, sir?" he asked hesitantly.

"*What* others?" demanded Darcy.

"There's the tailor, for one," the boy said quickly, "and the cobbler. They's goin' to come tomorrow fer payment. Me pa was goin' t' come tomorrow, too, but he heard Wickham tonight at the pub talkin' 'bout goin' home early in the mornin' so's me pa sent me right away."

Darcy's face went white with fury. "It would be their own fool's fault for taking credit for such large amounts from a young man with no references," he said. "However, I am not unsympathetic to their plight. You and I will go to the village now and ensure each man has received his due."

The boy looked at Darcy in astonishment. "Yer goin' to pay?"

"Yes," said Darcy firmly. "I cannot allow a man to lose his livelihood because a childhood acquaintance made use of my name."

Darcy donned his coat and hat. He and the boy left the room, which Darcy closed and locked securely.

"What is your name?" he asked as they walked quickly towards the village.

"Peter, sir," the boy said, running to keep up with Darcy's long stride.

"Well, Peter, I hope that this will be a lesson to your father and others in the village. Just because someone is a student here at school does not mean they are honest. Even those of the peerage will not often pay their debts."

Peter did not respond, and the two continued towards the village. Upon arrival, Darcy went to each place of business. Many had closed for the night, but Peter was able to find the owners of the establishments. Darcy paid each amount in full, leaving behind a stern warning not to give credit to Wickham in the future. He also insisted on collecting the vowels of each debt paid as evidence.

The look on the tailor's face was one of relief and gratitude as he looked at the money Darcy handed him. "God bless ye, sir," he said as a small, disheveled girl peered out from behind the man. His wife, clearly in the family way, stood behind him in the doorway, holding the hand of yet another child.

At last, the deed was done. Night had long since fallen, and Darcy knew it was almost time for curfew. He walked Peter towards the pub, where he saw a drunk Wickham stumble out the door with his friends. He considered confronting his friend, but one look at Wickham's unsteady gait told him that such a conversation would be fruitless. Instead, he returned to his room and fell into an uneasy sleep.

After a restless night, a knock on the door told him the carriage had arrived to carry both him and Wickham home. Darcy was somewhat surprised to see that Wickham was already in the coach, but he kept his thoughts to himself.

"Darcy, there you are! Let's get moving, shall we?"

Wickham's smile looked somewhat unnatural, and Darcy smirked when he saw the green pallor on his friend's face.

"Rough night?" he asked loudly.

Wickham winced, making Darcy smile in satisfaction. "Not at all, old boy. I'm just eager to be home. Shall we get going?"

Darcy looked at his friend in mock confusion. "Don't you have some unfinished business in town? Perhaps some unpaid debts?"

Wickham turned pale underneath his green pallor, causing his usually handsome features to take on an ill-favored appearance. "No, nothing like that. I took care of it all yesterday."

Darcy felt rage well within him at the realization that his friend had intended to leave without paying any of the tradesmen, but he forced it down. "Excellent, then. Let's be on our way."

Wickham sighed in poorly concealed relief as Darcy tapped on the roof of the carriage. The coachman snapped the reins, and off they went towards Derbyshire.

The few days it took them to journey home passed slowly. Wickham, once he recovered from his hangover, did his best to entertain his friend with stories and anecdotes from the semester. He appeared to not notice that his stoic friend was more solemn than usual.

Darcy, on the other hand, heard little of what Wickham was saying. He kept picturing the thin face of the tailor's daughter looking up at him from behind her father's legs. Her dress was worn and threadbare, and by the amount Wickham had attempted to leave unpaid, she might not ever receive another dress. Entire families could be ripped apart by unpaid debts, forcing the families to starve or even to sell their children.

At first, Darcy was inclined to hide the situation from both his father and Wickham's. The longer they travelled, however, the more indignant Darcy became on behalf of the tradesmen. *His own father is a member of the working class*, Darcy thought in anger. *How could he behave in such a way?*

Then he imagined the looks on the men's faces as he told them the truth about George Wickham. His heart ached at being the one to cause sorrow to men whom he loved and admired. Mr. Wickham was just as much a father figure to Darcy as his own father.

Fitzwilliam had just resolved to keep the knowledge to himself when suddenly he heard his father's words to his mother all those years ago. *A man should never, ever avoid meeting his obligations.*

Suddenly, it was clear to him. *Wickham tried to avoid his obligations this time. He may have also done it while in London. If this goes unchecked, how many lives could he ruin by leaving unpaid debts? Not to mention consorting with barmaids, as Peter hinted. No, I have a duty to protect those beneath me. That includes making sure Wickham does not feel free to continue taking advantage of others.*

Immediately, Darcy felt as though a weight had been lifted from his shoulders. *If the roles were reversed, Father would rather be informed of my behavior than to be in the dark. Why should this be any different?*

Firm in his decision, Darcy resolved to seek a private word with his father and Mr. Wickham the day after he arrived home. His heart light at being able to share his burdens, the remainder of the journey passed somewhat more tolerably than the beginning. He only hoped it was not too late for the older gentlemen to reform his friend's character.

Chapter 5

Oxford, 1804

William Collins looked around nervously. He had arrived at Oxford and was about to be shown to his dormitory. Having never stayed so much as a single night away from Longbourn and the Bennet family, he was understandably feeling out of his element.

Mr. Bennet had offered to accompany the young man, but as his adopted father was a Cambridge man and therefore of little use in a foreign location, William did not want both men to be away from the family for such a long period of time. Heaven forbid they *both* lose their lives in a carriage accident!

Now, standing uncertainly outside the main buildings of the university, with his trunk at his feet, William found himself wishing he had accepted Mr. Bennet's offer of companionship. Although he had gained a fair amount of confidence in his last eight years as a beloved member of the Bennet family, he still felt at times like the terrified boy awaiting his father's return after an evening of drinking.

He shifted nervously from foot to foot as he awaited a servant to fetch the dean. At last, an elderly man with a kindly face came bustling out of the building.

"Collins?" he called in a strong voice that belied his years.

"Th-that's me," stammered William, clearing his throat. "Although I prefer William."

The man stopped and fixed him with an odd look. "Most of our students use their surnames."

"Then please call me Bennet, which is the name of the man who raised me."

The dean quirked an eyebrow, and William held his breath nervously. Finally, the old man nodded and said, "I think that should be fine."

William let out a sigh of relief, lifted his trunk, and carried it towards another building that appeared to be the dormitories. His large frame, combined with years of horseback riding around his estate to check on tenants, had kept his body fit, although he still tended towards a sizeable girth around the middle.

After entering the building, William followed the dean up the stairs to the third floor, where the older man knocked on one of the many identical doors. The door opened, and a small young man opened it and peered out.

"Oh, Dean Stokes," he said with wide eyes. "What brings you here?"

"I've come to introduce you to your new roommate, William Bennet Collins."

Wide eyes grew bigger as he looked William up and down. "Pleasure to meet you, Collins," he said, opening the door wider. "I'm James Stanley.

"Hello, Stanley," said William with a friendly smile. "Please, call me Bennet. I'm glad to meet you!"

The tension in Stanley's face eased at William's kind demeanor. He beckoned them to enter, and William carried his trunk into the room.

"I will leave you two to become acquainted," Dean Stokes said, and he turned and went down the stairs, closing the door behind him.

William looked around at the small room which held two beds, two desks, and two closets. Stanley's items had already been unpacked and spread neatly throughout the room. As William opened his trunk and began unloading his items, Stanley watched him with wide eyes.

"I hope you're not a messy person," Stanley blurted out nervously after a few minutes of silence.

"Not with five female cousins in the house!" William replied with a smile. "The Bennet girls take up so much space, so if I left anything out, it was immediately claimed as the property of someone else."

"*Five* girls?" Stanley asked in amazement.

"And a finer group of girls you'll never meet," William said easily. "I went to live with them when I was ten, and they immediately embraced me as one of their own."

"Are they all older than you?"

"Younger, actually. The eldest, Jane, is fifteen and will come out next year. Lydia is the baby, and she's eight now."

"I don't have any sisters; just an older brother," Stanley said wistfully.

"What's he like?" William asked, settling himself on the bed now made up with linens he brought from home.

"Mean," said Stanley, then covered his mouth in horror.

William's eyebrows rose, and he looked at his roommate in concern. "How do you mean?"

Stanley looked at him, somewhat frightened. "Well, he is the heir, and he likes to get what he wants, even if it doesn't want to be given."

"Ah, I see," William said. "My father was much the same way. It's a shame to see all that potential wasted on someone with poor self-control."

This unexpected comment made Stanley look at William in astonishment. "My father says that it's his due as the heir."

William shook his head. "What does your mother say?"

"Not much," Stanley said sadly. "She is too afraid of my father."

Again, Stanley looked terrified at having shared something so personal with so little acquaintance. William's heart went out to the young man, and he gave him a kind smile. "I'm the heir to my cousin's estate, and I have always seen it as a responsibility, not an entitlement."

"You're the heir to an estate?" Stanley's mouth fell open. "But why are you at Oxford in the residences of those who plan to take orders?"

"I have always wanted to be a pastor," William said simply. "I feel called to help others, and my uncle Bennet, who is the current master of the estate, will be healthy for many years still. I have no desire to live a life of idleness when I could do good in the world."

Stanley sat in silent astonishment. Finally, he said, "My father wanted to purchase a commission for me. He thought it would make me stronger. My mother was able to convince him to allow me to take orders. She doesn't stand up to him often, but when she does, he listens."

"That is the mark of a good husband," William said. "My father was not that way. He espoused many of the beliefs that your brother appears to have, but it was not tempered by my mother's goodness, unfortunately."

"What happened to your parents?"

"They're dead," William said simply.

The two young men sat in silence, then Stanley said, "I'm glad you're my roommate. I didn't know what to expect, but I was praying that you would be kind."

William smiled warmly at his new friend. "That was my prayer as well. It appears the Lord has answered both our prayers."

Stanley smiled in return and sat up a little straighter. The defeat that burdened his shoulders seemed lifted, and suddenly William felt very hopeful about his time at Oxford.

Twelve-year-old Lizzy let out a sigh. "I miss William."

Jane looked up from her needlework and smiled at her sister. "I believe we all do," she said, nodding at eleven-year-old Mary, who stared morosely out the window.

Lizzy looked at her middle sister sympathetically. William had only been gone for a few weeks, and already Mary had seemed to wilt away over his absence. Prior to his departure, the two had often spent most of their time in conversation about the scriptures and religious works. His absence left a larger void in Mary than in the other Bennet girls.

Shaking her head to clear off her doldrums, Lizzy turned towards her sister. "Mary, would you like me to teach you how to play the pianoforte?"

Mary jumped slightly, startled at being addressed directly, and spun to face her sister with large eyes. "Really?" she asked in astonishment.

"Why not?"

"Lizzy, do you think yourself able to teach Mary? You did not spend much time with the music master," Jane said gently.

"Well, it is not my fault he decided to run away with one of his students!" Lizzy exclaimed. "I know all the notes and can play simple tunes. The only reason I am not a true proficient is that I do not take the trouble to practice," she added with mock conceit, lifting her nose in the air and looking down it at her sister.

Mary giggled and said, "Thank you, Lizzy. I believe I would enjoy that. May we start tomorrow? I would like to write to William and let him know!"

Lizzy smiled in acquiescence at Mary, who hugged her and ran off to her room. Jane looked at Lizzy and said, "That was very kind of you, Lizzy."

Waving her hand, Lizzy said, "I believe I shall benefit just as much as Mary, if not more so, because I will be forced to practice and improve."

Jane merely nodded in agreement and bent over her needlework again. She had become very focused on her household skills, as their mother had declared Jane was to come out to society the following year.

Elizabeth left Jane to her work and walked up the stairs to the nursery, where her mother would be with ten-year-old Kitty and eight-year-old Lydia. Along the way, she contemplated the way in which her parents had dealt with a child who was now old enough to come out in society.

Initially Mrs. Bennet had wished to have Jane come out at fifteen years old, but Mr. Bennet and William had convinced the woman that shy Jane would benefit from another year at home to learn how to run a household as well as her mother did.

This bit of flattery on her management skills was combined with William's statement that "none of the girls need be married off quickly. If all should choose to be old maids, I would gladly support them here at Longbourn forever!"

Although William had become one of the family the moment he came to Longbourn, Mrs. Bennet was still frequently concerned over her daughters' matrimonial prospects. The longer William had lived with them, the more her fears had abated. Still, she was very aware that a single woman had little place in English society, and her greatest desire was to see her daughters wed to men who would provide them with a life of ease.

Mr. Bennet, having left his indolence behind at his heir's arrival, worked to focus his wife's fears in a productive direction. When she spoke of her wishes to see her daughters married, he would make a remark that would motivate her to make changes. When she bemoaned the lack of marriageable men in the neighborhood compared to young ladies, Mr. Bennet would reply, "Our daughters would need to be very accomplished in order to attract any man's attention away from our neighbors," or "No man would wish to marry a spoiled child. It is good Lydia has time to grow out of that."

Her husband was pleased to see that these comments had pushed his wife in a more positive direction. While she would always be the same flighty woman he had married, her energies and nerves could be used in productive ways rather than causing turmoil and chaos.

As Elizabeth approached the nursery, she heard Lydia throwing yet another tantrum. She opened the door to Kitty in the corner, with tears in her eyes, on her mother's lap, holding a doll tightly to her chest. Mrs. Bennet was making soothing noises at Kitty while looking helplessly around the room.

Toys were strewn from wall to wall, and in the middle of the disarray was Lydia, who was lying on the floor, kicking her legs and screaming. "It's not fair!" wailed the child. "I want it! Make her give it to me!"

Mrs. Bennet hesitated and looked at Kitty, "Perhaps, Kitty, you could share your doll?"

Kitty shook her head emphatically as fat tears rolled silently down her eyes. "No, Mama! Please don't make me! Last time she played with Florence, she ripped a hole in the dress and stained her leg with tea."

"But I want it!" screamed Lydia, who had paused briefly to hear the conversation.

Mrs. Bennet looked wildly around the room, then finally saw Elizabeth. "Fetch your father," she mouthed.

Elizabeth turned and flew down the stairs towards her father's study. At this time of day, she knew he would have returned from visiting tenants and now be making notes in the estate's ledgers. It was a routine he regularly followed with William, and although the heir was away at school, Mr. Bennet was motivated to continue managing the estate in his stead.

After knocking on the door, she heard her father call for her to enter. She opened the door and said, "Papa, you must come quickly! Mama needs your help with Lydia."

"Where is the governess?" he asked in frustration.

"It is her half-day, Papa," Elizabeth replied. "Besides, she cannot teach all of us at one time, even if she were here."

Mr. Bennet let out a slow breath and said, "I simply do not know what to do with that child. The more she is corrected, the worse she behaves."

Not knowing how to respond, Elizabeth simply waited. He gave another tremendous sigh and lifted himself from his chair. "Very well, then," he said, straightening his waistcoat. "What is the trouble this time?"

Elizabeth explained the situation as best as she could while they climbed the stairs. Mr. Bennet's face grew increasingly grim as the noise from the nursery increased. They entered the room to find Mrs. Bennet offering different toys to Lydia, who responded by throwing them across the room and screaming in rage.

"Enough!" bellowed Mr. Bennet.

At the sound of her father's voice, Lydia froze. All eyes turned to Mr. Bennet as he surveyed the room with a grim look in his eye.

"That is quite enough out of you," he said sternly, fixing his gaze on Lydia. "This behavior has gone on quite enough and will no longer be tolerated. You are behaving worse than the youngest Lucas boy, and he is only two years old."

Lydia's wide eyes narrowed, and she opened her mouth to protest.

"Silence!" Mr. Bennet's voice thundered across the room. "You will *not* speak another word."

He turned to his wife and said, "Madam, would you kindly explain the situation?"

Mrs. Bennet hastily explained that Lydia had demanded to play with Kitty's doll, which had been a birthday present several months earlier from her uncle Gardiner. Lydia had taken the doll without permission earlier in the week and caused some damage, which led to Kitty's refusal to allow Lydia to play with it at all. This sparked Lydia's tantrum, which included throwing anything that her mother had used to attempt to pacify and distract Lydia.

Mr. Bennet's lips grew thinner in anger as he listened to his wife. Turning to his youngest daughter, he said, "Well, young lady? What have you to say for yourself?"

Lydia tossed her head and said, "Papa, it's not fair that she has a new doll while I do not! I am the youngest, and I should be allowed to play with it. She's getting too old for dolls, anyway."

"I see," Mr. Bennet said in a mild voice.

Certain she had convinced her father to her way of thinking, Lydia cast a triumphant glance at Kitty. Tears filled Kitty's eyes, and she looked pleadingly at her father.

"Lydia makes a valid point," he said, and Elizabeth gasped in dismay. "Kitty is getting older. For that reason, I think she should be moved out of the nursery and into a room with Mary."

Silence followed this announcement. Kitty's eyes lit up with excitement, and she said, "Really, Papa?"

He smiled kindly at her and replied, "Yes, my dear. It is clear that Lydia cannot be trusted, and it is unfair to you to have your things at risk. You and Mary shall share a room, and Lydia will be left in the nursery herself."

"La, what do I care?" Lydia said, tossing her head. "It means I shall have all the best toys for myself."

Mr. Bennet turned upon her, and her smug expression faltered at the look on his face. "Certainly not," he stated firmly.

She wilted slightly as he waved his arm around the room and continued, "You have demonstrated that you have no respect for toys or anything else. The nursery will be cleared immediately of all toys, which your sisters will choose from. The remaining items will be given to the tenants, who I am certain know how to treat them properly. All that will be left is your bed and a few items of clothing."

Lydia scrunched her face and opened her mouth, letting out a piercing scream of fury. It was immediately silenced when Mr. Bennet walked across the room, picked her up, sat on the bed, bent her over his knee, and gave her bottom one sharp smack.

Mrs. Bennet, Kitty, and Elizabeth gasped in shock. Not once had Mr. Bennet ever physically disciplined his daughters or his wife, although many men did so. Whether due to indolence or a gentle nature was unknown, Mr. Bennet had reached his limits with his youngest child.

Lydia's wail turned into sobs. Mr. Bennet gently lifted the child from his lap and placed her on the bed next to him, saying, "Lydia, your behavior is wild and uncontrollable. You cannot be allowed to continue in this manner or you will end up no better than a common fishwife."

He wrapped his arms around her in a hug; then he stood and crossed the room to his wife. "Mrs. Bennet, I believe it is time we hired a governess, for our youngest, who will specialize in her deportment. I only pray she is not beyond redemption."

He then rang the bell for Hill, who came quickly, having been listening in the hallway. She gave her master a deep curtsy of respect.

"Hill, I trust you heard the changes I am making to Kitty, Mary, and Lydia's room arrangements?"

"Yes, sir," she said, struggling to hide a smile of satisfaction.

"Please make sure they are completed before dinner. I will not subject Kitty to one more night at her sister's mercy."

Hill bobbed a quick curtsy, then immediately left the room to issue instructions to the maids and footmen. Her departure was immediately followed by Mary and Jane entering the room.

"What on earth?" gasped Jane when she spied her sister crying on the bed.

Mr. Bennet looked at his wife, Kitty, and Lizzy. "I shall leave you to explain the situation, Lizzy, as you have a bit more wit than the rest and should quickly regain the use of your tongue."

At this sardonic comment, Lizzy shook her head and said, "Of course, Papa."

"I shall be in my study, writing letters of inquiry for a firm governess, should there be any further need for my presence." Mr. Bennet gave Lydia a stern look, which caused her to shrink back and shake her head vehemently.

As he left the room, Lizzy began to explain in approving tones to Jane and Mary all that had occurred. He smiled as he heard Mary exclaim cheerfully at having Kitty share her bedroom.

Perhaps I ought to involve myself in the children's discipline more often! he thought as he descended the stairs and settled himself at his desk.

Chapter 6

Derbyshire, 1807

"Darcy, I came as soon as I heard. I am so sorry."

Darcy looked up and saw Wickham enter the door to his father's study. *My study*, he thought as another burst of sorrow welled up in his chest. The new master of Pemberley rose from the chair behind the desk and asked, "What are you doing here, Wickham?"

Ignoring Darcy's question, Wickham walked around the desk and wrapped his arms tightly around his friend. Darcy stood stiffly for a moment, then lifted his arms to return the embrace.

"Where else would I be?" Wickham answered after several moments.

Darcy stepped back from his friend and collapsed heavily into the chair behind the desk. "Your graduation from Cambridge is in two days. I expected you at school!"

"Nonsense," Wickham said firmly, crossing the room.

Darcy watched silently as his friend poured two brandies and brought them to the desk. He settled himself in the chair across from Darcy and pushed one of the brandies towards him. "You were there for me at my father's death; I certainly wasn't going to abandon you now."

Darcy nodded. "Thank you. I know your graduation was important to you."

"Pshaw," responded Wickham, waving his hand. "The certificate is what matters, not the ceremony."

The two remained silent, the brandies untouched on the desk, which prompted Darcy's mind back to those days of Wickham's rebellion.

After Wickham's disastrous first year at university, Darcy swore once again he would never allow himself to become inebriated, which led to him frequently declining even the mildest of alcoholic beverages.

Wickham's decision to eschew port, brandy, and other strong drinks did not come until the end of that summer, between his first and second years at Cambridge. Darcy remained true to his convictions and revealed all of Wickham's actions, including the unpaid debts he had attempted to escape.

The reaction from Mr. Darcy and Mr. Wickham were beyond anything either young man would have expected. Wickham originally attempted to charm his way out of the predicament when he was confronted, but the incontrovertible evidence in the form of the notes Darcy had purchased soon prompted Wickham into a petulant sulk.

"What does it matter if I claim to be Darcy's brother when none of us knows if it is false?" he burst out in anger after a quarter hour of lecturing.

Mr. Wickham turned white, whereas Mr. Darcy turned red.

"That may be the case," Mr. Darcy said coldly, "but no matter your parentage, you do not get to treat the livelihoods of men so disdainfully." Mr. Darcy turned to Mr. Wickham and said, "I believe my godson has not yet learned to appreciate the labors of those in the lower classes. Perhaps this summer can be a learning opportunity for him."

"I quite agree," said Mr. Wickham in a severe voice.

Wickham seemed to finally realize he had pushed too far, but his protests and pleas for a second chance were ignored. That very day, Wickham found himself in the cottage of Mr. Alvin Sykes, one of Pemberley's tenants who had recently broken his leg.

With only three young daughters under the age of eight, the recently widowed man had given over to heavy drinking. One day,

71

while inebriated, Sykes attempted to repair the roof of his cottage, lost his balance, and fell off. His eldest daughter had to fetch help, and the apothecary insisted the man remain in bed for three months, without any alcohol or laudanum.

Mr. Darcy had originally planned to hire a young man to take care of Sykes's farm, and Wickham's need to see for himself what hard work entailed made him an excellent candidate. Without so much as a by-your-leave, Wickham found himself dropped off by a mule cart. The three girls were then taken to stay with the pastor and his wife for the summer, leaving only Sykes and Wickham.

Thus began Wickham's reformation. At first, the young man rebelled at the grueling labor required to plow fields, care for livestock, and manage the household. He quickly learned, however, that if he did not work, he did not eat. Between witnessing Sykes's alcohol withdrawals and enduring firsthand the difficult life of the majority of Englishmen, Wickham ended the summer as a changed man.

His return to Pemberley the week before returning to Cambridge was a welcome relief for Darcy, who had spent his own summer studying at the hand of his father. Darcy dreaded the foul mood with which Wickham would return and feared their friendship over forever. However, when Wickham saw Darcy after three months of backbreaking work, his eyes filled with tears and all he could utter was, "Thank you. Thank you."

Darcy's astonishment turned to pleasure and relief at the return of his friend's former behavior. It was as if the year at Cambridge had never occurred—the two young men were once again the best of friends, and Wickham's newfound maturity and humility made him an excellent companion.

Old Mr. Wickham was gratified to see the changes in his son, and they came not a moment too soon. One day, while attempting to protect a tenant's young wife from her husband's beating, Mr. Wickham was struck on the head by the drunken man and died instantly. The man was prosecuted for his crime and hanged, much to the relief of his wife, who returned to her father's home to await the birth of her first child.

Darcy and Wickham delayed their return to Cambridge in order to bury old Mr. Wickham. The two friends stood silently with Mr. Darcy as the pastor conducted the funeral service. As the casket was lowered into the ground, Wickham collapsed to the ground and wept piteously. Darcy sank to his knees and placed his arms around his friend.

The lads were soon joined by Mr. Darcy, who embraced his godson and his son as they knelt in the mud by the grave. Wickham's muffled sobs were joined by the Darcy men's silent tears as they mourned one of the greatest men they had known.

A sudden noise at the door startled Darcy out of his memories. Wickham, too, jumped slightly as the housekeeper entered, carrying a tea tray. Spying the two glasses of brandy, she said, "My apologies, Master Fitzwil—I mean, Mr. Darcy. I shall take this away."

"No, no, Mrs. Reynolds," he urged, wincing inwardly at the appellation that had belonged to his father not three days before. "Please bring it in. I doubt we shall actually be drinking the brandy. We simply made it available, but neither of us has much stomach for it. Tea and biscuits sound much more appealing."

"I don't know why I even poured the stuff," agreed Wickham. "Why do you keep it in here, anyway?"

"My father liked being able to offer it to neighbors and visitors. He felt it was the gentlemanly thing to do, though you know he never drank it himself."

"Makes sense," Wickham said. "Probably best to keep it around, though Lord knows it will probably go bad long before either of us finishes it."

As the men spoke, Mrs. Reynolds approached the desk with the tea tray. She frowned at the mess of papers, looking for an empty spot on which to place the tray.

"Sorry, Mrs. Reynolds," said Darcy, shoving some papers to the side. "I don't even know what to do with all of this. I can't make heads or tails of anything."

Mrs. Reynolds set it down and said, "And I don't see why you should. You shouldn't be worrying about this, sir. At least wait until the funeral is over."

"I can't," Darcy said glumly. "There are some things that can't wait until tomorrow. The planting needs to begin, and if I wait too long, summer's heat will come and ruin it all. It's already been delayed because I can't figure things out, and there is no time to hire—let alone train—a new steward."

"A new steward?" Wickham said in surprise. "Whatever happened to what's-his-name?"

"Mr. Gordon's mother fell ill, and he left last week to tend to her. I received a letter yesterday that she has since passed on and left him a small inheritance, so he will not be returning. He is unaware of Father's death, or I believe he would have come back to help me. He knew Father was capable of handling the planting on his own, but I don't have the knowledge."

"Then hire me."

Fitzwilliam looked up at his friend, confused. "You? But what about your grand tour?"

"What about *ours,* you mean?" Wickham retorted.

"There is no possible way I could leave now, even if I were not in mourning," Darcy said, gesturing to the desk in front of him. "Not only do I have to manage Pemberley, but I could not abandon Georgiana at this time to make merry on the continent."

"And I refuse to go without my best friend; I'd have no fun without you," Wickham said firmly. "In which case, I will stay here as steward for as long as you and Georgiana need me. I daresay I know more about Pemberley than Gordon ever did."

Relief shone in Darcy's eyes. "In that case, you're hired. Only you must stay here in Pemberley and not in the steward's house. You are more brother than friend."

"Stay in Pemberley with servants and my best friend or live alone at the steward's house? Tough choice, Darcy. I don't know how I will ever decide." Wickham smirked at his friend.

As intended, Darcy chuckled. "It's the least I can do for ruining your graduation and your grand tour."

"Nonsense. There is nowhere else I would rather be," Wickham said sincerely. "Now, let's take a look at these papers, shall we?"

The two friends began systematically going through the former Mr. Darcy's desk. They spent the next several weeks looking over ledgers from previous years, riding the estate, and settling bills. They paused only to attend the funeral and spend time with Georgiana several times each day. The quiet twelve-year-old was rapidly approaching womanhood, and it was clear that she had taken the death of her father very hard.

Wickham and Darcy devoted hours to her amusement, and her every wish was immediately granted. She was a modest girl by nature, so it was rare for her to make a request. Her only desire was to begin taking lessons from a piano master, as she had far surpassed her governess's ability to teach. Letters were immediately sent out, and soon Pemberley was filled with hours of melodious sounds coming from the girl's fingertips.

A month after Mr. Darcy's funeral, Darcy and Wickham came to the conclusion that they would need to visit each of the Darcy properties in person in order to gain a full understanding of each estate and its needs.

"Think of it as our own grand tour!" said Wickham excitedly. "We can spend a fortnight in each location and return in time for the harvest here at Pemberley!"

Darcy had to admit that he found the idea appealing. "What about Georgiana?"

"We'll bring her with us," Wickham said. "After all, depending on whom she marries, you may choose to gift her an estate. She should be allowed to have her choice and could only do that if she sees all of them."

"When she marries?" Darcy repeated in surprise. "She is but twelve years old!"

"And that is three-quarters of the way to the age when most maids are thinking about husbands," Wickham pointed out.

Darcy let out a tremendous sigh. "I will need to speak with my cousin Richard. He has been assigned as her second guardian."

"Is he coming to visit?" Wickham asked.

"Yes, he just returned from the continent. His last battle injured his leg, and he has been recuperating at Matlock. I would invite him to join us for the summer, but I worry the travel will be too taxing for his healing."

"You could always make the offer and allow him to choose for himself which is best," Wickham suggested.

Darcy nodded in agreement, then said, "Each of the estates is in good enough condition for us to stay there, except for Larkwood."

"Is that the one in Northumberland?"

Darcy shook his head. "No, Staffordshire. The entire property is in a bit of disrepair as more tenants have moved to work in the cotton factories for a more stable income, and I do not know the condition of the manor house. From my father's records, it appears as though the local steward and butler had not sent a letter in quite some time. We may need to stay in an inn, and I would not like Georgiana subjected to such an environment for a long period of time."

"Staffordshire? Hmm..." Wickham mulled over the problem, then snapped his fingers and said, "I have it! I met a young man named Charles Bingley at Cambridge this past year. It was his first year, and as his family is from trade, I kept an eye out for him. I could write and ask if we could stay with his family until we determine if Larkwood is fit for residence."

"Would Mr. Bingley's family be willing to host a complete stranger?"

"I believe so. Bingley is of a friendly, open nature. He is eager to befriend and please those whom he meets, but in a genuine manner. He is not one to look to climb the social ladder. His father has built quite the inheritance and intends his son to purchase an estate with it upon his demise."

"A man without guile, it seems," Darcy said with a wry smile.

"Actually, yes, that describes him quite perfectly," Wickham assured his friend. "I believe he also has two younger sisters who are in finishing school but return home for the summer. He mentioned during the last week that he was eager to see them again. They would make good companions for Georgiana."

"Very well," Darcy said, "you may write your letter to Bingley. Perhaps we will have heard a response by the time Richard arrives. We can make plans then."

The letters to arrange the travel were dispatched quickly, and soon everything was arranged for their grand tour of the Darcy properties. Georgiana was eager, as she had rarely gone any farther than Lambton in her life. Major Richard Fitzwilliam arrived, gave his approval, and left again, as he was on his way to visit a military friend with whom he had served in Ramsgate.

Finally, the time had arrived for the Darcys and Wickham to begin their trip that would last about three months. Darcy could only hope it would all go according to plan.

Two months later

Darcy sighed in relief as their carriage pulled on the Staffordshire street where the Bingley's house resided. Their journey had been one series of mishaps after another, beginning with a broken wheel axle and ending with a sudden rainstorm that forced them to stop at an inn only an hour away from their destination.

Their arrival to Staffordshire, which was to be the last stop on their grand tour, had the three weary travelers in extremely high spirits. Georgiana had tolerated the journey remarkably well, due to

Wickham's hours of devotion for her amusement and the attendance of her governess.

Fitzwilliam had taken advantage of the travel time to finalize his notes from their prior stop and organize his thoughts for the next one. In each location, he had been very well pleased to find each manor and estate exactly according to the regular reports he received.

Larkwood was the estate that gave him the most trepidation, as there had been no report from its steward, butler, nor housekeeper in a six-month. Typically, Darcy would have sent a representative to bring back a report, but a combination of his father's ill health and death, the departure of the former steward, and the grand tour itself had delayed a visit. He was grateful that Wickham's friend was willing to let them stay there for an indeterminate amount of time.

The carriage pulled up in front of a well-maintained house, set comfortably amongst other fashionable houses on a street that was free of horse droppings. As the footman turned the handle to the carriage, the front door of the house was thrust open and a young man with a cheerful grin practically bounced down the stairs.

"Wickham, old chap! I'm delighted that you and your friends have arrived safely!"

Wickham exited the carriage, then turned to help Georgiana down. "Bingley, it's wonderful to see you."

The two men clasped hands, then Wickham performed the introductions. Bingley smiled at all of them, and he ushered them inside the house.

Darcy was pleased to note that the inside of the house was decorated in the latest fashion, although a bit more ornate than he preferred. It reminded him a bit of his aunt's, Lady Catherine's, formal sitting room, although that thought did more to unsettle him than give him any comfort.

A housekeeper began issuing directions to the maids and footmen about the luggage just as a young woman of perhaps twenty years of age came down the hall. "Charles, will you introduce me to your friends?"

"Of course!" Bingley beamed.

Introductions were made to Bingley's sister Caroline, who was younger than him by one year. She had recently come out into society the prior year and remained unwed after her first season. Darcy could quickly tell that she had adopted many of the mannerisms so common amongst the husband-hunting maidens in the ton.

Caroline was quickly joined by her sister, Miss Louisa Bingley. Miss Bingley, Charles informed them, was engaged to be married soon. Introductions were once again performed so Miss Bingley could know which guest was whom.

Upon learning Wickham was merely a steward, Caroline turned her back on the handsome man to converse more fully with Darcy. In response, Darcy continually directed the conversation to his sister and his need to get her settled from the journey.

Finally taking the hint, Miss Caroline issued a few unnecessary commands to the housekeeper, who was already beginning to usher the guests up the stairs towards their rooms. Bingley and Caroline followed, the latter continuing a stream of inconsequential chatter until Darcy politely excused himself and escaped into his sister's room.

Once alone, Darcy smiled reassuringly at Georgiana, who seemed quite overwhelmed by Miss Bingley and her chatter. "Do not be alarmed, dearest. I have no intention of falling prey to any machinations on this trip."

This comment startled a laugh out of Georgiana, who quickly covered her mouth and blushed in shame at having mocked her hostess.

"At the very least," Darcy said, "it will give you insight into the behaviors of many women in the ton. Although Miss Bingley is from trade, by this house and her dress, I imagine she has quite the dowry and was accepted into many houses from our circle."

"You will not leave me alone with her?" whispered Georgiana.

"Well," Darcy hesitated, "I must for at least one day when I go to

Larkwood with Wickham. I do not know the state of the house, and I would not feel comfortable taking you into an unknown situation."

When Georgiana bit her lip and looked away, he added, "Perhaps you could remain in your rooms while I am out. I can explain that you have developed a headache due to the travel."

Georgiana nodded vehemently, and Darcy laughed. He kissed her brow and left her to the ministrations of her maid while he went to his own rooms.

After assuring himself that his valet had everything in hand, Darcy went downstairs in search of Wickham. He found his friend-turned-steward in the drawing room, entertaining Bingley and his two sisters, along with an older gentleman whose appearance was so like Bingley's that Darcy knew immediately there was a familiar connection.

"Ah, Darcy!" exclaimed Wickham with a smile. "I was just telling the Bingleys about the time we snuck a pie that Cook had made for a dinner party your parents were hosting."

Darcy smiled wryly. "As I recall, *you* took the pie. I was the one who was unable to sit down for a week when my father was informed!"

The group laughed merrily. Bingley stood and said, "Mr. Darcy, may I present my father, Mr. Charles Bingley Sr."

Darcy bowed. "Thank you for allowing us to stay with you, sir."

Bingley senior crossed the room to shake his hand. "We are glad to host you," he said amiably. "I have appreciated the help your friend has offered my son at school. We are more than happy to return the favor."

Darcy returned the man's smile, then said, "I hope you do not mind if we go to Larkwood today. It has been many months since my father or I have heard from anyone there, and I am anxious to ascertain the state of things."

Bingley senior waved his hand dismissively. "Of course we do not mind! We know this is a business trip for you. You are welcome to leave your sister here with my daughters."

The man walked across the room to stand behind Miss Caroline. He placed his hands on her shoulder, and she leaned away slightly, then sat up straighter and offered Darcy a smile. "We would be delighted to have Miss Darcy join us," she said with an odd, tight smile.

Darcy looked at the man's hands. It almost appeared as if his fingers were digging forcefully into the girl's shoulders. But what reason would a man have to hold his daughter so firmly? *Perhaps she has a tendency to misbehave and he is reminding her to behave with decorum,* Darcy thought.

"I believe she has a bit of a headache after the travels and will keep to her rooms with her governess for the day, if that would not be an inconvenience," Darcy said.

"Not an inconvenience at all!" Bingley senior said jovially. "I will check on her personally later to ensure that all is well with her."

At this, Miss Caroline's eyes widened slightly in alarm, but she quickly bowed her head to look at her clasped hands. It was so brief that Darcy wondered if he had imagined the panic he saw in her face.

"I thank you," he said cautiously, "but I believe the governess has everything in hand. She will, of course, inform you if they are in need of anything."

Bingley senior's eyes narrowed slightly, but he smiled graciously. "Excellent!"

Darcy turned to Wickham, who had a slight frown on his face. "Shall we leave, then?" Darcy asked his friend.

Wickham nodded in agreement, and the two gentlemen took leave of their hosts. They mounted their horses and rode towards Larkwood, discussing various scenarios of what might be preventing the steward from sending any information.

What they discovered, however, was much worse than either of them expected.

Chapter 7

Darcy and Wickham stared at the Larkwood butler in disbelief. "You mean to tell me your master is in residence here?" Wickham asked incredulously.

"Certainly." The butler sniffed with disdain. "He is not at home at the present, but if you would leave your card, I will ensure that Larkwood's owner receives it."

Darcy raised an eyebrow and said, "May I inquire as to your master's name?"

The butler pushed his chest out slightly and said, "Mr. Darcy of Pemberley in Derbyshire."

Wickham burst out laughing, and the butler glared down his nose. Darcy smiled thinly and retrieved his card from inside a coat pocket. "I am afraid you may have been misinformed."

The butler looked at the name on the card, then paled. "I had not realized a relative of Mr. Darcy's was to visit. Please, allow me to show you to him in his study."

"I thought you said he was not at home," Wickham said sarcastically.

The butler showed the two men into the house. Darcy strode confidently ahead with Wickham, leaving the butler panting to keep up. After thrusting the door open, Darcy walked into the study. A thin man wearing spectacles looked up, startled. When he saw Darcy, he went pale. "Mr-Mr. Darcy," he stammered.

"Mr. Lowry," Darcy said coldly. "I have come to see why I have not received a report from you over the last year," he continued. "I was concerned for your safety, but here you are."

Darcy turned to the butler and said, "Send a footman to fetch the magistrate immediately."

The butler blinked in confusion. "I don't understand."

"Oh for heaven's sake, man!" exclaimed Wickham. "Mr. Lowry here is the steward. He has been passing himself off as Mr. Darcy, the *true* owner of the estate."

The butler gaped in astonishment at Mr. Lowry, who stared miserably at the desk. The truth was obvious, and the butler practically ran from the room to find a footman.

The magistrate quickly arrived, and Mr. Lowry was taken away. Wickham began reading over the estate books, which were in surprisingly good order. While Wickham looked at the finances, Darcy summoned the butler and housekeeper to begin to untangle the monstrous web of deceit that had been woven in Larkwood.

Night fell upon the estate, and Darcy looked at his watch. "I need to return to the Bingley residence," he informed Wickham. "I do not feel comfortable leaving Georgiana overnight with strangers."

"She has her governess with her," Wickham pointed out.

"I still feel uneasy about it. I cannot explain why, but I simply need to return," Darcy said. "If you prefer to remain here, I understand."

Wickham looked sharply at Darcy and nodded. "I will come with you, then."

After leaving strict instructions with the butler not to allow anyone entrance to the house, Darcy and Wickham saddled their horses and made their way to the Bingley residence. The journey only took a quarter of an hour as they rode at full gallop.

The two men arrived at the Bingley residence not long after the household had retired to bed for the night. A surprised footman answered their knock and admitted them into the house. They quietly made their way up the staircase towards their rooms, but they stopped at the sound of a woman sobbing.

A door opened to their right, and Darcy pulled Wickham back

into the shadow of the hallway. Bingley senior exited Miss Caroline's room, her sobs following as he closed the door with a grin. He adjusted his bedclothes, looked around, and sauntered off to his rooms.

"The bastard!" Wickham said with clenched teeth. "You were right to return, Darcy. Georgiana is not safe here."

"None of the young ladies are safe here," Darcy said grimly. "We'll speak in the morning about what to do to help. Unfortunately, there are very few legal recourses."

"In the meantime, you should have Georgiana's governess stay the night in her room," Wickham said.

"Oh, I will."

The two men went to their respective chambers, but their sleep was haunted by the echoes of Miss Bingley's cries.

The next morning, on the way downstairs to breakfast, Darcy instructed his sister's maid to begin packing her things. "We will be staying at Larkwood. Please inform Miss Darcy we will leave as soon as she awakens and is dressed."

He continued on to the breakfast room, where he found Wickham and Bingley. He glanced around the room to assure himself of Bingley senior's absence—as well as that of any servants—then made eye contact with his friend and gestured towards their host's son.

Wickham nodded and said, "Bingley, we were delighted to find Larkwood in excellent condition. Darcy and I plan on removing there with his sister sometime today. We would like to invite you and your sisters to join us."

Bingley's face, which had fallen at hearing of their departure, brightened immediately. "I say, that is very kind of you! I accept on behalf of myself, but I will need to speak to my father about my sisters' attendance."

Darcy and Wickham exchanged looks. After a few moments, Wickham said, "Bingley, you know I am your friend, right?"

"Of course!" Bingley immediately replied.

"I would never lie to you," continued Wickham.

"I never thought you would." A confused frown crossed Bingley's face.

Wickham hesitated, glancing once more at Darcy, then said, "Last night, when we returned from Larkwood, we came across your father exiting your younger sister's chambers. She was crying."

A sudden gasp caused all three men to jump. They spun around to face the door where a white and shaking Miss Caroline stood. When she saw their attention on her, she let out a low wail and ran from the room.

"Caroline!" shouted Bingley. He ran after her, pausing only to say, "I will return once I know what the devil is going on."

The door closed behind the young man, leaving Darcy and Wickham staring after the siblings in horrified silence. "Well, that did not go well," Wickham finally said.

"No, indeed," Darcy responded tightly. "I think it would be best for us to eat quickly while Bingley comforts his sister, then speak with him ourselves to assure him of our discretion and assistance."

The two men filled their plates from the sideboard and ate rapidly. Upon finishing, they made their way up the stairs. They heard shouting voices long before they reached the top.

"How could you *do* this to her?" Bingley's voice was filled with anguish and disgust.

Unwilling to interrupt the confrontation, Darcy and Wickham waited unnoticed at the entrance to the family wing.

"Come now, Charles," came the smooth voice of Bingley senior "You know you cannot believe what your sister says. She has always been high strung."

"You were seen leaving her rooms in the middle of the night," Bingley thundered. "I always knew Caroline and Louisa were desperate to stay at school over the holidays, but I never imagined it was because of your depravity!"

"What I do with my daughters is none of your business," snarled Bingley senior, the smooth façade giving way to the monster beneath.

"I am the head of this family, and I will do as I see fit. When I am dead, then you may deal with them how you wish."

"I am certain that can be arranged," Bingley said icily.

Darcy's eyebrows shot up, and he exchanged alarmed looks with Wickham. The two of them moved into the corridor. Bingley and his father were standing inches apart, faces read with fury. Miss Caroline stood at the door to her chambers, white-faced and trembling in her sister's arms.

Both Bingley men turned to see Darcy and Wickham. "Ah, gentlemen." Bingley senior's face and voice instantly became smooth and calm. "I apologize that you are witnessing a misunderstanding—"

"Don't bother, Father," Bingley spat out. "They saw you last night."

Bingley's senior's face went white, then red. "It doesn't matter," he snarled. "There's nothing anyone can do to stop me."

Bingley senior shoved his way past his two guests. As he reached the staircase, he turned around and opened his mouth to speak His sudden spin startled a passing maid, causing her to drop a pail of hot water that had been brought up the servant's staircase for a bath. The steaming liquid splashed over her master, who lost his balance and stumbled backwards.

Unfortunately for Bingley senior, stepping backwards meant stepping onto thin air. The man tumbled down, rolling backwards over himself until he reached the bottom step, where he lay unmoving.

The maid let out a piercing shriek and began to sob. Darcy, Wickham, and Bingley dashed down the stairs, treading carefully around the water before picking up speed again. The butler and a footman had already reached their master.

"Call for a doctor!" Bingley shouted, and a footman raced out the door. Darcy and Wickham knelt by Bingley senior, but it was clear there was nothing that could be done for the man. His neck lay at an unnatural angle and had no pulse.

"I'm so sorry," Wickham told Bingley, who stared at his father in shock.

Bingley looked down at his father, then up at his sisters, who were standing at the top of the staircase. "Is he… is he dead?" Miss Caroline asked fearfully.

"He is," Darcy responded after a moment's silence.

Miss Caroline burst into tears and collapsed to the floor. Miss Bingley, too, sank to her knees. Darcy saw his sister come to the staircase near the women, and Darcy hurried up the stairs to her. As he passed the weeping sisters, he heard one of them repeating in a whisper, "Thank you, Lord. Thank you."

Darcy sent Georgiana to her rooms, then turned to the terrified maid, who was still in hysterics. "I done killed 'im!" she wailed loudly in response to Darcy's questioning if she were all right.

These words startled Bingley from his shock. He looked down at his father, lips tightening in a disgusted grimace. He then came up the stairs and said, "You did *not* kill my father. It was an accident of his own making. You are not at fault, and I will make that clear to the magistrate."

As if summoned by Bingley's words, a knock sounded at the door, and the butler admitted both the doctor and the magistrate, who had met together for breakfast at the local inn. Statements were taken from all the witnesses, and the magistrate declared that it was an unfortunate accident.

After they left, Darcy gave the maid a guinea and told her she could rest for the day. This received an approving nod from the housekeeper, who bustled the young girl down to the kitchens. Bingley sent a missive to his father's solicitor, then asked a footman to fetch his sisters.

Darcy and Wickham went to excuse themselves, but Bingley said, "No, I would appreciate it if you would stay. I could use some support. I am at a complete loss, and you already know the truth of the matter."

"I am exceedingly sorry that our presence has caused this," Darcy said remorsefully as he and Wickham followed Bingley into a small parlor.

"No, do not apologize," Bingley said. "I can only feel gratitude that you did not stay silent. My poor, poor sisters. I had no idea, none at all."

"That is because we hid it," Miss Bingley responded.

The gentlemen turned in surprise, unaware that the Bingley girls had entered the room.

"Why would you not tell me?" Bingley asked, his voice breaking slightly.

"What could you have done?" Miss Caroline let out a harsh laugh. "Until we are married, we are under our father's control. Although now that he is gone, I do not think I ever want to marry."

"That is why I accepted Mr. Hurst's offer," Miss Bingley said softly. "I was going to take Caroline with me on the wedding trip, then insist she remain with me afterwards. Hurst's family has enough connections that Father could not have denied it without harming the business."

"Do you still wish to marry him?" Bingley asked softly.

Miss Bingley hesitated, then said, "Yes. To call off the engagement would forever ruin my reputation. He is kind, although he does drink to excess. I suppose we will have to delay the wedding, though, until the mourning period has passed."

"No!" cried out Miss Caroline. All eyes turned towards her. "I cannot bear to stay here—in this house, in those rooms, in that bed— one moment longer."

She buried her face in her hands.

"If I may," Darcy said with hesitation, "you could all be my guests at Larkwood. The estate seems to be in very good repair. It would allow you to leave this house and the memories while also allowing Bingley to be nearby to arrange things."

"I say, Darcy," replied Bingley with surprise, "that is very kind of you. What do you say, girls?"

The Bingley sisters looked at one another, then Miss Bingley said, "Thank you for your offer, Mr. Darcy. May we discuss things in private with our brother?"

"Of course!" Darcy instantly replied.

He and Wickham removed themselves from the room. While Wickham went to direct the loading of the carriage with their luggage, Darcy sought out his sister. Being full young, she did not understand all of what had occurred that day. Darcy simply told her that there had been an accident. She was very sorry for the Bingley family, as she knew what it was to be an orphan.

"I think it very good of you, brother, to invite them to stay with us. They must be quite distraught."

Darcy gently explained that Mr. Bingley Sr. was not as kind to his daughters as their own father had been, so his death was in some ways a relief. This knowledge caused Georgiana even more sorrow for the two young ladies, and she instantly resolved to be as good a friend as she could be.

A knock at the door brought their conversation to a close. Darcy left Georgiana to finish her preparations and joined Bingley in the hall.

"My sisters and I would like to join you at Larkwood today," Bingley said. "We will remain until it is time for me to return to school. Hurst will request a common license, and they will be married before I leave. Caroline will go with them."

"That sounds like an excellent idea," Darcy said. "Rest assured, you and your sisters will find peace and healing with us. I know I am a stranger to you, but you can trust in my discretion."

Bingley nodded. "I cannot begin to thank you enough."

"There is no need. The loss of a father is difficult enough, but with these circumstances, the matter is that much more painful. I am glad to do what I can."

One year later

"Are you certain you wish to do this, Bingley?" Darcy asked his friend as they exited their carriage at an inn.

The two men, accompanied by Wickham, were on their way to

Staffordshire. Bingley had recently finished his second year at Cambridge, and his two friends offered to stop by the school on their way to Larkwood for a quick visit. Darcy and Wickham were desirous to see that all was in order with the new estate manager, and Bingley wanted nothing more than to sever all ties to the county.

"Yes," Bingley said firmly. The men entered the inn and requested a private room for supper.

"I'm sorry, gentlemen," the innkeeper said regretfully, "but it has already been taken by a young man who arrived here about ten minutes before you. If you'd like, I can see if he would be willing to share it."

Darcy nodded in acquiesce, and the innkeeper sent a servant down the hall. While they waited, Bingley continued, "I want nothing more to do with Father's company. There wasn't enough time to sell it last summer before going to school. Now that all the arrangements have been made to bring the business up to snuff, I want to remove any trace of that man's influence in my life."

Bingley, horrified by what had been happening to his sisters, had vowed to do all he could to improve their lives. He increased their dowries, although Miss Caroline—who was now Miss Bingley after her elder sister's marriage to Mr. Hurst—still fiercely declared she had no desire to marry. The increased dowry provided enough income so she could establish her own household, should she ever choose to do so.

For the time being, however, Bingley's plan to sell the family business and purchase an estate was the last step in his journey to purge his father from his life. After the sale, he would continue at Cambridge for his last two years. Upon graduation, he would begin a search for an estate to lease.

The servant returned and whispered to the innkeeper, who once again approached the three friends. "The gentleman, a Mr. William Collins, says he would be delighted to have your company for dinner."

Darcy nodded, and the three gentlemen followed the servant

down the hall. As they walked, they continued their conversation.

"I think you are making the right decision," Wickham said. "You are getting a fair payment for your father's business, and this will allow you and Miss Bingley to make a fresh start in a new place."

"I just need to find an estate to let for a year," Bingley said glumly. "Most available estates are in disrepair."

This comment was made just as they entered the room, where a tall, heavy-looking man of around twenty-two sat at the table, tucking into a meat pie. He stood as they entered the room, then motioned for them to be seated at the table. As they took their seats, the young man requested that the servant to bring more food and drink for his guests.

"Delighted to make your acquaintance," he said cheerfully. "My name is William Collins."

Darcy, Wickham, and Bingley all introduced themselves. "Thank you for allowing us to join you," Darcy said formally as a servant arrived with more food for the increased party.

"Not at all, I assure you! I do hate eating alone, but I could not bring myself to eat out in the inn, either."

"It makes you too easy a mark," Wickham said approvingly.

"I also do not drink alcohol very often, and it was flowing a little too freely out there for my taste," Collins admitted with a frown.

Darcy and Wickham looked at one another in astonishment. "We do not drink, either!" Wickham exclaimed.

"Ah, it is always nice to meet a fellow teetotaler," Collins said with another smile.

The four fell into a casual conversation while they ate. The three friends learned that Collins had recently graduated from Oxford and was taking orders. "I'm the heir to my cousin's estate in Hertfordshire. He raised me after my parents died, but I have always felt called to the church. I am hopeful my cousin will live for many more years, so I will be taking the living near our home."

"Does your cousin not have any children?" Bingley asked.

"Five daughters," Collins said with a smile. "Unfortunately for them, the estate is entailed away from the female line."

"What brings you to Staffordshire, then?" Bingley asked congenially.

A shadow crossed Collins's face. "I was born here," he said after a brief hesitation. "My parents died when I was eight years of age, and I have not returned here since. I thought after graduation I would spend the summer here, then return to Hertfordshire."

"Where will you stay?" Wickham inquired.

"At one of the local inns, I imagine," Collins shrugged.

Wickham looked at Darcy, then said, "You must join us at Darcy's estate, Larkwood!"

Darcy's eyes widened, then he shot a glare at his friend. It was too late to object, however. "There is plenty of room," he said through gritted teeth.

Collins looked at the three men in surprise. "Why, that is quite generous of you indeed! I'm afraid I would not make for a pleasant companion, however. My memories of Staffordshire are not entirely pleasant, and I may be prone to needing solitude for quiet reflection. I would not want to put a damper on your house party."

At these last words, Bingley snorted into his cup. His companions stared at him as he began to laugh, the sound of which was tinged with a hint of mania. After a long minute, Bingley composed himself enough to say, "I apologize. It's simply that my last memories of being here are quite horrible as well, and I have been dreading making this visit. The closer we get to my late father's residence, the more depressed I feel."

"*Bingley,*" Darcy hissed sharply, darting his eyes at Collins. He had been unaware of his friend's feelings, as the younger man had spent their travels behaving with his customary jovial nature. For Bingley to be so expressive in front of a stranger about such a sensitive matter meant he was not as carefree as he appeared.

Bingley returned Darcy's glower with one of his own. "I decide whom I can trust. I *need* to speak about this with someone who can help me understand my father's sins. Who better than a man of the cloth?" Turning to Collins, he said, "Please join us."

Collins nodded hesitantly, his eyes scrutinizing Bingley. "Very well," he said slowly. "I cannot deny that I would appreciate some company. It would keep me from my morose thoughts. I only ask, in return, that you are honest with me about the nature of your visit."

This request made Darcy sit up straighter and sharply at the newly ordained man of the cloth. "I trust that such communications would be kept private?"

Collins's eyes widened slightly at the harsh tone. "Naturally," he assured them. "In fact, I will tell you my story first. Afterwards, you may decide how much you wish to tell me."

The four gentlemen spent the next quarter hour in quiet conversation. No one spoke as Collins related the story of his mother's health and his father's abuse. At the end of his narrative, Bingley shared all that was discovered in the final hours of his father's life.

At the end of Bingley's recital, Collins sat back heavily in his chair. "I see why you are struggling to return," he said to Bingley. "And why you were wary of my intentions," he added with a nod to Darcy.

The four sat in silence for several long moments. Finally, Collins said, "I think I will join you, my friends. I believe I can help you as much as you can help me during this journey."

Chapter 8

After dinner, Mr. Bennet sat by the fire in the sitting room with his wife and several daughters. The silence was soon interrupted by a high-pitched, girlish voice.

"My dear Mr. Bennet," said his wife, "have you heard that Netherfield Park is let at last?"

Mr. Bennet replied that he had not.

"But it is," returned the lady, "for Mrs. Long has just been here, and she told me all about it."

Mr. Bennet made no answer.

"Do you not want to know who has taken it?" cried his wife impatiently.

"You want to tell me, and I have no objection to hearing it," Mr. Bennet said sardonically as he turned a page in his newspaper and winked at Lizzy.

This was invitation enough.

"Why, my dear, you must know, Mrs. Long says that Netherfield is taken by a young man of large fortune from the north of England; that he came down on Monday in a chaise and four to see the place, and was so much delighted with it that he agreed with Mr. Morris immediately; that he is to take possession before the next assembly."

"What is his name?"

"Bingley, I believe."

"Is he married or single?"

"Oh! Single, my dear, to be sure! A single man of large fortune; four or five thousand a year. What a fine thing for our girls!"

"How so? How can it affect them?"

"My dear Mr. Bennet," replied his wife, "how can you be so tiresome! You must know that I am thinking of his marrying one of them. Well, all save Mary, of course."

"Is that his design in settling here, Mrs. Bennet? For he will be much sorry to hear that I only have four of my five daughters left."

"Design! Nonsense, how can you talk so! But it is very likely that he *may* fall in love with one of them, and therefore you must visit him as soon as he comes."

"I see no occasion for that. You and the girls may go, or you may send them by themselves, which perhaps will be still better, for as you are as handsome as any of them, Mr. Bingley might like you the best of the party."

At this wry comment, Elizabeth let out a burst of laughter, which she quickly turned into a cough that she covered with her handkerchief.

Mrs. Bennet laughed along with her second daughter. "You flatter me, my dear Mr. Bennet. When a woman is a grandmother, she should no longer think of her own looks and should instead focus on those of her daughters. Besides," she added with a small smirk at her husband, "if I were to run off with Mr. Bingley, who would keep Mrs. Hill from cleaning and organizing your study when you are out for the day visiting tenants?"

At this witty retort, Mr. Bennet chuckled and arose from his seat. He crossed the room and kissed his wife on the head fondly. "Depend upon it, my dear. I would miss you for much more than that."

Elizabeth smiled fondly as her mother blushed. Taking advantage of her mother's good mood, Elizabeth excused herself for a walk. As she donned her boots and bonnet, she smiled at the thought of how very differently the conversation could have gone had William not come to live with them over a decade prior.

Although she had only been four years of age, Lizzy had a very clear memory of when she met her cousin William Collins. It had been a terrifying experience for her, and it was indelibly fixed in her memory.

While she did not have a firm recollection of his appearance, she would never forget the nights for weeks after his arrival when the entire household awoke to his haunting screams of fright. The nightmares he experienced after his father's savage beating had convinced Lizzy that men who imbibed to the point of losing control were not men who could be trusted with the care of a woman or child. She was grateful her father and William were both very cautious in how much liquor they drank on the rare occasions they indulged themselves.

As Lizzy wandered down the path towards Oakham Mount, she thought absent-mindedly about William, who was now not only her cousin but also her brother.

Although he was almost of age to go to school when he came to live with the Bennets, William Collins was not mentally or emotionally ready to be sent away. Mr. Bennet did not have fond memories of how boys treated one another at Harrow, and Eton was much the same. As a result, Mr. Bennet personally instructed the young man until he was much older.

The time spent in the Bennet's home did much to heal William's soul. In a safe, comfortable environment, the young man thrived. While he would never be the most handsome or clever of men, he had a warm, gentle character. The servility that marked his behavior in the first year of his move to Hertfordshire was gradually replaced with confidence and kindness.

When William reached his majority, he continued to express a strong interest in taking orders and serving his Lord. In this, he was supported by his cousin Mary, who also felt a pull towards the words of the Almighty. Although she was seven years his junior, the two cousins became close through their common interests and could often be found pouring over the Bible as well as the diverse works of

Fordyce and Wollstonecraft.

When William returned from visiting Staffordshire after his graduation from Oxford at the age of twenty-two—only three years prior—he was surprised to discover his cousin Mary to be a nearly grown woman of fifteen years old. The friendship they enjoyed soon blossomed into romance, and the two were joined in matrimony the following year. Upon their marriage, William chose to take the last name of Bennet in honor of the family who raised him and from whom he would be receiving an estate. In order to avoid confusion, however, the majority continued to refer to him as William or Collins.

Most recently, Mary had given birth to a boy, Samuel Collins Bennet, named in honor of his grandmother Mrs. Samantha Collins. This birth secured the Longbourn estate for another generation of Bennets. Until such time as William would take over the management of Longbourn, he and Mary lived in the local parsonage, where William had been granted the living upon his graduation when the former curate retired.

Elizabeth smiled at the recollection of visiting Mary and Samuel the day before; Samuel had recently begun crawling, and Mary was constantly fetching the child from getting into things he ought not. Mary had confided in her that she thought she might be increasing again, which was both a surprise and a joy.

"Please do not tell Mama," Mary had begged, "as I cannot bear to think of her raptures over another grandchild when I feel so ill!"

"I won't say a word," Elizabeth assured her sister. "Would you mind if I wrote to Aunt Gardiner about it?"

Mary smiled and shook her head. "Not at all. I know how close you are to her. Just be sure to tell her to *not* make mention of it to Mama. Her delight will make my illness worse!"

Making a mental note to ask Cook to prepare some gingerbread for Mary, Elizabeth finished her climb up Oakham Mount. As she gazed down into the valley below, she saw three riders crossing Netherfield's largest pasture, one of whom was far in the lead. She smiled in response to the laughter she heard coming from the gentlemen and hoped they would prove to be as amiable in person.

Noting the high position of the sun, Elizabeth turned back towards Longbourn, taking one last look at the riders below.

"I say, Darcy, I do believe you cheated!" Bingley exclaimed with laughter as he caught up to his friend.

"How could I have cheated when you are the one who chose the horse?" Darcy protested in return.

"It's practically witchcraft the way you can get a horse to do your bidding," Wickham retorted as he followed behind Bingley. Turning to the younger man, Wickham added, "He was the same when we were boys. No matter which horse I chose for him, he would always best me."

Bingley shook his head in mock frustration. "Maybe I should choose a pony next time!"

The three men burst into laughter again, then urged their horses into a trot through the trees as they headed back towards Netherfield.

"What do you think, Darcy?" Bingley asked his friend eagerly. "Does it meet with your approval?"

"I daresay it does," Darcy answered, "but I hardly need give my approval when Wickham here has already assured the both of us that the estate was worth the price."

"When a gentleman is in desperate need of funds due to gambling, he is much more willing to negotiate terms," Wickham said modestly.

"I hope you did not give him too hard of a time," Bingley said in concern. "I would hate to take advantage of someone's misfortunes."

"Losing your inheritance with gambling is hardly a misfortune," Wickham said disdainfully. At Bingley's shocked expression, he added, "But no, you are paying a fair price to lease a good estate."

"It's a good thing Collins mentioned Netherfield in one of his letters," Bingley said. "I cannot wait to see the look on his face when we show up at the assembly tomorrow!"

"How do you know that he is not already aware of our visit?"

Darcy asked.

"Because he is an old, married man who avoids gossip in all forms!" cried Wickham.

"I may also have told him that we were settled in at Pemberley for the winter," Bingley said sheepishly.

Wickham's laughter caused Darcy's horse to startle and rear up. Bingley let out a shout as Darcy, who had carelessly loosened his hold on the reins after the race, went flying backwards and landed hard directly on his hind end.

Bingley and Wickham quickly dismounted. Wickham grabbed the horse's reins and calmed him while Bingley rushed to Darcy's side. "Are you all right, Darcy?" he gasped out.

Darcy began to rise, then groaned in pain. "I daresay I shall have a bruised *derrière* for quite a while, but there seems to be no permanent damage."

"You'll do anything to get out of dancing at an assembly, won't you?" Wickham chortled.

Darcy glared at his friend. "You keep your mouth shut. It was your levity that caused it in the first place." He turned and looked at Bingley. "Come on, then. Help me up."

Bingley reached out and helped Darcy up, biting back a grin as Darcy muttered a few choice oaths aimed at Wickham.

"You could always remain at Netherfield," Bingley suggested. "I am certain that Caroline would be more than happy to keep you company."

Darcy turned his glare towards the younger man. After her father's death, Miss Bingley had taken up residence with her sister, Mrs. Hurst. Upon Bingley's graduation, he had established a house in town and invited Miss Bingley to be his hostess. The young woman who once declared to never have any interest in marriage had changed her opinion, setting up Fitzwilliam Darcy as the hero in her story who had rescued the damsel in distress. His gentlemanly behavior had induced in her a type of hero worship, and he was the recipient of her sincere, devoted attentions.

Sadly, for the young lady, Darcy was not interested in marrying her. While he admired her for her fortitude and recovery, he did not have the same amount of affection for her that she had for him. There were very few similarities in their desires: she enjoyed town, while he preferred the country; she enjoyed going to parties, and he preferred to remain at home with a book.

Since he knew there was no chance of affection developing on his side, he took great pains to never give her any encouragement. He had seen friends in marriage of unequal affections, and such marriages were not agreeable to either party. No, he would not marry Miss Bingley for the simple fact that she thought herself in love with him whereas he knew he was not in love with her.

Despite his best efforts, Miss Bingley seemed unable or unwilling to recognize the lack of interest in her beloved. She continuously sought to make herself agreeable to him. It saddened Darcy; because he knew of the horrors she had endured, he could not bring himself to overtly reject her. He only hoped that her feelings would soon wane or that he would find someone to marry before her attentions became too obvious.

Bingley, of course, knew of his sister's admiration, but—like Darcy—he could not bring himself to crush her tender heart. Darcy had informed both of his friends that nothing would persuade him into matrimony with Miss Bingley, and Bingley was in whole-hearted agreement. She would not be able to make Darcy happy, which in turn would cause her to be miserable.

Darcy's groan of pain reminded his two friends that they would need to assist their friend in returning to Netherfield. Darcy rapidly discovered that walking was just as painful as riding, so they made their way on horseback to Netherfield as carefully as possible.

The following evening, Elizabeth Bennet looked around the assembly room at her friends and neighbors. She had just arrived her parents,

Jane, and Kitty; Mary would be coming later, while Lydia still had one more year until she would be allowed to come out to the neighborhood. Although she was saddened to miss out on the merriment, she was placated with permission to stay with her baby nephew at the Collins's home so Mary and William could attend.

After greeting Sir William, Elizabeth crossed the room to find Charlotte Lucas. She was eager to hear about the new tenants of Netherfield; her father had been too occupied with estate matters to pay his respects, and rainfall had prevented her from visiting Charlotte.

The two girls chatted amiably about the variety of rumors that had been circulating ever since the notice that Netherfield Park had been leased. Charlotte did not have much more information than Elizabeth, as Sir William's visit had gone unreturned. The Netherfield gentlemen were said to have returned to London in order to escort a large party to visit.

Suddenly, all chatter stopped as the doors opened to admit the newest members of Meryton society. Elizabeth looked over the newcomers, and her eyes fixed on a tall man with a somber visage moving stiffly alongside three other gentlemen and two ladies.

"The tall one must be Mr. Darcy," whispered Charlotte. "The younger man with the smile is Mr. Bingley, and he is accompanied by his two sisters. The elder sister is married to Mr. Hurst, the older gentleman. The very handsome one is Mr. Wickham, who is Mr. Darcy's steward."

Sir William, as master of ceremonies, bustled forward and began to introduce Mr. Bingley and his group to the partygoers. Elizabeth watched with interest, but her attention was called away by her mother's frantic beckoning. Rolling her eyes, Elizabeth joined her family, and her mother hissed, "What do you think, girls? Are they not the handsomest men you have ever seen? And the taller one has ten thousand a year!"

Elizabeth attempted to quiet her mother, but her efforts were in vain. Mr. Bingley's smile faltered slightly as they approached the Bennet family, and Elizabeth could tell they had heard her mother's vulgar remarks.

Introductions were made, and Mrs. Bennet put Jane forward as a desirable dance partner. Mr. Bingley immediately solicited her hand for the next two dances, and Jane blushed with pleasure. Mr. Wickham was already leading Charlotte Lucas to the floor, so Mrs. Bennet turned to Darcy, who said with clenched teeth, "Thank you, madam, but I rarely dance."

Darcy then gave an extremely short bow, excused himself, and walked stiffly across the room. "Well!" huffed Mrs. Bennet in annoyance. "Have you ever met such a proud, disagreeable man?"

Elizabeth murmured in agreement but was almost immediately collected by one of the Lucas boys, who had requested the dance with her. They enjoyed a lively reel, then he escorted her to some chairs on the side of the room while he went in search of his next partner.

She had been obliged, by the scarcity of gentlemen, to sit down for two dances; and during part of that time, Mr. Darcy had been standing near enough for her to overhear a conversation between him and Mr. Bingley, who came from the dance for a few minutes to press his friend to join it.

"Come, Darcy," said he, "I must have you dance. I hate to see you standing about by yourself in this stupid manner. You had much better dance."

"I certainly shall not. You know how I detest it, unless I am particularly acquainted with my partner. At such an assembly as this, it would be insupportable. Your sisters are engaged, and there is not another woman in the room whom it would not be a punishment to me to stand up with."

"I would not be so fastidious as you are," cried Bingley, "for a kingdom! Upon my honor, I never met with so many pleasant girls in my life as I have this evening; and there are several of them you see uncommonly pretty."

"You are dancing with the only handsome girl in the room," said Mr. Darcy, looking at the eldest Miss Bennet.

"Oh! She is the most beautiful creature I ever beheld! But there is one of her sisters sitting down just behind you, who is very pretty, and I dare say very agreeable. Do let me ask my partner to introduce you."

"Which do you mean?" and turning round, he looked for a moment at Elizabeth, till catching her eye, he withdrew his own and coldly said, "She is tolerable; but not handsome enough to tempt me; and I am in no humor at present to give consequence to young ladies who are slighted by other men. You had better return to your partner and enjoy her smiles, for you are wasting your time with me."

Elizabeth gaped in astonishment. She felt the heat rise in her face and heard a rushing in her ears. Torn between following the man to give him a piece of her mind or retreating from the room in tears, she took a few deep breaths.

Just as she regained her equilibrium, she heard a voice shout, "Collins!"

Elizabeth looked up to see her brother-by-marriage entering the room with Mary. Almost immediately, Collins was surrounded by the Netherfield gentlemen—save Mr. Hurst, who was securing a glass of punch at the refreshment table. Even the dour Mr. Darcy had a small smile on his face.

"What...? How...?" sputtered Collins.

"Surprise!" cried Bingley cheerfully. "Aren't you glad to see us?"

Elizabeth's eyes widened in surprise as her tall, heavyset cousin beamed with a smile she had only seen twice before: once on his wedding day and again when his eldest son was born.

"I cannot believe you all are here!" Collins exclaimed with heartfelt delight. "Mary! Look who it is!"

Mary smiled and said, "I can see that your friends are here, but I am afraid I have never had the pleasure of making their acquaintances."

Collins blushed slightly and said, "Oh, of course! These are the gentlemen who allowed me to stay with them when I visited Stafford-shire. Mr. Bingley, Mr. Wickham, and Mr. Darcy. Gentlemen, this is my wife, Mary."

Bingley then introduced his sisters and Mr. Hurst, who had since joined the group with his libations, to Mr. Collins, and the entire group moved across the room, which had fallen into quiet whispers. Collins led them over to Mrs. Bennet, where he reintroduced "his beloved mother" to the gentlemen.

Elizabeth was gratified to see Mr. Darcy pale slightly upon hearing Collins's relationship to the woman he had disdained earlier. He was still holding himself stiff and aloof, barely uttering a word or two at a time.

Her musings were interrupted by Charlotte's appearance at her side. "You did not tell me your family was acquainted with the Neth-erfield party!" she said in mock anger.

"I had no idea myself," Elizabeth cried defensively. "William never said a word to any of us."

Charlotte laughed. "Based on your cousin's expression, I think he had no idea of the acquaintance either. He certainly looked surprised when he came into the room."

"I supposed this means I must bear their company," Elizabeth said with a touch of bitterness.

"You do not like them?"

"It is not so much a matter of *them* as it is *him*. Mr. Darcy seems to think himself quite above his company."

"Well, my dear Eliza, he does have good reason. I understand from my mother that he has ten thousand pounds a year, plus a large estate in the north and half of Derbyshire."

"Then Derbyshire should keep him," retorted Elizabeth. She sighed and said, "Well, no matter. The other members of the party seem amiable enough. Jane certainly seems well pleased with at least one of them."

And indeed, Jane was very pleased with Bingley. Since their first two dances, he had scarcely left her side, other than to greet Collins. The two of them stood speaking quietly next to Mrs. Bennet, who was involved in conversation with Mr. Wickham and Kitty.

"Will you introduce me to them?" Charlotte asked Elizabeth abruptly.

Elizabeth looked at her friend in confusion. "Have you not already been introduced?"

"Well, yes, by my father. But it is not the same as being introduced as a particular friend of the family."

"Charlotte, are you trying to catch a husband?" Elizabeth began to laugh, but she immediately stopped when Charlotte's face crumpled.

"Oh, Charlotte," she whispered. "Pray, do not mind me and my foolish tongue. I would be happy to present you as a dear friend of the family to anyone you wish to encourage."

Charlotte blinked a few times, clearing her eyes of the tears that had pooled in them. "I am twenty-seven years old, Lizzy," she said, her voice catching. "It is not often that so many eligible men come into the neighborhood at once."

"I know." Elizabeth put her arms around her friend. "Let us go join my mother, and I will proudly declare that you are one of the best women of my acquaintance."

Elizabeth took her friend's arm, and the two girls crossed the room. "Hello, William, Mary," she said, nodding at each of them.

Collins turned from speaking with Mr. Darcy and said, "Ah, Lizzy! Come and meet my friends!"

"We have already been introduced," Lizzy said coolly to Darcy. Then, remembering her manners, she added, "Allow me to present my dear friend, Miss Charlotte Lucas."

Darcy gave a brief nod in response. Collins's eyes widened slightly at his friend's curtness, but he quickly turned so that Mrs. Bennet and Mr. Wickham could be part of the conversation. "Mr. Wickham, this is Miss Lucas, a close friend of the Bennet family. She is in the particular confidence of my sister, Lizzy."

Wickham smiled and said, "Yes, Miss Lucas and I shared a charming dance together! I have not yet had that pleasure with Miss Elizabeth, however. May I have the next two?"

Lizzy shot a look at Charlotte, whose smile was fixed on her face. This was not going at all the way it was supposed to!

"Of course," Lizzy said warmly. "Although I hate to leave Charlotte."

"We cannot have that," Wickham said, sending another charming smile toward Charlotte. He called to Bingley, who reluctantly left Jane's side. Upon being reintroduced to Charlotte, he immediately asked her to dance, and Elizabeth was satisfied she had done her best.

The remainder of the evening passed enjoyably for all except Mr. Darcy, who wished for nothing more than his bed and a dose of laudanum. Even Miss Bingley was caught smiling sincerely during a set with Wickham, who made every effort to bring joy to the face of each lady with whom he danced.

Chapter 9

The next morning, Elizabeth awoke earlier than her customary time. Although she had been up late at the assembly, the words "not handsome enough to tempt me" haunted her dreams. The crow of the rooster finally signaled the dawn—and the fact she could safely go for a walk. She had been staring at the ceiling for what seemed to be hours.

Elizabeth moved carefully so as not to disturb Jane, who had crawled into bed with her last night to discuss Mr. Bingley. "He's just what a young man ought to be, Lizzy," Jane had said. "He's sensible, good-humored, and lively."

Elizabeth put on an old dress and headed for the kitchens. She snatched a bun from the tray, gave Hill a small smile, and headed out into the brilliant sunlight. The birds seemed unaware of their friend's unusual scowl; their songs echoed in the morning air, and eventually the scowl on Elizabeth's face faded away.

The walk up to Oakham Mount did much to clear Elizabeth's head. Although her pride was still wounded from Mr. Darcy's remarks, she determined that she would no longer give the man any power over her. *After all*, she thought as she gazed down into the valley, *what are men to the beauty of nature?* A nearby squirrel chittered at her as if in agreement.

Slowly, Elizabeth made her way back to Longbourn. She knew there would be much discussion that day over the events from the previous night, and she was disinclined to think about the inhabitants of Netherfield any longer than necessary.

Elizabeth was surprised to find Collins and Mary already at the house, along with baby Samuel. "What brings you so early?" Elizabeth asked with a smile, taking her nephew from his mother.

"William wanted to hear everyone's impressions of his friends," Mary said, giving her husband a gentle smile.

"If they are such good friends, how is it that we have not heard of them before?" Kitty asked, joining the group in the breakfast room. She was followed by Lydia, who immediately filled her plate with bacon and eggs.

"I would be interested to hear this story as well," Elizabeth said, burning with curiosity. "The only one of your friends we have met in the past is Mr. Stanley—and that was only at your wedding, even though you have been acquainted for years!"

Collins sat at the table and buttered a slice of bread. "I met Darcy, Wickham, and Bingley when I went to Staffordshire after graduation. Darcy's father had passed away a few years prior, and he and Wickham were extremely occupied with estate matters. Bingley's father had also just passed away, and he was travelling for business as well. We met at an inn, discovered we had much in common, and they invited me to join them at Darcy's estate while I visited my birthplace."

"I thought Mr. Darcy's estate was in Derbyshire." Elizabeth frowned.

"He owns several estates; Pemberley, his home, is in Derbyshire. He has another—Larkwood—in Staffordshire," Collins explained.

"He must be quite rich!" exclaimed Lydia, just as her mother entered the room with Mr. Bennet and Jane.

"Who is rich?" Mrs. Bennet demanded to know.

Collins cleared his throat and looked somewhat sternly at Lydia. "Yes, it is true that Darcy is the owner of multiple estates and has a substantial income. Wickham acts as his steward, though they have been friends since childhood. Bingley, the son of a wealthy tradesman, is looking to purchase an estate. All these facts, however, do not make them of any more worth. What I value most about them is their character."

Lydia looked at her plate, a bit shamefaced. Elizabeth spoke hastily to give her youngest sister some time to regain her composure. "You did not answer as to why we have not met them before."

"Indeed!" cried Mrs. Bennet. "Really, William, it is too cruel of you! Why have you not put my daughters into the paths of these rich men?"

William shot Elizabeth a look as if to say, *Now do you understand why not?*

Elizabeth bit back a smile as he said, "They have been much too occupied with personal and business affairs to come this far south. I did, however, mention Netherfield being empty in one of my last letters to Bingley. I had no idea he would come to the place without informing me first."

"What a good joke!" cried Lydia, clapping her hands and bouncing slightly in her seat.

Elizabeth and Jane smiled at one another over Lydia's childish actions. Although her behavior had improved significantly since the day their father had turned her over his knee, she still had more energy and enthusiasm for life than all her sisters combined.

The chatter continued until everyone had finished breakfasting, at which point they retreated to the parlor wherein they would await the traditional call from the Lucas family. As expected, Lady Lucas and her daughters—Charlotte and young Maria—arrived to discuss the events from the night before.

"You began the evening well," Mrs. Bennet said kindly to Charlotte, who blushed faintly under the praise. "You were Mr. Wickham's first choice!"

"Yes, and Jane was clearly Mr. Bingley's favorite," responded Charlotte with a smile at Jane.

"She most certainly was," Mrs. Bennet said with a satisfied smile. "I believe he admired her very much. How could he not with her beauty?"

"Mama, please," Jane said quietly, her face red with embarrassment.

Ignoring her daughter, Mrs. Bennet continued. "Now as for Mr. Darcy! Well, I must say I have never met a more disagreeable man."

"Madam!" exclaimed Collins, who had sat quietly in the corner of the room. "Mr. Darcy is one of the most honorable gentlemen of whom I have had the pleasure to meet!"

Mrs. Bennet flushed. "He slighted poor Lizzy, you know."

All eyes turned towards Elizabeth, who frowned at her mother. "Now, Mama, how did you hear about that? I did not tell anyone, especially once I discovered William's connection with the man. I would not have my brother embarrassed by the poor behavior of someone with whom he claims a strong acquaintance."

Ignoring the subtle hint, Mrs. Bennet declared, "Mrs. Long heard every word!" and proceeded to share the entire conversation between Bingley and Darcy. She finished by saying, "Now, I know my Lizzy isn't quite the beauty Jane is—after all, no one could be—but no one can say Lizzy is merely tolerable unless he is either blind or peevish."

By the end of the tale, Mr. Collins's lips were pressed together in a firm line, and more than one member of the group had an angry expression on their face. Mrs. Bennet nodded in satisfaction at the reactions to her story.

"And that was the end of it!" Lizzy laughed, desperate to change the topic of conversation. "I assure you, I will not allow his words to upset me. I greatly enjoyed meeting the acquaintance of others in the party, and the assembly was delightful in every way!"

Smiles formed on the faces of those in the room, and the discussion moved away from Mr. Darcy and his behavior. Elizabeth let out a sigh of relief and took a sip of her tea. While she listened to a conversation between her mother and Lady Lucas about Mr. Wickham's prospects, Collins moved across the room to join Elizabeth at the settee.

"My dear sister," began Collins, settling his large frame next to her slight one, "I cannot begin to apologize for my friend's behavior. I do not know what came over him, but I beg you to know that this would be the first time I have heard any kind of ungentlemanly behavior from the man."

"I am sure it is so," she hastened to assure him, although she privately had her doubts. She had not missed the way the man winced when Collins had clapped him on the shoulder in welcome.

Collins smiled at her. "You forget, Lizzy, that I know you. You will be polite because he is my friend, but you will not actually change your opinion of the man."

Elizabeth smiled back. "Perhaps," she admitted.

"All I ask is that you keep an open mind about him. I believe Aunt Gardiner would tell you the same, were you to ask in your next letter to her."

"I will keep an open mind," she assured him. *But I will not promise anything. He must prove that he is worthy of my cousin's friendship. William is the kindest man I know; I would hate for his generous nature to be taken advantage of by a man whose pride will not even allow him to dance with me!*

The ladies of Longbourn soon waited on Netherfield, and the visit was returned in kind. Jane's gentle nature and pleasing manners soon caused Miss Bingley and Mrs. Hurst to declare their new friend "the sweetest girl in the world."

While Jane accepted their friendship with the greatest pleasure, Elizabeth was not so persuaded. She thought she detected a hint of artificiality in their smiles whenever they conversed with her, and more than once, she witnessed a supercilious look whenever their mother joined the conversation.

Collins often accompanied the Bennet women to visit Netherfield—at least whenever his duties in the parish would allow it. When he was in attendance, the men often retreated into the study. If he were not in attendance, the men were often out shooting or touring the grounds of the estate.

Elizabeth had a sneaking suspicion that the Bingley sisters were doing all they could to keep their brother from her sister. Whenever Bingley happened to call at Longbourn along with his sisters, they often kept their visits short. If he did not accompany them, however, the ladies' conversations with Jane would last long past the traditional fifteen minutes.

After one such call, Elizabeth made mention of her suspicions to Charlotte Lucas, who agreed with Elizabeth's assessment.

"Bingley does like your sister, undoubtedly. However, if she does not show more affection than she does, she may lose him."

"Show more affection?" exclaimed Elizabeth in astonishment. "My dear Charlotte, if he cannot see her regard for him, then he must be a simpleton."

"But remember, Eliza, that he does not know Jane's disposition as you do. She should make the most of every half hour she has in his company."

"Your plan is a good one," replied Elizabeth, "if her only desire were to be married. As yet, she cannot be certain of the degree of her own regard, and she does not know his character."

"If she were to marry him tomorrow, I should think she had as good a chance of happiness as if she were to have studied him for an entire year. Happiness in marriage is entirely a matter of chance, and it is better to know as little as possible of the defects of the person with whom you are to pass your life."

"You make me laugh, Charlotte, but you know you would never act this way yourself!"

"Believe me, Eliza, if any gentleman had spent as much time with me as Mr. Bingley has with Jane, the banns would be posted already."

"It has barely been a fortnight!"

"Yes, and she has danced four dances with him at Meryton, seen him one morning at his own house, dined in his company four times, and received two calls at Longbourn. That is more than enough time to get a measure of his disposition."

Elizabeth laughed at her friend's earnest statement, although she was not entirely certain if Charlotte truly believed what she was saying.

Occupied in observing Mr. Bingley's attentions to her sister, Elizabeth was far from suspecting that she was herself becoming an object of some interest in the eyes of his friend. Mr. Darcy had at first scarcely allowed her to be pretty; he had looked at her without admiration at the assembly; and when they next met, he looked at her only to criticize.

What Elizabeth was not aware of was the great amount of physical pain Darcy had felt at the assembly. His fall from the horse left him unable to walk well, and the stiffness continued as the days progressed. He had dismissed her as not handsome enough to tempt him, but the truth was that *no* woman could have persuaded him to dance when he could scarcely put one foot in front of the other.

No sooner had he made it clear to himself and his friends that she had hardly a good feature in her face, he discovered her beauty greatly enhanced by the intelligent expression in her dark eyes. This made way for other discoveries, such as the lightness of her form when she danced, the joy in her laughter, and her easy playfulness towards others.

He began to wish to know more of her, and an opportunity presented itself at Sir William Lucas's home, where a large party was assembled to dine. Included in the company was Colonel Forster, the leader of a militia regiment who was to remain in Meryton the entire winter.

Darcy watched nearby as Elizabeth conversed with the colonel. Eager to hear what was causing her eyes to brighten during the conversation, he took an inadvertent step closer to her. In doing so, he drew her notice.

"Did you not think, Mr. Darcy, that I expressed myself uncommonly well just now in requesting Colonel Forster to host a ball for us in Meryton?"

Darcy could not help but appreciate the spark of defiance in her eyes, and he flattered himself that she was looking for a reason to include him in her conversation.

"A ball is one of the many topics of conversation with which a woman can express herself vociferously without judgment of society," he said. "However, some may prefer rational conversation to dancing as the order of an evening."

"You are quite severe on us," Elizabeth retorted, eyes flashing dangerously.

Charlotte interjected, "And now it is your turn to be teased, Eliza. I am going to open the instrument."

Darcy watched in consternation as Elizabeth was led to the piano. Her performance was pleasing, but by no means was she a prodigy. The warmth of tone and expression as she sang and played, however, caused him to feel as though he had rarely heard any performance give him such pleasure. *That her bosom rises each time she draws breath has no influence on my admiration*, he told himself. *I am as impartial and objective as I always am.*

After Elizabeth completed her songs, Mary took her seat at the piano. "Oh, Mrs. Collins, will you play a jig?" begged young Maria Lucas, who had just come out.

Mary smiled and nodded, seamlessly switching to a lively tune. Darcy looked on in indignation at such a mode of passing the evening. So great was his annoyance that he failed to notice Sir William approach him.

"What a charming amusement this is for young people, is it not, Mr. Darcy?" the jovial man inquired.

Darcy simply nodded.

"Your friends perform delightfully," Sir William continued, gesturing towards Jane and Bingley on the floor, accompanied by Wickham and Charlotte. "I have no doubt you are adept at the science as well."

"It is a compliment which I never pay to any place if I can avoid it," Darcy responded shortly, acutely aware of the ache that lingered in his backside.

At that moment, Elizabeth walked past the two gentlemen. Sir William seized upon the opportunity and cried, "My dear Miss Eliza, why are you not dancing? Mr. Darcy, you must allow me to present her to you as a very desirable partner! You cannot refuse to dance, I am sure, when so much beauty is before you!"

Elizabeth quirked an eyebrow at the word "beauty," and Darcy blushed slightly. *Did she hear me that night?* Realizing there was nothing else he could do—embarrassing himself by admitting his pain and its location was unacceptable—he requested the honor of her hand.

"Indeed, sir, I have not the least intention of dancing. I entreat you not to suppose that I moved this way in order to beg for a partner," she said, eyes widening then narrowing in turn.

"Nonsense, my dear!" cried Sir William. "You excel so much in the dance, and who could object to such a partner?"

Elizabeth looked away archly and turned, begging to be excused. She crossed the room and offered to turn the pages for her sister.

Darcy was unoffended by her resistance; in fact, he was in some shock. He had never had a woman refuse his offer to dance before! Miss Bingley, who had remained close to her sister, immediately moved to his side. "I can guess the subject of your thoughts," she said with a winning smile.

"I should imagine not!" he said in surprise.

"You are considering how insupportable it would be to pass many evenings in this manner. I am quite of your opinion. The society here is nothing compared to the elegant manners found in town!"

"You are entirely wrong, I assure you. My mind was more agreeably engaged. I have been meditating on the very great pleasure which a pair of fine eyes in the face of a pretty woman can bestow," he responded coolly.

"Indeed!" she exclaimed, face alit with joy. "Might I inquire as to whom the eyes belong?"

"Miss Elizabeth Bennet," he said shortly, then mentally kicked himself.

"I... I see," she said, face falling. Out of the corner of his eye, he saw her blink rapidly. "I wish you every happiness," she choked out before fleeing from his side to her sister's.

Darcy's compassion was unmoved; indeed, his feelings were those of some satisfaction. Although he had no serious intentions towards Elizabeth, it was no hardship to put an end to Miss Bingley's imaginations once and for all. He was so busy congratulating himself that he failed to notice Elizabeth's glittering eyes taking in the entire scene.

From her place at the piano, Elizabeth could only guess as to what had occurred between Darcy and Miss Bingley. It had been clear to Elizabeth since their first acquaintance that Miss Bingley had tender feelings towards the man. *What could he have said to cause such a poised young lady to flee his side in tears?* Elizabeth wondered.

Although she had little fondness for Miss Bingley and her false friendship towards Jane, Elizabeth could not help but feel compassion for the lady. She resolved then to show the utmost kindness to the woman in future meetings.

Chapter 10

Elizabeth's resolution to be more kind to Miss Bingley was almost immediately put to the test the following week. Miss Bingley and Mrs. Hurst had sent an invitation to Jane for a private dinner while the gentlemen dined with the officers. Mrs. Bennet, upon spying rain clouds, insisted Jane travel on horseback.

Mr. Bennet was out with Collins at the time, and there was no one else to take Mrs. Bennet in hand before Jane was forced to leave. Mrs. Bennet eagerly saw her daughter off with many cheerful predictions of rain. Her hopes were answered; not long after Jane left, the rain began and continued throughout the entire evening.

Mr. Bennet and Collins were quite upset with Mrs. Bennet when they returned from the fields, but by then, there was nothing that could be done. The next morning at breakfast, Elizabeth received a note wherein Jane said that she was feeling unwell with a sore throat and headache.

"Well, my dear," said Mr. Bennet, when Elizabeth had read the note aloud, "if your daughter should have a dangerous fit of illness—if she should die—it would be a comfort to know that it was all in pursuit of Mr. Bingley and under your orders."

"Oh, Mr. Bennet," his wife said scathingly. "People do not die of little trifling colds. She will be taken good care of. As long as she stays there, it is all very well."

Elizabeth, feeling anxious about her sister, determined to go to Netherfield on foot. Her mother bemoaned the state of her dress, but Elizabeth refused to be moved.

"Three miles in some dirt is nothing, and I will be fit enough to see Jane," Elizabeth declared.

"We will go as far as Meryton with you," said Kitty. "Lydia and I wish to visit Mary and our Aunt Phillips."

"As well as see the regiment," Lydia said with a twinkle in her eye.

The three set off, and soon they were at Meryton. Lydia and Kitty waved goodbye as they entered Mary's home, and Elizabeth set out towards Netherfield on her own. Impatient to see her sister, she crossed fields and jumped over stiles into puddles. She arrived at the estate with muddy boots and a flushed face.

The butler showed her to the breakfast parlor, where the entire party was assembled. Bingley and Wickham received her with good humor while Miss Bingley eyed her petticoat with a slight sneer. Elizabeth asked after her sister, and she was saddened to hear that Jane had slept ill and was very feverish.

Bingley personally escorted Elizabeth to Jane's room, where she found her sister in bed with a violent cold. Mr. Jones had prescribed some draughts and bedrest, but in spite of that, her head ached acutely. Elizabeth spent much of the day in Jane's room, and eventually they were joined by Miss Bingley and Mrs. Hurst.

When the clock struck three, Elizabeth felt she must leave. Miss Bingley offered the carriage, but Jane expressed such dismay at her sister's absence that the invitation was converted into an offer to stay for the duration of Jane's illness. Elizabeth gratefully accepted, and a servant was dispatched to fetch clothing for her stay.

An hour later, Miss Bingley and Mrs. Hurst retired to change for dinner, and shortly thereafter, Elizabeth herself was summoned down to eat. She had much preferred to stay with her sister, but Jane felt that it would be rude to avoid the company.

The dinner was surprisingly cheerful, with Wickham and Bingley carrying much of the conversation. The ladies laughed frequently as the two gentlemen related several humorous experiences. Even Darcy was seen showing a few wide smiles, which somewhat unnerved Elizabeth.

Shortly after completing her meal, Elizabeth excused herself to check on Jane and retire for the evening. As she left the room, she heard Miss Bingley say to Darcy, "What could she have been thinking, scampering about the county because her sister has a cold? She looked positively wild! With her hem six-inches deep in mud, I'm sure her behavior must have affected your opinion of her fine eyes, Mr. Darcy."

Elizabeth froze, awaiting his answer. "Not at all," he said mildly. "They were brightened by the exercise."

Gasping softly, Elizabeth rushed up the stairs. She was grateful to find Jane asleep because she needed time to compose herself. *Fine eyes? Surely he must have been jesting, as I know from his own words that I am not handsome enough to even tempt him to a dance.* Having settled on this explanation, her sleep was still interrupted with dreams of Darcy's unnerving gaze following her around the room.

The next morning passed much as the previous day had: the gentlemen went out shooting and the ladies passed the time with Jane. After luncheon, however, Jane quickly fell asleep. Miss Bingley and Mrs. Hurst excused themselves to the music room, and Elizabeth was left to her own devices.

Having heard Wickham tease Bingley about his lack of library compared to Pemberley's, Elizabeth was not hopeful of finding any diversion in the room. She soon grew bored with needlework, however, and set forth in search of something to occupy her time.

Elizabeth scanned the dusty shelves of the Netherfield library. To her surprised delight, she found a copy of Mrs. Radcliffe's *Romance of the Forest* stuffed between two books on animal husbandry. *Well, at least there is a slight connection between the two subjects*, she thought a bit naughtily, then blushed and looked around as if someone could read her thoughts.

She had been eager to read Mrs. Radcliffe's novel, but her father rarely approved book purchases that did not in some way improve his children's education. A gothic novel was certainly not something he would allow.

Within minutes, Elizabeth was lost to the harrowing adventures of Adeline with the La Motte family. She was so engrossed in her tale that she failed to notice Darcy enter the room.

Darcy, on the other hand, was immediately aware of Elizabeth's presence on the window seat. Her feet were tucked underneath her dress, and one finger anxiously twirled an errant curl in between turning the pages.

Selecting a book from the shelf, Darcy took a seat on an over-stuffed chair directly across the room. He attempted to read, but his eyes kept straying to the lady directly across from him. Upon discovering that he had read the same page three times without actually comprehending the information, he gave into the temptation to simply stare at her.

Several minutes passed in silence, with only the occasional gasp or turn of the page from her lips. Becoming uncomfortable in his seat, he shifted slightly. The movement caused her to startle and drop her book.

"Mr. Darcy!" Elizabeth exclaimed. "I did not hear you enter the room, sir!"

"My apologies," he replied formally. "It was not my intention to startle you. I was merely perusing the latest reports on crop rotation."

She laughed nervously and bent to pick up her book. This allowed him an unintentionally provocative view of her form, which caused him to shift uncomfortably again.

"Are you using crop rotation at your estate?" she asked.

"A bit," he responded. "Are you familiar with the practice?"

"Yes, Papa and William have been determining which plants will grow best in our climate as many of the pamphlets they have read apply more to the northern counties."

Darcy nodded in agreement. "I would be happy to discuss what I have learned with them, if they are interested. The majority of my estates are in the north, so my information may not be of any more use than what they have already read."

"That is kind of you, sir. I will pass that along to them." She hesitated, then ventured, "I am somewhat surprised you have not spoken about this already with William, given your friendship."

Darcy smiled slightly. "Our friendship is of a peculiar kind. I believe he and Bingley share the most in common with one another."

Elizabeth bit her lip, causing his heart to jump slightly. She opened her mouth as if to inquire more but was interrupted.

"Oh, Mr. Darcy! Here you are!" Miss Bingley's cloying voice entered the room before she did. She stopped upon seeing Elizabeth in the room as well. "Oh, Miss Eliza—I had not realized you were in here as well. Is Jane quite well enough for you to abandon her company for that of Mr. Darcy's?" she tittered.

"I left her sleeping comfortably with a maid, who will fetch me if she awakens or appears uncomfortable," Elizabeth said with a small smile.

Miss Bingley wrinkled her nose. "How... wonderful." She then turned attention to Mr. Darcy and smiled coyly. "I am sorry my brother has such a poor collection of books for your entertainment. Hopefully you will not think too harshly of my abilities as hostess."

"Not at all, madam," Darcy said. "I have brought several from my own personal collection, and I find there are some on these shelves about estate matters that I have not seen before."

"Oh, how odious it must be, to always be thinking of your estate! Certainly, as a gentleman of some means, you must find time to enjoy with your friends," Miss Bingley responded.

"Yes, I have enjoyed my time with Bingley very much," he responded coolly.

Miss Bingley's face fell at this, and Elizabeth's heart could not help but twinge in sympathy for the lady. It was clear that she admired Mr. Darcy very much, but it was also equally clear that he did not return her regard in the slightest.

He need not make his disdain so obvious! she thought, fists clenching her book tightly.

The slight movement caught Darcy's eye. *She is just as annoyed about our private conversation being interrupted as I am*, he thought with satisfaction.

Elizabeth couldn't bear to see Miss Bingley's sorrow. "I cannot thank you enough for allowing me to stay with my sister. You are an excellent hostess," Elizabeth said.

Miss Bingley blinked in surprise. "Why, thank you, Miss Elizabeth. Your sister is a dear, sweet girl. It is a shame she feels so unwell.

"Poor Jane does not recover quickly when she is ill," Elizabeth said. "I am grateful at how quickly you called for Mr. Jones. Your thoughtfulness does you great credit."

A genuine smile crossed Miss Bingley's face for the first time since she had arrived in Hertfordshire. "It is the least I can do."

At that moment, a footman knocked on the door. He cleared his throat and said, "Begging your pardon, Miss Elizabeth, but the maid has asked me to inform you that your sister has awakened."

"Oh, thank you!" Elizabeth said. She laid the book to the side, then paused. "Miss Bingley, would you mind if I took this book to my rooms? I would like to finish it before I leave Netherfield."

"Of course," Miss Bingley responded graciously. "I will accompany you to see your sister, if that is all right?"

"Certainly!" said Elizabeth with surprise. The day prior, Miss Bingley had done all she could to avoid the sick room once Elizabeth had arrived.

The two ladies left Mr. Darcy in the library and went above stairs.

A maid was sent to fetch Mrs. Hurst, and the four women enjoyed a comfortable conversation. Elizabeth recalled the vow she made at Lucas Lodge to be kinder to Miss Bingley, and she made every effort to sincerely recognize the young woman's admirable qualities.

She can be quite witty when she isn't trying to show herself above her company,

Elizabeth thought as Miss Bingley described an ardent—yet foolish—suitor she had the year prior in London, who was more in love with her fortune than her person.

Just as Elizabeth was feeling more kindly disposed to the woman, Miss Bingley said to Jane, "I imagine that you have not had the same opportunities to meet gentlemen of quality, given your uncle's address."

Jane blinked in surprise and responded, "While it is true that we have not been exposed to as much society as you have, I have had many opportunities to meet amiable young men, especially through my cousin William."

"And you have remained unattached?" Miss Bingley inquired delicately.

"My sister and I have promised each other that only the deepest of love will induce us to matrimony," Elizabeth interjected hastily. "Jane has had many suitors over the years, but none that have stirred her heart."

Jane blushed slightly and looked down while Miss Bingley eyed her thoughtfully as she took a sip of tea. She put down her teacup and said, "Allow me to speak plainly, Miss Bennet. I worry about my brother. He is a very good man, and I want the best for him. Being the son of a tradesman, he needs to marry into the best circles for the sake of his children. However, his genuine nature makes him vulnerable to the machinations of those who seek to marry him for fortune. A few smiles, a few compliments to his dancing, and he's a lost man."

Here, Miss Bingley hesitated and bit her lip. She glanced at Mrs. Hurst, then pressed forward. "Our family life was not a happy one, and I do not know how Charles escaped from school or our father with his character intact. I will not allow him to fall victim to a fortune hunter who pretends to love him, only for him to be miserable the remainder of his life."

Jane and Elizabeth stared at Miss Bingley, jaws agape. Jane took a shaky breath. "I greatly esteem and admire your brother," she said carefully. "I am not able to say any more than that. I can promise, however, that I would not show *more* than I feel, nor could I—in good conscience—accept an offer of marriage from someone whose feelings I could not return in equal measure."

A brilliant smile crossed Miss Bingley's face. "Excellent," she said. "Had you answered in any other way, I would have done everything in my power to remove my brother from your presence—regardless of the fact that he is good friends with your cousin."

Having said her piece, Miss Bingley excused herself from the room, with Mrs. Hurst following behind.

Elizabeth looked at Jane in bewilderment. "What exactly occurred just now?" the younger sister asked the elder.

A satisfied smile crossed Jane's face. "I believe, Lizzy, Miss Bingley just proved that *I* was correct in my assertions that she is a true friend."

Elizabeth gasped in mock outrage and threw a pillow at her sister's smirk. "Bravo, Jane! I do believe this is one of the few times that you bested me in matters of character observation!"

Jane giggled, then began to cough harshly. Elizabeth hastily fetched a glass of water, which her sister sipped gratefully. After swallowing, Jane said, "I believe, however, that the time with my new friend has sapped what little strength I had."

"Yes, I should leave you to rest." Elizabeth kissed her sister on the forehead and tucked the blanket up around her. She left the room and whispered to the maid to wait until Jane awoke, at which point Elizabeth should be fetched.

The maid nodded in understanding. Jane was asleep before the door even finished closing behind Elizabeth.

Elizabeth began to walk towards her own room, but before she reached the door, Darcy came down the hallway towards her. "I believe the dinner bell is about to ring," he said, extending his arm.

She placed her hand on his elbow, and a jolt of energy seemed to burst from the connection. Startled, her eyes flew up to meet his.

They were dark and piercing, and she blushed under their intensity. Something tugged deep in her stomach—a sensation she had never before experienced.

"Have you had an enjoyable day?" she asked a bit breathlessly. *What is wrong with me,* she asked herself.

Darcy's face was inscrutable. "Yes, it was tolerable, I suppose."

What is it with him and that word? Does he truly just view life as something to be tolerated? she wondered.

They reached the parlor just in time for the butler to announce that dinner was ready. Bingley escorted Elizabeth in, and Wickham followed with Miss Bingley on his arm. Mr. Hurst took in his wife, and Darcy followed at the end.

Dinner passed in much the same manner as the evening before, with Wickham and Bingley jovially conversing about shared experiences.

"Where was Mr. Darcy when this was occurring?" Mrs. Hurst inquired at one point.

Wickham laughed and said, "He was there with us! He told us we were fools to try to race the horses down that lane, but in the end he followed along."

"Yes, to be on hand to fetch a doctor... or the mortician," Darcy shot back.

The dinner party erupted in mirth, and it was some time before Wickham could calm himself enough to say, "But that is Darcy for you. He will tell you the truth—especially when he thinks you are an idiot—but he will be there to help you when he is proven correct."

Darcy smiled wryly and lifted his glass in acknowledgment. "I will always be there for my friends."

Dinner soon ended, and the ladies left the gentlemen to their port. Following Miss Bingley to the music room, Elizabeth was pensive. *I cannot make out Mr. Darcy's character at all.*

The ladies entered the room and were surprised to find a maid helping Jane settle in comfortably by the fire. "I did not know you were to join us," Elizabeth exclaimed. "Are you certain you should be out of your room?"

"Stop fussing, Lizzy," Jane scolded. "I feel much better after my afternoon rest and dinner tray. I wished to enjoy the company of our gracious hosts." Jane smiled at Miss Bingley, who smiled sincerely in return.

As if summoned, the gentlemen entered the room at that moment. "Miss Bennet!" Bingley cried in excitement. "I am delighted to see you downstairs looking so well!"

Jane blushed at his exuberance as he took a seat next to her. He spent several minutes assuring himself of her comfort. As he did so, Hurst lay down on a sofa and almost immediately fell asleep. Wickham took a seat next to Miss Bingley and Mrs. Hurst, leaving Darcy to sit at a writing desk to begin a letter.

Elizabeth, left to her own devices, began to wish she had thought to bring the novel she'd discovered in the library. She was eager to discover what would happen next to the poor heroine and the man who loved her. Instead, she began mentally composing her next letter to her Aunt Gardiner.

A burst of laughter came from the other side of the room, and Miss Bingley covered her mouth in an attempt to stifle the unladylike guffaws coming from her mouth. "I cannot believe it, Mr. Wickham! Did you truly say that?"

Elizabeth looked around the room. Bingley gazed at his sister, his face a mix of concern and tender regard. Darcy was frowning severely at the group, and Hurst gave a loud snort in his sleep.

What could he have against Wickham's attentions to Miss Bingley? Elizabeth thought in consternation. *It is clear he does not return her regard, so why would he object to his friend commanding her interest? I truly cannot make him out at all.*

Her musings were interrupted when Miss Bingley said, "Miss Eliza, do say you will take a turn about the room with me! Mr. Wickham here would have me believe the most ridiculous of things, and I feel I must escape."

Wickham scoffed in mock outrage, and Elizabeth laughed. "Very well, I would be happy to help you make your escape."

The two ladies slowly made their way around the room. After a few seconds, Miss Bingley said, "Mr. Darcy, won't you join us?"

Darcy looked up from his letter, startled. "I thank you, but no. I am afraid that it would defeat the purpose of your walk."

"My purpose, sir? I'm afraid I don't know what you mean," Miss Bingley responded.

"You have chosen this method of passing the evening for one of two reasons. You are either in each other's confidence and have secret affairs to discuss, or you are aware that your figures are to the greatest advantage in walking. If the first, I would only be in your way; and if the second, I can admire you much better from here."

Elizabeth stared at Darcy in shock while Miss Bingley let out a peal of laughter. Bingley looked up in confusion, and Wickham repeated Darcy's words to him and Jane in between snorts.

"Oh, shocking speech!" cried Miss Bingley. "I've never heard anything so abominable! How shall we punish him, Miss Eliza?"

Elizabeth fumbled slightly for a response. Mr. Darcy's uncharacteristic teasing had completely thrown her off her balance. Finally, she said, "I think the best thing to do would be to laugh at him. You are all such good friends; surely you must know of something!"

"Upon my word, I cannot think of a thing," declared Wickham, having finally calmed himself enough to speak. "How can you tease such calmness of manner and presence of mind?"

"Mr. Darcy is not to be laughed at?" Elizabeth's eyes flashed at him. "That would be a great loss to me, for I dearly love to laugh."

"Wickham gives me more credit than is due." Darcy shot a look at his friend. "The wisest and best of men can be mocked by those whose first object in life is a joke."

Affronted, Elizabeth replied coolly, "Certainly, there are such people, but I hope I am not one of them. I hope I never make a mockery of that which is good. Follies and nonsense do divert me, and I laugh at those. But I suppose those are precisely what you lack."

"That would not be possible for anyone," Darcy retorted. "But it has been the study of my life to avoid those weaknesses which often expose a man to ridicule."

"Ah, I see," said Elizabeth. "Such as vanity and pride, perhaps?"

"Yes, vanity is a weakness indeed," he answered. "But pride—where there is real superiority of mind, pride will always be kept under control."

Elizabeth turned away to hide a smile. He had proven himself to be what she had thought from the first: too arrogant to be able to see himself as such.

The tension in the room held for some moments until Wickham coughed uncomfortably. "Well, now that that's settled, perhaps we could hear some music, Miss Bingley? I do not believe Miss Bennet has had the opportunity to hear you perform since she arrived."

Miss Bingley agreed with alacrity and hurried to the piano. Elizabeth returned to her seat, acutely aware of Darcy's intense gaze for the remainder of the evening.

Chapter 11

The following morning revealed a much-improved Jane. She came down for breakfast, and this success motivated the sisters to request the carriage in order to return to Longbourn. Bingley protested vociferously, but Jane and Elizabeth were quite firm.

Although Jane was loath to leave the company, Elizabeth could not be more eager to escape Darcy's presence. She reminded Jane that if they stayed at Netherfield for much longer, their mother would come to assure herself of her eldest daughter's health. The potential for embarrassment outweighed any benefit in residing in the same house as Mr. Bingley—at least, in Jane's mind.

The Netherfield party bid farewell to the Misses Bennet with mixed emotions. Darcy was becoming increasingly aware of the danger of paying too much attention to Elizabeth Bennet. Miss Bingley was sorry to see her new friends leave, but she knew the friendship could develop through frequent visits between the two estates. Bingley only wished he could contrive a reason for Miss Bennet to remain at his side permanently.

Elizabeth sighed with relief as Netherfield Park faded from sight. "Oh, Jane, I have never been more glad to leave a place in my life!"

"Really?" Jane asked in astonishment. "I found the visit to be quite delightful! Surely you must admit that Miss Bingley's company is vastly superior to Lydia's."

Amused, Elizabeth said, "I would not inform Lydia of your opinion, if I were you. Unless you wish to awaken one morning with your hair missing."

Jane laughed, and Elizabeth continued speaking over the sound. "Truly, Jane, I found the entire party delightful, except for Mr. Darcy. There is something about him that makes me uneasy. I do not trust that his friendship with William is on equal footing, and I cannot like the way he disdains Miss Bingley's feelings towards him."

Jane nodded slowly. "Mr. Bingley mentioned at one point that he was aware of his sister's feelings for Mr. Darcy, but Mr. Darcy has told Mr. Bingley that he will never make her an offer of marriage."

"How cruel," Elizabeth cried, her eyes narrowing on behalf of her new friend.

"Perhaps," responded Jane, "but it is less cruel than giving her false hope."

Elizabeth huffed and sat back on the seat, refusing to concede the point. The remainder of the journey was spent in silence, each lady's thoughts revolving around a gentleman at Netherfield.

Upon their return home, they found Collins in the drawing room with their mother and Mary.

"Elizabeth! What can you have been thinking, bringing your sister home when she has been so ill?" cried Mrs. Bennet. "She should have stayed at least a sennight at Netherfield in order to recover her strength! How else will she be able to catch Mr. Bingley?"

Elizabeth rolled her eyes towards Collins, who smiled at them. "I'm glad to see the rumors of your imminent demise are grossly exaggerated, Jane," he said.

Mrs. Bennet stared blankly as Elizabeth and Mary giggled. "Well, they have come just in time for my news," Collins continued. "I just received a letter from my friend, Stanley."

"The one who stood up at your wedding?" Kitty asked.

"Yes, Kitty. He writes to ask if he may visit for a time. Would it be all right if he stayed here at Longbourn? There is more space than at our parsonage, and with Mary in a delicate condition—"

"Mary!" shrieked Mrs. Bennet. "Are you with child again? Oh, my clever girl! Another grandchild!"

Mary glared at her husband, who winced sheepishly. "Yes, Mama," Mary said, interrupting her mother's effusions. "However, I have only just felt the quickening."

"Be that as it may," continued Collins hastily as Mrs. Bennet opened her mouth to speak, "it would be of great benefit to us if he could stay here."

"Does he bring his wife with him?" Mrs. Bennet blinked innocently.

Collins smiled ruefully and said, "No, madam, he is unmarried."

"Well, of course your friend is welcome to stay with us!" she exclaimed with delight. "Such a charming young man he was at the wedding, I remember. Very eager to please, as I recall... and so handsome."

Mary hid a smile at this description of Stanley, who possessed somewhat awkward and plain features, as well as an obsequious nature.

"Yes, well, his family is not as accommodating as mine was growing up," Mr. Collins said. "He is accustomed to having to flatter in order to gain an iota of kindness."

"What is his profession?" Elizabeth asked curiously.

"He also took orders, like me. He was recently appointed to a living at Hunsford, in Kent. His patroness is somewhat difficult to please, from what I understand from his letters. He does his best to help those under his care while catering to her ladyship's many demands," Collins replied.

"His own living? Well, if he is your age and unmarried still, he must be in want of a wife! What a fortunate thing for you, Lizzy!" Mrs. Bennet exclaimed.

Elizabeth looked up at her mother, startled. "Whatever could you mean, Mama?"

"Why, I am thinking of you marrying him, you silly girl! It is not very often you have a single gentleman in your home for... how long did you say he will be staying, William?"

"A fortnight, I believe," he answered.

"There a fortnight!" Mrs. Bennet smiled with satisfaction. "That will be plenty of time for you to make him fall in love with you. I would have him for Jane, but she is for Mr. Bingley."

Elizabeth looked at her mother in horror. "No offense to your friend, William, but I am not at all interested in marrying him! I do not know him, and I am not sure I even like him as anything other than my dear brother's friend!"

"Pssh, what does liking have to do with marriage?" Mrs. Bennet said sharply, waving a hand in the air. "Besides, he writes letters to William and you write letters to your Aunt Gardiner—you already have something in common."

Elizabeth blinked at this bit of inanity, but her mother continued her tirade. "Mark my words, I will see you married to Mr. Stanley! Otherwise you will be stuck here at Longbourn as an old maid, tending to Mary's children until you die."

With that declaration, Mrs. Bennet swept from the room, calling for Hill. "Oh, Hill! We must begin making preparations for our guest immediately!"

Mary and Collins looked at Elizabeth with sympathy.

"When is he coming?" Elizabeth asked glumly.

"He arrives in two days," William said, stifling a laugh.

An hour before Mr. Stanley's arrival at Longbourn, Lizzy feigned a headache. "Oh, Mama, I feel as though I may vomit from the pain," she said, gagging slightly.

Mrs. Bennet took one look at Elizabeth's face and immediately sent her to her bedroom. "We cannot have you making a poor impression on our guest! Imagine if you were to cast up your accounts in front of him? He would never have you!"

Pleased with herself, Elizabeth spent the evening and the entire next day finishing the novel she had smuggled into her trunk from

Netherfield. "I can see now why Lydia and Kitty are wild for these stories," she said to herself as she fanned her reddened face. "It is almost sinful the way it makes me feel."

She soon drifted off to sleep, but it would not be a peaceful one.

Elizabeth was in a dark forest, hiding from a wicked uncle who was trying to marry her to a wicked lord. Cornered by his footmen with no chance of escape, she was about to throw herself off the cliff.

Suddenly, a gentleman in a mask rode in on a white horse. He swept her into his arms and carried her away to safety. As they galloped towards his hidden estate in the trees, she felt his strong arms holding her tightly. The same familiar tugging in her stomach began to grow until the desire for something—she knew not what—filled her entire body.

At the gates of his home, he leaned in to kiss her. "Wait! I do not know who you are," she said. She lifted her hands to the back of his head and untied his mask. As it fell away, she looked into the face of... Fitzwilliam Darcy.

Elizabeth awoke with a gasp. Her heart was pounding, and she could barely catch her breath. Then she began to laugh. *What a ridiculous dream! Mr. Darcy would never be so gallant, or so romantic.*

For the next few hours until daylight, she drifted in and out of a restless sleep. Her mind would simply not let go of the desire she had felt to have him kiss her.

Finally, sunlight burst over the top of Oakham Mount. Elizabeth dressed, put on her boots, and escaped through the kitchen door. She walked to the top of Oakham Mount, certain that the climb would banish the odious man from her thoughts. When that failed, she returned to the wooded area near her house and traipsed across trails for over an hour.

After missing breakfast and completely exhausting herself, Elizabeth returned to Longbourn. To her surprise, she saw the Lucases' carriage at the front. She slipped in the back door, quickly changed her dress, and hurried down to the drawing room.

As soon as she entered, Charlotte hurried to her side. "Eliza," she whispered, "I must speak with you privately."

Elizabeth didn't hesitate. "Mama, I am going outside with Charlotte to show her the new flowers."

She whisked her friend out the door before Mrs. Bennet even had a chance to open her mouth.

Once outside, Elizabeth turned to her friend. "Well?" she asked, raising an eyebrow.

Charlotte bit her lip, hesitating. Elizabeth furrowed her brow. "Charlotte, what is it?" she asked in concern.

"I am to be married," Charlotte blurted out. She clamped her lips together and looked at Elizabeth anxiously.

Elizabeth burst into laughter. "Oh, Charlotte!" she said, wiping a tear from her eye, "I thought there was something truly the matter. What a good joke!"

"It's not a joke, Lizzy!"

Charlotte's unusually angry voice pierced through Elizabeth's mirth. She gaped at her friend. "I don't understand," Elizabeth said uneasily.

"I am getting married. The banns will be read this Sunday, and the wedding will take place just after Michaelmas," Charlotte repeated.

Elizabeth opened and closed her mouth several times, mute. After a moment, she sputtered, "To whom?"

"To Mr. Stanley."

Elizabeth stared at her friend, blinking in dismay. "Charlotte, surely you must be joking!"

"No, Elizabeth, I am not!" Charlotte responded heatedly. "I will be Mrs. Stanley in about a month."

"But you've only just met!" Elizabeth cried out. "Charlotte, what do you know of him? His character? Other than he is unfortunately plain and—"

"Enough, Elizabeth!" interrupted Charlotte angrily. "I will not hear another word spoken against him. For your information, we were seated next to one another at Mary's wedding. I found him to be an intelligent conversationalist, very complimentary towards myself, and—most importantly—his wife will be mistress of her own home."

"You've... you've been courting all this time? Without telling me?"

"Of course not, Elizabeth. I would have shared that with you. I asked Mr. Collins after his friend several months ago. Around the same time, Mr. Stanley was granted the living and wrote to Mr. Collins to see if I was still unmarried. He believes we will complement each other very well, and I have heard nothing of him that gives me unease."

"I cannot believe William would—"

"What, Lizzy? What wouldn't your cousin do? Help his friend find a responsible, caring woman to help with his parishioners and make his home comfortable? Recommend a spinster to a man who is looking for a wife because he knows the man will treat the woman kindly? I am *old*, Eliza, and I am tired of watching younger ladies dance while I sit to the side with the matrons, with my mother looking at me in despair."

Here Charlotte stopped speaking, breathing heavily. There were several moments of silence as the two friends stared at one another. "Why can you not be happy for me?" Charlotte whispered, her voice breaking.

"Oh, Charlotte!" Elizabeth flung herself at her friend, and the two women embraced tightly. "I am so sorry. If you are happy, then I am happy."

Several sniffles and two ruined handkerchiefs later, the girls walked arm in arm back into Longbourn. They entered the parlor, where Mrs. Bennet was attempting to persuade Mr. Stanley into sitting next to Kitty. Elizabeth looked at him in some surprise; she had not even noticed he was in the room before Charlotte had taken her out.

Charlotte looked at Mr. Stanley and nodded, who beamed back. Elizabeth noted with pleasure that the happiness seemed to reach into his eyes. His plain face had wrinkles that could only come from years of smiling.

"Mrs. Bennet," he said, crossing the room to stand by Charlotte, "I am delighted to inform you that Miss Lucas has done me the honor of accepting my offer of marriage."

Mrs. Bennet's eyes widened, and her face paled. Her mouth opened, but no words came out.

"Congratulations!" cried Elizabeth warmly, offering her hand to Mr. Stanley. "You could not have chosen a better woman to be your wife."

Mr. Stanley's beaming face broke into a full smile. "I feel fortunate that she has accepted my offer, and I look forward to when I can introduce her to my parish and my patroness. Lady Catherine de Bourgh told me I needed a wife, and I am most fortunate in my choice!"

Elizabeth's eyes met Charlotte's, who blushed slightly. "I am certain Lady Catherine will have every cause to approve. My friend is the most excellent of ladies."

"Indeed, she is!" he enthused.

Once congratulations had been offered by each member of the Bennet household—including Collins and Mary, who had arrived shortly after the announcement—Mr. Stanley and Charlotte departed in order to pay other calls in the neighborhood.

Once the carriage could no longer be heard, Mrs. Bennet collapsed onto the sofa. "Oh, what is to become of you, Lizzy? Charlotte has stolen your husband!"

Collins immediately protested, and Elizabeth exclaimed, "Mama! Charlotte has done no such thing!"

"Those Lucases," the matron sniffed, "Such artful people, they are. Well, I suppose he is only a parson, after all. At least my daughter has married the heir of an estate."

Elizabeth rolled her eyes at Collins, who shook his head.

"I married William because I love him, Mama," Mary said in exasperated tones.

"Well, who wouldn't love the heir of Longbourn?" Mrs. Bennet retorted.

It was a familiar argument—one that had been repeated many times over the years. Mrs. Bennet had been and always would be a simple woman. *I simply cannot understand why Papa chose her, out of all the women he must have met,* Elizabeth thought ruefully.

Jane, who had been sitting quietly in the corner with her embroidery, gently changed the subject, and the remainder of the day passed somewhat more calmly.

Three days later, Mrs. Bennet and her four unmarried daughters sat in the drawing room. A knock was heard at the front door, and the Netherfield party was announced.

"Mr. Bingley!" Mrs. Bennet exclaimed with a winsome smile. "How glad we are to see you! Here, please, come be seated."

Bingley was shown to a spot on the settee near Jane while the rest of the guests were left to find their own seats. Mr. Wickham and Miss Bingley sat across from Jane. Mrs. Hurst—who had come without her husband—joined Kitty and Lydia at the table, where the young girls were refinishing one of Jane's old bonnets.

Darcy strode towards the window and stared out at the lawn, his hands clasped behind, with his back to the room. Elizabeth was sitting on a small stool next to him, head bent over a letter from her Aunt Gardiner.

Not only did his position place him in proximity to Elizabeth, but he surprisingly enjoyed the additional advantage of seeing her face in the window's reflection. She bit her lip and smiled softly, causing his heart to swell within him.

What can he mean by coming to visit, then ignoring the room? Elizabeth huffed. *Why must he inflict his presence on us when it is clear he has little desire to be here?*

Her musings were interrupted by a loud squeal from across the room. "Oh, Mr. Bingley, what an excellent idea!" Mrs. Bennet clapped her hands with glee.

Bingley blushed and said, "I am glad you approve, madam. I had hoped my idea of a ball would be well received."

"I do not see who could object!" Lydia exclaimed. "If only I were allowed to come out. I would dance every dance."

"I believe you would," Mr. Bingley smiled kindly at her. "If I am still at Netherfield when you are of age, I will gladly hold another ball that you can attend."

Lydia's squeal was identical to the one her mother had emitted only moments before. Elizabeth winced slightly at the sound. Out of the corner of her eye, she saw Mr. Darcy's lips tighten in annoyance.

"Will you be inviting the militia?" Kitty asked eagerly.

"I had not thought—" began Bingley.

"Oh yes, you must invite the officers!" Mrs. Bennet declared. "After all, it would not do to have too many ladies at your ball. A man in regimentals always makes for a handsome dance partner. I recall being in love with a redcoat myself, once, when I was in my youth…"

Elizabeth's face burned as her mother prattled on. When the lady paused for breath, Mr. Bingley hastily interjected by saying, "If it is not too early, I would like to solicit your hand for the first two dances, Miss Bennet."

"That is very kind of you, sir!" cried the young lady's mother. "Of course my Jane will be happy to dance the first set with you, and any other dance you would request as well! Thank the gentleman, Jane."

Elizabeth felt as though her face would catch fire. Jane went red, then white. She murmured something indiscernible to Bingley, who gazed at her with adoration shining in his eyes.

Darcy's face grew increasingly grim as the conversation progressed. After Bingley's request, Wickham took the opportunity to ask Miss Bingley for the first set to open the ball. The young woman blushed prettily, glanced at Darcy, and then accepted.

Bingley and Wickham then proceeded to request dances from all the ladies in the room. After it was all arranged, Darcy turned around. "I believe you said we had a few more calls, Bingley?" he asked pointedly.

"Ah, yes, I'm afraid we do," admitted Bingley. "I hope to see all of you next week, on the twenty-sixth of November!"

"We would not miss it for the world," assured Mrs. Bennet energetically.

The Netherfield party departed, and the conversation turned towards the multitude of preparations that would need to be made over the coming week.

Chapter 12

The day of the Netherfield ball finally arrived. The ladies of both Longbourn and Netherfield had spent hours of preparation, Miss Bingley in particular. The result was spectacular; the guests gasped in amazement as their carriages approached the manor. Each window blazed with hundreds of candles, and the hedges were adorned with ribbons and flowers.

When it was the Bennets' turn to disembark, they were greeted warmly by Bingley. "Miss Bennet, you look radiant," he said as he kissed her hand.

Jane flushed prettily and murmured her thanks. She turned to Miss Bingley. "I have never seen a house so beautifully decorated."

Miss Bingley smiled and said, "We are so glad you were able to attend."

Another family arrived, so the Bennets continued on into the ballroom. Elizabeth stared around in amazement. Beautiful hothouse flowers lay across delicate tablecloths with centerpieces that rivaled anything she had ever seen. Candles were lit every few feet on intricate pedestals.

"Oh, Lizzy," Jane said in awe. "Have you ever seen anything so beautiful?"

"Miss Bingley is extremely talented," Elizabeth replied.

The two sisters continued their examinations until the musicians began to warm up their instruments. Bingley approached and extended his arm. "Shall we, Miss Bennet?"

Elizabeth smiled as she watched her sister move to the dance floor to open the ball. Bingley was certainly making a statement of his interest by requesting Jane instead of his sister for the first two dances.

Wickham and Miss Bingley stood next to them in the line. Elizabeth looked around and spied Kitty. "As the ladies outnumber the gentlemen, would you care to stand up with me?" she asked her younger sister.

The two joined the dance floor, and the evening officially began.

Several dances later, Elizabeth left the floor in search of refreshments. As she talked with Charlotte Lucas, she felt someone stand next to her. She turned and was surprised to see Mr. Darcy at her side. "May I have the next two dances, please, Miss Elizabeth?" he requested.

Elizabeth opened her mouth in surprise. "Why, I had not... that is, yes, sir, you may."

He strode away, and Charlotte began to laugh at her friend's stupidity. Elizabeth glared at her but could not help laughing herself. "It is not amusing! I do not know why he asked me to dance, the hateful man."

"Come now, Eliza. You must not turn away a man with ten times your father's consequence," replied her friend in amusement.

Across the ballroom, Darcy watched Elizabeth with a small smile. *It appears she is as eager to dance with me as I am with her,* he thought with satisfaction.

There was still much left of the current set, and he was free to observe her at his leisure. When she had walked into Netherfield, with her hair piled in elegant curls on top of her head, he had forgotten how to breathe. He had never been much for women's fashion, but he gave the Almighty thanks for whichever seamstress had developed the current style of ball gowns. Her dress displayed every bit of her curves to perfection, and the low neckline caused his eyes to stray farther below than was gentlemanly.

It was all he could do to prevent himself from putting his hands on her right then. Instead, he forced himself to wait until asking her to dance so as not to give rise to any expectations. For all her charms, he was keenly aware of her lower station. That did not mean, however, that he could not enjoy the feeling of having her in his arms for a dance.

Finally, the music ended. He crossed the room and extended his arm. She took it, and once again, a jolt shot between them. They were silent as they reached the center of the floor.

Elizabeth felt as though every eye in the room was focused on her. She heard whispers increase as friends and neighbors watched in shock while the proud Mr. Darcy, who had never once stood up with anyone outside his own party, began to dance with Elizabeth Bennet.

After several minutes of silence, Elizabeth said, "The ball is very well attended, is it not? There are quite a number of guests."

"Yes," was all he said.

After another minute, she said, "Mr. Darcy, I believe it is your turn to speak. I have remarked on the number of couples. Perhaps you could share your opinion on the decorations or even observe that private balls are much more pleasant than public assemblies."

"Do you speak as a rule when dancing?" he inquired.

"Sometimes. One must have some conversation, or it would look odd to be entirely silent for half an hour together. Although perhaps we should start having conversations arranged so that strange partners might escape with saying as little as possible to one another."

He gave her a sharp look. "Are you consulting your own feelings on the matter, or do you think to gratify mine?"

"Both," Elizabeth replied archly, "for I have seen a great similarity in our characters. Each of us has a social, taciturn nature, and we are both unwilling to speak unless we have something to say that will amaze the whole room."

"That bears no resemblance to your own character, I am sure," he said shortly.

He made no answer, and they were silent again as they went down the dance. Suddenly, she asked, "So tell me how you came to be acquainted with the Bingley family. I understand from my cousin William that the encounter was unusual, but it made you into the best of friends."

Darcy's face darkened. He could not say a word, and Elizabeth began to question whether he would suffer a fit. Finally, he answered, "Mr. Bingley and his sisters allowed us to stay in their home while I travelled. Their father passed away while I was there, and I helped Bingley resolve the business side of the issue."

Elizabeth flushed slightly and opened her mouth to respond, but at that moment, Sir William Lucas appeared close to them. He stopped with a bow and said, "I congratulate you, Mr. Darcy! I have never seen such superior dancing outside of St. James's court. Allow me to say I hope to have this pleasure repeated—especially when a certain desirable event shall take place."

At these words, Sir William looked significantly at Bingley, who was standing up for the second time with Jane. Near them, Wickham was in deep conversation with Miss Bingley, to the exclusion of all others.

Darcy's face darkened as he looked towards both couples. He bowed in acknowledgment to Sir William, then recovered himself and continued to lead Elizabeth in the dance.

"I apologize," he said, "but Sir William's interruption has made me forget what we are speaking of."

"It is of no matter," Elizabeth said quietly in embarrassment. "You were merely answering a question I had asked. I remember you saying once at Netherfield that a superior mind will always be able to regulate pride."

"I did."

"Do you consider yourself to have such a superior mind?"

"May I ask, Miss Bennet, to what these questions portend?"

"Merely to make out your character, sir," she replied. "I am having difficulty understanding the type of person you are, especially as a friend. I have seen such different characteristics in you that I am puzzled."

"I wish, Miss Bennet, that you would not sketch my character at this time. I fear the distraction of the ball would do either of us little credit."

"But if I do not take your likeness now, I may never have another opportunity," she retorted.

Darcy was not given a chance to respond as the music ended. He bowed, she curtsied, and he returned her to her mother before retreating to a corner of the room.

Collins approached Darcy and said, "Well now, I was surprised to see you dancing with my sister!"

Darcy looked at his friend in concern. "Why would that surprise you?"

"Well, I know for a fact that dancing is a compliment you never pay to any place if you can help it."

Darcy blinked at the familiar words he had said to Sir William. *But Collins was not even present at that event. How could he...?*

"Besides," continued Collins, a bit stern, "you also once proclaimed her not handsome enough to tempt you into dancing."

Darcy's jaw dropped. "What? I never..." his voice trailed off. "Wait, I *did* say that. Why the devil would Bingley repeat such a thing?"

"He did not," Collins replied. "The lady overheard you herself."

Darcy's eyes widened, and he groaned in frustration.

"I take it you no longer think she is merely tolerable?"

Gritting his teeth, Darcy shook his head. "I consider her to be one of the handsomest women of my acquaintance."

Collins smiled. "Well, you will have much to do in order to repair her opinion of you."

"There is little point," Darcy said bitterly. "I am to leave for London tomorrow in order to spend the holidays with Georgiana, then on to Pemberley for the spring planting. I do not believe I will return to Hertfordshire."

Collins's smile dimmed. "I see. Are you certain that is what you wish?"

"I wish circumstances were different," Darcy replied. "As much as I admire her, I cannot allow myself to become attached to someone whose circumstances in life are so decidedly below my own."

Darcy cursed himself the moment the words left his lips. Collins's face hardened slightly. "Perhaps it is best you are leaving tomorrow after all," he replied.

"Collins, I—"

"No, Darcy, I understand. Just remember, my friend, that life can be quite lonely if position is more important than love."

Collins walked away before Darcy had a chance to respond. Miserably, Darcy watched Collins approach his wife and kiss her cheek. Mary blushed in response, and a twinge of jealousy welled up in Darcy's chest. He pushed it down, then went in search of Bingley.

Elizabeth watched Collins walk away from Darcy, shaking his head. *What could have been the trouble?* she wondered.

She quickly put it out of her mind when she saw Kitty stumble slightly. "Are you all right, Kitty?" she asked.

"I feel a bit warm," Kitty admitted.

"And little wonder!" Elizabeth said with a laugh. "Between all the candles and the fact that you have not sat out a single set, you are due for a rest! Come, let us find some fresh air."

Elizabeth escorted her sister out of the ballroom and into a small garden below a terrace. They sat together on a bench, enjoying the cool November air, looking at the stars in the clear night sky.

Their solitude was interrupted by a voice coming from above. The ladies looked up to see Darcy standing at the open French doors that led out to the terrace.

"This is a terrible idea," Darcy said.

"I don't believe it's your decision," Bingley retorted.

"But her history! Her family! Surely you can see the difficulties that could arise in your future felicity with such a match," Darcy responded.

Elizabeth gasped quietly. "Are they speaking about Jane?" Kitty inquired in confusion.

Hushing her sister, Elizabeth listened more closely.

"I think a man has the right to determine how he will be happy," Wickham responded testily.

The three men stood in silence for several minutes, then Darcy said, "Just be certain of her affection. It would not be the first time a woman chose to marry for convenience rather than feeling. Perhaps you should go with me to London tomorrow and think things over."

Elizabeth let out an unladylike growl. At the noise, the gentlemen fell silent. Darcy looked out the window, and the girls shrank back on the bench into the shadows.

Fortunately, they were unnoticed, although Darcy closed the window and the remainder of the conversation was muted.

Elizabeth was shaking. Whether from cold, anger, or fear of being caught, she did not know. What she did know was that Mr. Darcy, in all his arrogance, was trying to persuade Mr. Bingley from pursuing her beloved elder sister!

"Let's go inside," Elizabeth seethed.

The ladies quickly returned to the ballroom. Shortly after entering the room, Bingley and Wickham returned through another door. Elizabeth noticed that Mr. Darcy did not accompany them nor did he reappear for the remainder of the ball.

"Good riddance. I hope I never lay eyes on that hateful man ever again."

The morning after the ball, the inhabitants of Longbourn slept in until much later than their usual hour of arising. They finally congregated in the breakfast room well past the noon hour. Elizabeth yawned as Lydia, the only one to have gotten a good night's sleep, rattled away with questions about the event.

"What was it like? What dresses did they wear? I imagine the lace on Miss Bingley's dress—"

"No lace!" cried Mr. Bennet. "Please, my dears, I beg you to postpone your discussion about the evening until after I have gone to my

146

book room!"

Lydia agreed, but only if he would eat more quickly. He gave her a small smirk and took a bite of food, chewing it with slow, exaggerated motions. His youngest daughter, in response, turned to ask her mother to describe the feathers in Mrs. Hurst's hair.

"I yield!" cried Mr. Bennet, chewing rapidly again.

The table broke out into merry—but tired—laughter. Mr. Bennet finished eating and excused himself, at which point Lydia and Kitty fell into a conversation about the ball gowns seen at the dance.

A maid knocked at the door and brought in a tray. "The post has just come, ma'am," she said to Mrs. Bennet.

Mrs. Bennet sifted through the sealed envelopes, removed a few, and sent the rest with the maid to take to Mr. Bennet. "Jane!" she suddenly shrieked. "There is one here for you from Netherfield!"

Jane took the letter and quickly read through it. "It is from Miss Bingley. It seems the party at Netherfield has decided to visit London until after Christmas, which they wish to spend with their families in town. They will return after the holiday, however."

Kitty looked at Elizabeth, who compressed her lips into a firm line.

"Oh no!" wailed Mrs. Bennet. "Jane, how could you allow him to leave without securing him first?"

Jane blinked in astonishment at her mother.

"Mama," protested Elizabeth, "you know that Jane has little control over whether a gentleman courts her. Besides," she added, hiding her doubts, "she says they will return in January."

Kitty stared at Elizabeth, who flashed her eyes in return. *Kitty, if you dare say anything, I will steal all your ribbons and slash your dresses.*

Fortunately for Kitty, she could read Elizabeth's expression—even if she could not read her mind. "Do not worry, Mama, Jane," Kitty said kindly. "I am sure Lizzy is right."

Mrs. Bennet sniffed. "I do hope so."

Jane folded the letter quietly and put it into her pocket. Her pale face caused no small amount of concern for Elizabeth, who quickly said, "Jane, would you like to take a turn around the garden with me?"

Without waiting for a response, Elizabeth stood and, pulling Jane by the arm, exited the breakfast parlor.

Once outside, Elizabeth said, "Now, Jane, what are you not telling me?"

Jane burst into tears. "I do not know why he would leave! Last night he spoke quite warmly with me about how much he enjoyed Hertfordshire and how he had never met more pleasant people in all his life. He looked at me quite intently when he said it, and he never mentioned leaving for town!"

"I can only guess there is some matter of pressing importance that calls him there," Elizabeth assured her sister. "Additionally, we do not know which member of the Netherfield party in particular has a need to go to town. Perhaps Mr. Hurst or Mr. Darcy has business there, and he did not wish to go alone."

Jane sniffled. "That could be possible. Mr. Bingley is rather accommodating that way."

"And once he has travelled all that way, with it being so close to the holidays, he may wish to take advantage of the proximity to his family and friends."

"There is some logic in what you say," Jane admitted.

"I do not think Miss Bingley would lie to you about her brother's intentions; not when she has been so honest and forthright with you in the past. And it shows a great sense of friendship for her to write to you directly and inform you of the specific dates of his travel."

Jane wiped her eyes and smiled at her sister. "Thank you, Lizzy. You are the best of sisters."

Elizabeth returned the smile until her sister left her side. Then her face darkened. *Don't make a liar out of me, Mr. Bingley.*

Chapter 13

The following weeks passed uneventfully, except for preparations for Charlotte Lucas's wedding to Mr. Stanley. The Bennets paid frequent visits to Lucas Lodge in order to put together flower arrangements and sew linens for Charlotte's future home. As Sir William had not been a member of the gentry for long, Charlotte did not have much prepared to be a gentleman's wife.

"Besides, we did not think I would ever be married," she confided quietly to Elizabeth one day. "I have spent more time helping Maria with her trousseau in the past rather than tending to my own."

"Did you not wish to delay the wedding until after the holidays in order to complete everything? Will you not miss your family?" Kitty asked.

"No, Mr. Stanley is anxious to be married quickly. It seems Lady Catherine—that is his patroness—is of the opinion that a married rector is preferable to a single one." Charlotte looked around the room and discreetly lowered her voice. "In any case, I think I would much rather have a short engagement so as not to hear my mother's raptures over the situation."

Elizabeth and Kitty stifled giggles while Jane looked on with a sad smile. Elizabeth looked in concern at her sister, who appeared to be in a depression since Mr. Bingley's departure. Jane had recently received a second letter from Miss Bingley, who informed them that it appeared the business would take a bit longer than anticipated. Whereas Miss Bingley had originally hoped they could return to Netherfield in January, circumstances dictated that it would not occur until March. The reason being, Miss Bingley explained, that something had occurred within the Darcy family, and the Bingleys' assistance was requested by Mr. Darcy.

Elizabeth frowned when she read this, but she assured Jane that Miss Bingley had once again offered honest truth in the past, and she would continue to do so in the future. What Elizabeth did not say was that she strongly suspected Mr. Darcy of doing all he could to keep his friend in town and away from Jane.

Finally, Charlotte's wedding day arrived. Elizabeth had never seen her friend as radiant as she did when she walked arm in arm with her new husband out of the church.

At the wedding breakfast, Elizabeth approached her friend and embraced her. "I could not be happier for you, my dear friend."

Charlotte returned the embrace. "Thank you, Eliza." She hesitated, then said, "I must confess, I am a bit nervous at meeting Lady Catherine. My father and Maria will come to me in March. Will you promise to be one of the party? I daresay I will wish for your company just as much as theirs."

"If my father allows it, I will happily come," assured Elizabeth.

The two friends hugged once more, and Elizabeth stepped back to allow Mrs. Long and her nieces time with Charlotte. It was the most joyous wedding celebration Elizabeth had ever attended.

Elizabeth anticipated she would miss her friend greatly, but there was scarcely any time between Charlotte's departure for Hunsford and the Gardiners' arrival for the holidays.

Every year, Mr. Gardiner, his wife, and their children travelled to Longbourn to celebrate with family. Mr. Gardiner was the younger brother of his two sisters, Mrs. Bennet and Mrs. Phillip. The time he spent at boarding school was what prevented him from turning out as silly as either of his sisters. At school, he quickly showed a keen knack for business. Instead of replacing his father as the Meryton solicitor—a position which was later filled by Mr. Phillips—Mr. Gardiner chose to set up shop in London.

While not wildly successful, Mr. Gardiner's business earned enough money for him to take a wife. The two met when he was on a business trip in Derbyshire. Mrs. Gardiner was the daughter of a minor gentleman, with a comfortable dowry. She liked the ambition and dedication she saw in Mr. Gardiner, and the two were quickly married. They owned a large home on Gracechurch Street, where he could be close enough to his family during the workday.

Jane and Elizabeth were frequent visitors at Gracechurch Street, especially once William came to stay with the family. This eased Mrs. Bennet's burdens while allowing the two girls to enjoy a sensible mother figure. Mrs. Gardiner's influence on her nieces helped them to see how a gentleman's daughter was to truly behave. This was something they could not learn from their mother, whose father worked for his living.

The Gardiners and their four children descended on Longbourn with all the enthusiasm one could expect from children who had been in a carriage for hours. They spilled out of the door the moment it was opened and were greeted by hugs and smiles from their cousins.

Mrs. Bennet ushered them all inside out of the cold winter air, and the children were immediately sent to the nursery where they could work out all their pent-up energy. This was one of Lydia's favorite times of year ever since Kitty had come out, leaving Lydia alone in the nursery.

After settling their children and freshening up, Mr. and Mrs. Gardiner joined their nieces in the drawing room. After exchanging greetings, Mrs. Bennet settled into conversation with her brother while Mrs. Gardiner took Elizabeth to the side for a quiet tête-à-tête.

"Now tell me, Elizabeth," said Mrs. Gardiner. "What is happening with Jane and Mr. Bingley? Your weekly letters have been detailed, but now that I have seen Jane for myself, I am convinced something else must have happened."

"Oh, Aunt!" sighed Elizabeth. "I am very worried about her. Miss Bingley has written to say that they will not return until planting. Jane is sure that he will never return and that Miss Bingley is just too kind to say so."

"What do you believe?" asked Mrs. Gardiner curiously.

"I think Miss Bingley is telling the truth. There may be events or business that she does not feel comfortable writing in a letter. It could also be that Mr. Darcy is not being entirely honest about the situation in order to keep Bingley from Jane."

Mrs. Gardiner listened with interest as Elizabeth recited everything she and Kitty had heard that night at Netherfield. After finishing, Mrs. Gardiner sat thoughtfully for a few moments. "I think you may be correct, Lizzy."

"I was wondering, Aunt, if you thought it might be good for Jane to return with you to London after Christmas."

"To chase after Mr. Bingley?" Mrs. Gardiner said with a laugh.

Elizabeth joined in the laughter. "No! I simply wish Jane to have a change of environment without her mother or neighbors speculating as to Mr. Bingley's plans."

"I can see how that might make it difficult for Jane to recover," Mrs. Gardiner agreed thoughtfully.

"And if Jane happens to think it wise to call upon Miss Bingley while in town in order to continue the acquaintance, who knows what might occur?"

"I say, Lizzy, that is an idea worthy of your mother! Very well, I will ask Mr. Gardiner if Jane can join us."

Mr. Gardiner easily approved Jane's visit, and the remainder of the holiday passed by quickly. January arrived, and soon the Gardiners and Jane were loaded into the coach and conveyed to London.

It was only then that Elizabeth began to feel Charlotte's absence keenly. The loss of both her closest sister and friend made the days pass slowly. Letters were delayed in coming from both ladies as they settled into their new homes.

Charlotte's first letters were received with a good deal of eagerness, as Elizabeth was anxious to hear about married life, the parish, and Lady Catherine. Unsurprisingly, Charlotte's optimistic letters were full of nothing but praise for her husband and the people whom she had met. Slightly disappointed, Elizabeth accepted that she would have to make her own determinations about the situation herself.

After weeks of waiting, a letter finally came from Jane. Elizabeth was surprised, as the two sisters had frequently corresponded in the past when they were apart. The only news received from Jane had been a few lines to write that she had arrived safely and made plans to call on the Bingleys the following week.

Two weeks before Elizabeth's trip to Hunsford, a second letter from Jane finally arrived.

My dearest Lizzy,

I hope that all is well with you at Longbourn. I apologize for how long it has taken me to write you a letter. I kept putting it off, hoping that I would hear from the Bingleys before I sent it.

As I informed you before, I made plans to pay a call to the Bingley townhouse. A week of rain made that call impossible, and I was forced to delay my plans.

When a dry morning finally occurred, I immediately took my uncle's carriage to Grosvenor Street. Upon descending from the carriage, I knocked at the door and was met by a severe-looking butler, who informed me the family was not at home. Disappointed, I left my card with the Gardiners' address written on the back.

Upon turning around, I saw Mr. Darcy standing at the stairs. He seemed quite surprised to me. He asked after my family, to which I replied you were all well. We both stood somewhat awkwardly before I told him that I had come to pay a call on Miss Bingley.

He nodded and said he would be certain to inform them of my visit, but he also said there were pressing circumstances that kept them all very occupied. I nodded in understanding, and he helped me into the carriage. As I departed, I saw the butler open the door and immediately usher him inside.

I was hopeful that I would receive a note from Caroline explaining when a good time to call would be or to at least acknowledge my visit. As of yet, I have not received a note nor has their card been left at the Gardiner residence.

Lizzy, I hope you can agree with me now that I will probably never see Mr. Bingley again. I cannot say I blame them, however. Caroline must have seen something in my behavior that made her feel as though I did not truly care for her brother. I know I am not as forward as Kitty or Lydia, which may have led to a misunderstanding.

I will endeavor to banish every painful thought, however, and think only of the pleasures I have of being with my aunt and uncle. I eagerly await your visit when you come with Sir Lucas and Maria to break your journey here.

With love,

Jane

Elizabeth closed the letter in anger. *I truly cannot believe Miss Bingley would be so false a friend. There was truth in all her looks when we conversed at Netherfield. No, there is something more than meets the eye.* She thought for a moment. "Of course!" she exclaimed aloud, startling Kitty, who was working on a needlepoint next to her.

"What does Jane have to say?" Kitty asked.

Elizabeth read the letter aloud to Kitty, then said, "I think Mr. Darcy may have stolen the card Jane left for the Bingleys."

Kitty looked at Elizabeth in surprise. "I cannot believe he would be so wicked!" she cried.

"What else could be preventing them from calling on Jane?" Elizabeth demanded in return.

"Perhaps it is as Mr. Darcy and Miss Bingley have both said: urgent business keeps them very occupied at the moment."

"Well, it is very rude of them to not even send a note, then," Elizabeth huffed.

"I quite agree. Perhaps Jane should try visiting again?" suggested Kitty.

"I will attempt to persuade her to do so when I am there," Elizabeth replied.

Two weeks later, Elizabeth found herself doing just that as she and the Lucases stopped for a brief respite before continuing on to Hunsford. "But Jane," she argued, "perhaps Miss Bingley never saw your card."

"Are you suggesting the butler lost it?" Jane asked, bewildered.

"Or Mr. Darcy stole it," Elizabeth responded darkly.

"Lizzy!" exclaimed Jane. "Mr. Darcy has not done anything to deserve such harsh judgment! No, the only logical conclusion is that Mr. Bingley is no longer interested in me or I have done something to give the impression that I am not interested in him."

Elizabeth opened her mouth to respond, but she was stopped by Jane's harsh cry. "Enough, Lizzy! I cannot take another moment of this."

Chastened, Elizabeth watched as Jane blinked back tears.

"Please, Lizzy, allow me to move on," she pleaded. "I will be well, I promise. All will be as it was before. Let us not speak of it again."

Elizabeth's eyes filled with tears. "Very well, Jane."

The two sisters embraced, remaining in that position until Mrs. Gardiner summoned them to dinner. After eating, Mrs. Gardiner sat herself near Elizabeth in order to discuss the situation.

"I have written to my friends in Derbyshire to inquire about Mr. Darcy," Mrs. Gardiner began. "They all have nothing but good to say about him, both as a landlord and as a master. Like his father before him, he runs his estate dutifully."

"That does not mean anything," Elizabeth said stubbornly. "I also never saw him be cruel or unkind to a servant. I merely believe him to be arrogant and to think condescendingly of those beneath him."

"You could be right," Mrs. Gardiner said. "I have been concerned about Jane during this visit, and I do not understand why the Bingleys would ignore the acquaintance. I have tried to persuade her to attempt a second visit, but she refuses. I have never known her to be so stubborn. She struggles to keep up her spirits, and quite often she comes down for dinner with red eyes."

"When I return from Hunsford, if the Bingleys are not back at Netherfield, I will pay a call on them myself," Elizabeth declared.

"I think that might be for the best," agreed Mrs. Gardiner. "I would do so myself, but I have never made their acquaintance and would not wish to be considered impertinent."

The conversation was interrupted by Jane herself, and the subject of conversation changed.

"Lizzy, your uncle and I wondered if you would like to join us on a pleasure tour this summer," Mrs. Gardiner said. "We have not yet determined how far we shall go, but we wish to go as far north as the Lakes."

"Oh, my dear aunt!" Elizabeth exclaimed. "What delight! I would love to accompany you! I have long since wished to see the beauties of the north! You have quite removed any melancholy I may have been feeling. After all, what are men to rocks and mountains?"

Jane and Mrs. Gardiner laughed at Elizabeth, who quickly joined in their laughter.

"I would worry about my poor father with both Jane and myself absent for so long this year, but he has dear William to keep him company. With only Kitty and Lydia in the house, he might find that he prefers for his daughters to travel!"

It was on this happy note that Elizabeth went to bed that night. Jane's troubles, though heavy on her mind, were balanced with the delights of Hunsford and the Lakes. She had never had much opportunity to travel other than to and from London.

With Jane's insistence that Elizabeth no longer speak of the Bingleys, Elizabeth resolved to look forward to the future. In Hunsford, she would be free of any reminders of her sister's sorrows, and she was determined to make the most of every moment.

Chapter 14

Elizabeth looked out the window of the carriage in delight. Every object in the next day's journey was new and interesting, and her spirits were in a state of enjoyment. Jane had been cheerful that morning as she bid her sister farewell, which alleviated much of Elizabeth's concerns.

When they turned onto the lane to Hunsford, Maria joined her at the window to search for the parsonage. Finally, it came into view, with a garden sloping down to the road and a laurel hedge in front—exactly as Charlotte had described.

Mr. Stanley and Charlotte appeared at the door, and the carriage stopped at the small gate that led up to the house. In a moment, they were all out of the chaise, sharing hugs and smiles. The new Mrs. Stanley welcomed her friends with pleasure, and Elizabeth found herself satisfied with the genuine joy in Charlotte's eyes.

Mr. Stanley began to show his guests about the parsonage. He was about to lead them into the garden when Charlotte recommended they give them time to settle into their rooms first.

"And that is why I married you," Mr. Stanley said, beaming at his wife. "I would be lost to the niceties of society without your guidance."

The two shared a private smile, and Elizabeth was relieved to see that her practical friend seemed to be falling a bit in love with her husband, and he with her. *They may have married for logical reasons, but they are good companions for one another*, she thought privately.

The evening was spent talking over Hertfordshire news, much of which had already been written in letters. It was gratifying to see Charlotte express her contentment with her new situation in sincere tones. Elizabeth had been concerned her friend only wrote the best, without actually feeling any of it, but that proved to not be the case.

After a delightful visit, they all retired for the night.

About the middle of the next day as Elizabeth readied herself for a walk, she heard someone rush up the stairs.

"Oh, Lizzy!" cried Maria, "you must come immediately!! There is such a sight to be seen!"

Elizabeth dashed down the stairs after Maria. "Have the pigs got into the garden again?" she asked the young girl in vain.

She looked out the front window and saw a phaeton with two ladies at the front gate speaking with Mr. and Mrs. Stanley. "Is this all?" she cried in astonishment. "It is nothing but Lady Catherine and her daughter!"

"Oh, no, that is not Lady Catherine—it is Mrs. Jenkinson, who lives with them. The other Miss Anne de Bourgh. Who would have thought such a wealthy heiress could be so small?"

"Ah, I see," Elizabeth said in understanding.

After a short conversation, Charlotte and her husband returned to the parsonage. "How fortunate you ladies are!" cried Mr. Stanley upon seeing the two girls.

Elizabeth and Maria blinked at him, then turned to Charlotte.

"Miss de Bourgh has issued an invitation for the entire party to dine with them tomorrow," she explained.

Maria was in raptures. "I do not have a thing to wear!" she cried in dismay.

"Not to worry," Mr. Stanley said reassuringly. "Lady Catherine prefers to keep the distinction of rank. She will not be offended by your modest attire."

"Just put on whatever you have that's best," Charlotte said with a slightly exasperated look at her husband.

Elizabeth hid a smile at this evidence of Collins's assessment that his friend was eager to please those above him. She wondered if more of his sycophancy would be on display once he was actually in the presence of the great Lady Catherine de Bourgh.

She would not have to wait long to determine the accuracy of her hypothesis. The following day passed quickly, and soon they were on their way to Rosings. As the weather was very fine, they had a pleasant walk of about half a mile across the park. Elizabeth was pleased with the park, even though she felt it slightly more formal than her preference.

When they ascended the stairs to the hall, poor Maria was so nervous her hand fairly shook where it rested on her father's arm. Even Sir William appeared slightly pale, but Elizabeth's courage did not fail her.

The group reached the room where Lady Catherine, her daughter, and Mrs. Jenkinson were sitting. Her ladyship, with great condescension, arose to receive them. Introductions were performed by Mrs. Stanley, and bows and curtsies were exchanged.

Lady Catherine was a tall, large woman with strong features. It surprised Elizabeth to see how thin and small the daughter looked next to her mother. The girl's features, though plain, were insignificant, and she spoke very little, even after dinner was served.

The meal itself was impressive. Mr. Stanley sat at the bottom of the table and was asked to carve. He and Sir William ate and praised every dish, which Lady Catherine responded to with gracious smiles. Elizabeth did not have much of an opportunity to speak, as she sat between Charlotte and Miss de Bourgh.

When the ladies entered the drawing room, there was little to be done but hear Lady Catherine talk. She spoke without a single pause until coffee arrived. She minutely questioned Charlotte about every detail of managing her home. Once she was satisfied with Charlotte's answers, she turned her attention to Elizabeth.

Elizabeth felt all the impertinence of her ladyship's questions: how many sisters did she have? Were they older or younger? Had they a governess? What kind of carriage did her father keep?

In spite of her annoyance, Elizabeth answered every question with composure. The gentlemen soon joined them, and card tables were placed. Elizabeth sat to play with Maria, Miss de Bourgh, and Mrs. Jenkinson. Their group had very little conversation whereas the other table was filled with Lady Catherine speaking and Mr. Stanley flattering.

When at last Lady Catherine and her daughter had tired of games, the carriage was offered to Charlotte, who gratefully accepted it.

Sir William only stayed one week at Hunsford, but his visit was long enough to convince him of his daughter's comfort and security. Throughout his visit, Mr. Stanley frequently took his father-in-law out in the gig to show him the countryside.

Once Sir William left, Mr. and Mrs. Stanley returned to their usual employments. Elizabeth was gratified to see that her friend was being well treated by her husband. Although they spent much time apart during the day due to their various responsibilities, Mr. Stanley made a point to seek out his wife and assure himself of her happiness and comfort.

The entertainment of dining at Rosings was repeated about twice per week. Elizabeth soon saw that Lady Catherine was a most active landlord. There was nothing that occurred in the parish that was beneath her notice. Charlotte mentioned to Elizabeth one day that although the lady's suggestions were useful, for the most part, there were the occasional demands that did not make sense logically.

Elizabeth spent much of her time walking and exploring the grounds. The time of year had exceptionally fine weather, and she found a particular path that seemed to put her beyond the reach of Lady Catherine's curiosity.

A fortnight into her visit, with Easter approaching, Elizabeth was surprised to hear that Lady Catherine was expecting two guests: her nephews. One was the second son of an earl, and Elizabeth anticipated that both gentlemen would have similar manners to their aunt.

One evening, Mr. Stanley spied an ornate carriage pass by the garden on its way to Rosings. The following morning, he hastened to Rosings to pay his respects. To the ladies' surprise, he returned almost immediately.

"Make haste, my dear!" he exclaimed as he rushed into the parsonage. "Lady Catherine's nephews are on their way to pay a call at our home!"

"What?" exclaimed Charlotte. "Whyever for?"

"Apparently one of them is known to you," he said breathlessly. "A Mr. Darcy of Pemberley?"

Elizabeth froze. *No! Surely Providence would not be so cruel!*

She scarcely had time to compose herself before the doorbell was rung. Mr. Darcy and his cousin—a Colonel Fitzwilliam—were announced by the maid.

The two gentlemen entered the drawing room, and a fluttering erupted in Elizabeth's stomach. As much as she loathed the man, she had to admit that Mr. Darcy was exceedingly handsome.

For his part, Darcy could not believe it when he heard that Elizabeth Bennet was staying no more than a mile away from him as he visited Rosings. It was as though the heavens themselves had sent him a sign.

When he chose to leave Netherfield, his intention was to forget her entirely. As much as he wished it to happen, his mind and thoughts were full of her. He missed her kindness, her wit and intelligence, and the way her eyes sparkled when she bantered with him.

Even with all the business and difficulties he encountered in town, she was constantly present on the edge of his mind. With each decision—especially those about his sister—he asked himself, *What would Elizabeth say?*

To see her here, in the flesh, was more torment than he could stand. *All right, Lord,* he murmured in silent prayer. *You have more than made your point.*

His musings were interrupted by a low laugh. Elizabeth and Colonel Fitzwilliam were in quiet conversation, and something she said must have been humorous.

Eager to be in conversation with her as well, Darcy crossed the room and settled himself next to his cousin. "I trust your family is well, Miss Bennet?"

Elizabeth raised an eyebrow and said, "Tolerably, sir."

He winced slightly, Collins's words ringing in his ears.

"My eldest sister has been in town these three months," she continued. "Have you never happened to see her there?"

Darcy hesitated. "I believe I met her once, attempting to visit Bingley. She called around the same time as I had."

Elizabeth pursed her lips. "Ah, yes, that is right. It is a pity she could not find them at home. She was eager to renew her acquaintance with Miss Bingley."

"Alas, they are quite occupied with business," Mr. Darcy demurred.

"So my sister has been given to understand," Elizabeth replied doubtfully.

There was an awkward pause, then Colonel Fitzwilliam changed the conversation with the readiness and ease of a well-bred man. After their leaving, his manners were much admired by the ladies of the parsonage, and they anticipated with pleasure their next opportunity to visit with him.

It was some days, however, before another invitation was issued to dine at Rosings. It was Easter time, and Lady Catherine requested their presence for the first time in over a week. The invitation was accepted, of course, and at a proper hour, they joined the party in Lady Catherine's drawing room.

Her ladyship received them civilly, but it was clear that they were not her most honored guests that day. She was so engrossed by her nephews that aside from the greetings, she hardly paid the party from the parsonage any mind at all.

Colonel Fitzwilliam was extremely glad to see them, as any additional entertainment was a relief to him at Rosings. He once again sat himself with Elizabeth, drawing her into such an animated conversation that all eyes repeatedly strayed to them.

Finally, Lady Catherine could no longer tolerate the distraction. "I say, Fitzwilliam, whatever are you discussing with Miss Bennet?"

Stifling a laugh, he said, "We are speaking of music, madam."

"Of music! Why, had I ever learnt to play, I would have been a great proficient! As would have Anne, had her health allowed her. How is Georgiana, Darcy?"

Darcy went suddenly pale and looked at the colonel. "How is she?" he repeated stupidly.

"I believe, in her letters, she has told me she practices daily," the colonel interjected.

"Yes, but I wasn't asking if she wrote about her practice. I was asking Darcy to tell me whether she is proficient."

Darcy relaxed slightly and answered, "She is quite proficient, madam."

"I am very glad to hear that," responded Lady Catherine. "Pray tell her from me, when you see her next in town, that she cannot expect to excel if she does not practice more."

"I will tell her when next I see her," said Darcy, exchanging a quick look with Fitzwilliam.

"I have given the same advice to Miss Bennet here quite often. As Mrs. Stanley has no instrument, Miss Bennet is welcome to practice in Mrs. Jenkinson's room. She would be in nobody's way in that part of the house, and she would improve greatly if she would but take me up on my offer."

Darcy looked somewhat ashamed of his aunt's ill breeding and did not respond.

"Will you play for us, Miss Bennet?" requested Colonel Fitzwilliam.

Elizabeth laughed and agreed, saying, "Your aunt is correct, however, and I do not play so very well."

"I'm sure that cannot be so." The colonel smiled charmingly. "Allow me to turn the pages for you."

She began to play, and midway through, Darcy moved closer to the piano. It was not consciously done; her music and passion pulled him towards her like a siren's call.

Elizabeth saw his approach and arched an eyebrow. "Do you mean to frighten me, Mr. Darcy, by coming in all this state to hear me? I will not be alarmed, even if your sister is skilled. My courage always rises at every attempt to intimidate me!"

"I shall not disagree with you," he replied, "because I know you do not really believe I would wish to alarm you. And I daresay I have been acquainted with you long enough to know that you find great enjoyment in professing opinions that are not your own."

Against her will, Elizabeth laughed heartily at this description of herself, which caused her playing to falter. She resumed her playing, choosing a simple tune that would allow her to carry on the conversation unimpeded.

After a moment, she smiled at Fitzwilliam and said, "Your cousin will teach you that I am not to be trusted! It leaves me no choice but to retaliate, and I'm afraid that what I have to reveal about Mr. Darcy's character may be quite shocking."

"I am not afraid of you," Darcy retorted with a smile.

"Please tell me!" cried the colonel. "I should dearly like to know how my introverted cousin behaves amongst strangers!"

"Prepare yourself from something truly dreadful, Colonel. The first time I ever saw your cousin was at a ball. And what do you think he did? Everything but dance. He stood stiffly in a corner and refused to stand up with anyone even though gentlemen were scarce. I can say with confidence that more than one lady was sitting down in want of a partner."

Colonel Fitzwilliam looked at his cousin's dour face and laughed.

"While it is dreadful, it is not surprising. Anyone who knows Darcy can tell you that he does not like to stand up with strangers."

"Yes, and no one can be introduced in a ball," Elizabeth shot back.

Colonel Fitzwilliam's eyes widened slightly at her tone, and she took a calming breath. The song came to a close, and she began to excuse herself. Just as she went to stand, Mr. Darcy opened his mouth to speak.

"I have not the talent that some have," he said haltingly, "of conversing easily with others. I am not able to understand their tone of voice or appear interested in their concerns."

Here he paused for some moments, then braced himself and said, "I was also in a significant amount of pain that evening. The day before, I was thrown from my horse. The pain was quite intense, and I'm afraid my temper left much to be desired. I could scarcely walk, let alone dance."

He looked deep into Elizabeth's eyes. "I scarcely remember that evening, and I would have said anything to anyone in order to get them to leave me alone."

Elizabeth's eyes widened at this admission. "Why did you choose to attend, then? Certainly, your time might have been better employed resting."

"I did not wish to miss seeing Collins and his reaction to our surprise."

Surprised, Elizabeth did not know how to respond to this reasoning. On seeing her reaction, he said, "I may not have the most spirited of natures, but I surround myself with those who do because I value it."

"He can be quite jovial when amongst those with whom he chooses," Fitzwilliam interjected. "I never laugh so hard as I do when I am with Darcy."

"Even though much of the humor is directed at me, rather than with me." Darcy smiled wryly.

"Well, as you know, I dearly love to laugh," replied Elizabeth.

Darcy's eyes lit up, and his chest swelled with hope. Could it be that she had forgiven him for his intemperate words at the assembly? Did he have a chance? The look she directed at him was softer than he had ever seen before. Surely she could not disdain him as much as Collins had hinted—not after all this time.

He had spent the last four months since the ball at Netherfield in agony. Everywhere he turned, he saw her. Every conversation, he envisioned her participation with lively wit and an arch smile. Instead of separation cooling his ardor, it only fanned the flames into a blazing fire that burned within him every time he thought of her.

For her part, Elizabeth's chief feeling was that of confusion. Mr. Darcy was as open as she had ever seen him. Additionally, knowing of his injuries definitely put a different light on his aloof and stiff behavior when she'd met him. She resolved to consider the matter later when she was in the privacy of her bedroom.

Their private conversation was interrupted by Lady Catherine's presumptuous remarks on Elizabeth's performance. These were intermingled with many instructions on execution and taste, which Elizabeth accepted with graciousness and civility. At the request of the gentlemen, she remained at the instrument until her ladyship's carriage arrived to return the guests to the parsonage.

Chapter 15

Elizabeth sat by herself the next morning, writing a letter to Jane about the events the day prior. Mrs. Stanley and Maria were on business in the village, and Elizabeth was startled by a ring of the doorbell.

The door opened, and Mr. Darcy—and only Mr. Darcy—entered the room. He seemed just as surprised to find her alone as she was him. He apologized for the intrusion and explained he was given the understanding that all the ladies were at home.

They sat down, and she inquired after everyone at Rosings. Once the pleasantries had passed, there were several minutes of awkward silence. Each looked around the room, and Elizabeth desperately attempted to think of something she could say to him.

"How very suddenly you all quitted Netherfield last November!" she blurted out, then blushed. Forging ahead, she said, "I trust Mr. Bingley and his sisters were well when you left London?"

"Perfectly so, thank you."

After another moment of silence, she realized he would provide no further answer. "Last my sister heard from Miss Bingley, they were planning to return to Netherfield in March. Do you know if that is still the case?"

Darcy shifted somewhat uncomfortably in his chair. "I am afraid I am not in possession of any other information, Miss Bennet."

"If he means to be so little at Netherfield, perhaps he should give it up entirely. It would be better for the neighborhood if there was an occupant who was more... reliable."

Darcy shifted again. "I believe the nature of his business is quite unsteady. It is difficult to predict what will occur."

"Is Miss Bingley well? I only ask because Jane has not received any responses to her letters."

"I have not seen Miss Bingley in some time," he responded.

Elizabeth pressed her lips together, and the room fell silent again.

"Mr. Stanley seems quite fortunate in his choice of wife," Darcy finally said.

"Yes, indeed! He has met one of the few sensible women who would have made him happy. He is a great friend of my cousin, but does not have his... confidence," Elizabeth replied.

"It must be agreeable for her to be settled so near her family, as well."

"It is nearly fifty miles! I would not call that an easy distance!"

"And what is fifty miles of good road? Yes, I believe it is a very easy distance."

"I should never have considered it as her being settled near her family," Elizabeth exclaimed. "Indeed, I have felt as though she had gone to the other side of the world."

"It is proof of your own attachment to Hertfordshire, then. Anything beyond Longbourn is too far for you," he replied with a smile.

Thinking of Netherfield, she said, "I suppose a woman could be settled too near her family. The distance must be relative to the individual's situation and variety of circumstances. I do not think Charlotte considers herself very near her family, based on Mr. Stanley's present income."

Mr. Darcy scooted his chair closer and laid his elbows on his knees. He leaned forward and said intently, "You cannot have always been at Longbourn. You cannot have too strong an attachment."

Elizabeth sat back and looked at him in surprise. "On the contrary, sir," she replied coolly. "I love my family very much."

Darcy flushed slightly and said, "Of course you do."

At that moment, the front door opened, and in walked Charlotte and Maria. They looked surprised to see Darcy there. He stood and explained that he had thought them all at home. Charlotte offered to call for some tea, but he demurred and stated he was needed at Rosings. He bowed and departed swiftly.

"My dear Eliza!" exclaimed Charlotte once the gentleman had left and Maria had excused herself. "What could he mean, calling on you alone? He must be in love with you!"

Elizabeth burst into laughter. "My dear Charlotte," she mimicked. "Mr. Darcy is no more in love with me than the baker is!"

Although doubtful, Charlotte did not press the issue. Time would tell which of the two friends were correct.

Several days passed, in which Elizabeth enjoyed walking the lanes of Rosings in the fine spring weather. On her second walk, she encountered Mr. Darcy and dropped a hint that it was her favorite path so he would know to avoid it in the future. To her disappointment, he seemed to appear with regularity. To make matters worse, he would insist on accompanying her every time they crossed paths.

Their walks were often quiet, with Elizabeth attempting to make conversation. It was difficult, however, when Mr. Darcy only answered with short words.

"How do you find Rosings, Mr. Darcy?"

"Very well, Miss Bennet."

"I understand you visit every year?"

"Yes."

"Is it much changed since you came last year?"

"Not particularly."

After the second such walk, she gave up trying to engage him in active conversation. Instead, she began to expound upon the books she was reading, articles from that day's newspaper, and Longbourn's preparations for the planting season.

To her surprise, Mr. Darcy became more engaged when she rambled on than when she tried to draw him out with questions! Elizabeth simply could not understand the gentleman at all. He shared his own opinions of the same books and articles, and he compared Pemberley's methods to those of Longbourn in great detail.

To make matters more difficult, his explanation as to his behavior towards her at the Meryton assembly had done much to soften her initial prejudice against him. It seemed at odds, however, with the fact that he seemed to be deliberately preventing Mr. Bingley from continuing his acquaintance with Jane.

After about a week of coming across Mr. Darcy each day, she decided to take a new route to read Jane's latest letter in private. When a quarter of an hour had passed, she was surprised by someone on the path. It was not Mr. Darcy this time, but it was Colonel Fitzwilliam. She put away her letter and smiled at him kindly.

"I am making a tour of the park as I do every year," he said by way of explanation. "Would you care to join me?"

"I was about to return to the parsonage," she replied.

"Allow me to accompany you, then," he said, extending his arm.

The two walked in comfortable companionship. "How much longer do you plan on remaining in Kent?" she asked him.

"We will leave on Saturday; that is, if Darcy does not put it off again. I am quite at his disposal."

"It seems he arranges things just as he pleases," she replied, fighting to keep her voice light.

"He does like to have his own way," replied Fitzwilliam. "I believe we are all guilty of that at times, however. It is only that some of us have more freedom than others. As a second son, like myself, I have become accustomed to self-denial and dependence."

"I imagine a son of an earl does not have too much of an acquaintance with that!" Elizabeth laughed. "When have you ever been prevented from something you desired?"

"Well, perhaps I have not experienced hardships as some have, but I certainly cannot marry where I'd like, for example."

Elizabeth colored at this, wondering if the comment was meant specifically for her. She responded in a lively tone, "And what is the usual price for an earl's younger son? I imagine that, unless your brother is quite ill, you cannot go below fifty thousand pounds!"

Fitzwilliam laughed at her jest. "That seems about right."

"Perhaps Mr. Darcy asked you to accompany him so he could have someone at his disposal at all times," she continued with an arched smile. "I wonder if he does not marry so he can have that convenience at all times! But perhaps his sister fills that position; as he has sole power over her, he may do what he wishes with her."

Colonel Fitzwilliam grew serious, then he forced a smile. "No, I am afraid he is forced to share that advantage with me, as we share guardianship over her."

"Do you indeed? I wonder what sort of guardians you make," she said, amused. "Does your charge give you very much trouble? Girls that age—like my youngest sister—are sometimes a little difficult to manage."

Colonel Fitzwilliam looked so alarmed at this that she immediately added, "You need not be frightened! I am merely joking. The only thing I know of Miss Darcy is what I have heard from Miss Bingley."

Colonel Fitzwilliam went pale white. Confused, Elizabeth added, "My sister Jane fell ill while visiting at Netherfield and was there for some days. I was called to attend her, and during that time, Miss Bingley mentioned Miss Darcy was quite an accomplished young lady and a great favorite of hers."

The color returned to Fitzwilliam's face. "Ah, yes, I believe she is a good friend of my young cousin. They are quite often in one another's company. Their brother is a good friend of Darcy's as well."

"Oh, yes," Elizabeth replied drily. "Mr. Darcy takes a great deal of care of him."

"I suppose that is one way to say it," Fitzwilliam mused. "From something he said on our journey here, I have reason to think Bingley is much indebted to him. Something to do with rescuing him from a lady."

"I see," Elizabeth rasped. She cleared her throat and said, "Did Mr. Darcy give reasons for this interference?"

Fitzwilliam hesitated. "Well, I believe it is a circumstance that Darcy would not want to get back to the lady's family."

"You may depend upon my secrecy, sir."

"And to be honest, I am not certain that the friend Darcy spoke of even was Bingley. He simply mentioned that he had a friend who was considering marriage to a lady who was unacceptable."

"What do you mean?"

"I believe there were strong objections to the lady."

Elizabeth made no answer and walked on, her heart swelling with anger. After several moments, Fitzwilliam asked her if she was well.

"Oh, I am only thinking on what you have told me. Who was Mr. Darcy to be the judge?"

"You think him officious?"

"I do not see what right Mr. Darcy has to make decisions for his friend in matters of the heart," she said vehemently. "But," she continued lightly, recollecting herself, "as we do not know all the specifics, we should not judge your cousin so harshly. Perhaps there was not much affection in the relationship."

"Perhaps," he admitted, "but it would lessen my cousin's triumph very sadly!"

This seemed to be in such perfect alignment with her image of Mr. Darcy that she could not trust herself with an answer. Thankfully, the parsonage came into sight, and she could excuse herself to her room. Once there, she shut the door so she could think uninterrupted on all she had learned.

It must *be Mr. Bingley,* she thought furiously. *Who else could Mr. Darcy be able to influence so easily? Mr. Wickham had such a strength of character that I cannot imagine him falling susceptible to Mr. Darcy's machinations. Additionally, as this happened recently, it could only have been Mr. Bingley—Mr. Wickham did not appear to pay particular attentions to any unsuitable ladies.*

She had always been of the opinion that Mr. Darcy had done

something to keep his friend from her sister, and this was the evidence! There was incontrovertible proof coming directly from the man's own cousin! What could be more certain than that?

"There were some strong objections to the lady." Colonel Fitzwilliam's words echoed in her ears.

To Jane herself, there could be no possibility of objections! She is all that is good and kind! No, it must be that he is against my family because of our lower station in life compared to his own.

Elizabeth spent several hours contemplating this line of thought. The agitation and tears that were produced brought on a headache, which became more severe as the time for their dinner appointment at Rosings approached.

Charlotte took one look at her friend, saw that she was truly unwell, and insisted that Elizabeth remain at the parsonage in order to rest and recover. Mr. Stanley was somewhat apprehensive at the idea of offending Lady Catherine, but his wife reminded him that Lady Catherine would not wish someone who was potentially ill to be in company with Miss de Bourgh. This immediately changed Mr. Stanley's position, and he wished his wife's friend every hope of improvement while they were away.

After they left, Elizabeth went to her desk and removed every letter that Jane had written to her since her arrival in Kent. There was no specific complaint, but almost every line was written with a lack of Jane's typical cheerfulness.

This review of the letters served to escalate Elizabeth's anger towards Mr. Darcy. She could not think of him without feeling utter abhorrence, and it was in this frame of mind that she heard the doorbell ring.

Darcy stood nervously at the door of the parsonage. When Elizabeth did not arrive at Rosings with the rest of the party, his heart stopped. He had planned to make his request for her hand that evening, but now her illness had ruined all of his plans.

He had spent the entire day wrestling with himself. He knew that in the past she had not had the highest opinion of him, but certainly, she had accepted his apology for his intemperate words. He yearned to make her part of his life, in spite of the turmoil that existed in his family. *Not in spite of*—because *of*, he reminded himself.

Upon entering the room, he barely took in her pale face. He hurriedly asked after her health, not noticing her cold response. After several minutes of silent pacing, words began to pour from his mouth.

"I have struggled in vain, but I can no longer repress my feelings. You must allow me to tell you how much I ardently admire and love you. I beg of you, relieve my suffering and become my wife."

Elizabeth stared at him in shock, flushing a deep red. *Did he just say what I think he said?*

He took her silence and maidenly flush as encouragement and continued speaking. "In declaring myself, I am aware that I am going against the wishes of my family, my peers, and I dare say, my own better judgment. The fact that your family has connections so decidedly beneath my own has given me great cause for concern. Indeed, as a rational man, I cannot help but see that a union between us will come as reprehensible for many among my acquaintance. Furthermore—"

"Allow me to stop you there, sir."

Darcy's mouth froze open.

Elizabeth's frigid tone penetrated the chaos of his mind. "In cases such as these, I believe convention would dictate that I express gratitude for the honor of your feelings—but I cannot."

Now it was Darcy's turn to stare in shock.

"I have never desired your good opinion, and you have certainly granted it most unwillingly. I am sorry to cause you pain, but it was unconsciously done. I hope that the wrestle over these emotions will cause your heartache to be of short duration." With that, she pressed her lips tightly together and fell silent.

Darcy, upon realizing she would not continue speaking, said in a voice of forced calm, "And this is all the reply I am to receive? Why, with so little attempt at civility, am I rejected? Although I should not ask, as it is of little importance."

"And *I* might inquire," she retorted hotly, "why you chose to tell me you liked me against your will and your better judgment! You said it with so evident a desire to offend and insult me, which would give just cause to incivility, if indeed I was uncivil."

As she said these words, Darcy's face lost all color. He did not interrupt her; indeed, such an attempt would have been fruitless in the face of her released emotions that had been bottled up for so long.

"I have *every* reason in the world to think ill of you! What do you think would tempt me to accept the man who has ruined the happiness of a most beloved sister? You cannot deny that you attempted to prevent Jane from continuing an acquaintance with the Bingley family. Not only did you do all in your power to separate them—and thus exposing them to the derision of the world—but you continued your treachery by hiding Jane's visit to their home in London."

"I did not—"

"I heard you, sir. My sister Kitty and I heard you the night of the Netherfield ball. We were in the gardens, and you were in a room with an open window. We heard you tell Mr. Bingley that Jane was not a suitable match because of her family and her history."

She paused momentarily. When she saw he displayed no evident feeling of remorse, she continued with fury. "But it is not merely this on which my rejection is founded. Almost from the moment of your acquaintance, I determined you were not a true friend to my cousin William. He spoke so highly of you, and you have treated his friends and family as though they were lower than the dirt on which you tread. In what imaginary act of friendship can you defend your rudeness towards the community in which he lives?"

"And this is your opinion of me!" Darcy burst out. "I thank you for explaining so completely. My faults, according to this calculation, must be great indeed. But perhaps these offenses might have been overlooked had I not injured your pride by concealing my struggles and offering you flattery. But I abhor deceit. Nor am I ashamed of the feelings I shared—they were natural! Could you expect me to rejoice in the inferiority of your connections? To congratulate myself on the hope of a family whose condition in life is so decidedly beneath my own?"

The fury on Elizabeth's face became so intense that Darcy visibly flinched. "You are mistaken, sir," she said in a voice that shook with rage, "if you suppose the manner of your declaration affected me in any way other than removing any guilt I might have felt at refusing you, had you behaved in a more gentlemanlike manner."

He startled at this, but she ignored his reaction. "You could not have made me an offer of marriage in any way possible that would have tempted me to accept it."

Again, his astonishment was obvious, and he looked at her with a mixture of disbelief and mortification.

"From the very beginning," she pressed on, "your manners showed me the full extent of your arrogance, conceit, and selfish disregard for the feelings of others. I had not known you more than a week before I could safely say that you were the last man in the world whom I could ever be prevailed upon to marry."

"You have said quite enough, madam," Darcy said hoarsely. "I perfectly understand your feelings, and now have only to be ashamed of what my own have been. Forgive me for wasting your time."

With a whirl of his coat, Darcy fled the parsonage, leaving the door to slam shut behind him.

The turmoil of Elizabeth's mind was now excruciating. She had no idea what to think or do. She ran to her room, flung herself on the bed, and cried for a full half hour.

As she reflected on every horrid moment of the evening, her surprise continued to increase. *How could he have been in love with me all this time? So much so that he was willing to marry me in spite of his abhorrence to the idea.*

She continued in very agitated reflections until she heard the sound of Lady Catherine's carriage bringing her friends back to their home. She extinguished her candle and feigned sleep until she finally fell into disturbing dreams.

Chapter 16

Elizabeth awoke the next morning, feeling as though she had not slept at all. The memories from the previous evening immediately flooded into her consciousness, and she closed her eyes again in an attempt to blot them out. She sat up in bed and winced at the pain behind her eyes.

In spite of her aching head, she resolved to leave for a walk immediately after breakfast. She ate quickly and excused herself before Charlotte could comment on her pallor.

The five weeks she had so far spent in Kent enabled her to learn the paths almost as well as she knew the ones in Longbourn. She began to turn down her favorite path but remembered that she frequently encountered Mr. Darcy there. Instead, she turned another direction and headed into the trees.

After walking for some minutes, she spied a gentleman moving amongst a grove of trees. Afraid it was Mr. Darcy, she turned to head in the opposite direction when she heard her name called. She closed her eyes in resignation and turned towards him.

As she feared, Mr. Darcy approached her. Upon reaching her, he extended a gloved hand, which held out a sealed letter. She instinctively took it, then immediately chastised herself.

"I have been walking for some time in hopes of meeting you here. Will you do me the honor of reading that letter?" he asked with a look of haughty composure.

Without waiting for a response, he bowed and strode away.

Elizabeth placed the letter in a pocket and walked deeper into the trees. She intended on ignoring the letter at first. *What could he have to say to me, the hateful man?* However, curiosity soon overtook her, and she removed the envelope from its hiding place. With no expectation of pleasure, she began to read.

Be not alarmed, madam, on receiving this letter. It will not contain any repetition of those sentiments and offers that were so disgusting to you last night. I write without any intention of paining you, but my conscience demands you be made aware of circumstances as they truly are.

Two offenses of a very different nature were detailed by you. The first, that I had willingly separated Bingley from your sister. The second, that I am not a true friend to your cousin. I was unable to address either with composure last night. I only hope your sense of justice will allow me to acquit myself via this letter. The offenses, though on the surface appear to be distinct, are in fact intertwined.

I first made the acquaintance of Mr. Bingley four years ago when I visited Staffordshire. Mr. Wickham, my steward and close friend, was acquainted with him from school. My father had passed away, and the manager at one of my estates had ceased all correspondence during my father's illness.

Upon arriving at Mr. Bingley's home, we soon discovered his father leaving Miss Bingley's chambers in the middle of the night. I will not offend your sensibilities by further explanation. All I can say is that his attentions were not appropriate for a father to make towards his daughter. Wickham and I informed Bingley, who confronted his father. During that confrontation, Mr. Bingley Sr. ran away and bumped into a passing maid, causing him to fall down the stairs to his death. We all witnessed the tragedy.

That day prior, I had discovered the steward of Larkwood—a Mr. Lowry— had been passing himself off as myself! He was living as Fitzwilliam Darcy, master of the estate. A magistrate was sent for, and I never saw the man again. The Bingleys removed themselves from their home and resided with me for the summer while I set things to right at my estate.

The following year, Bingley, Wickham, and I returned to Staffordshire to conclude some business. The journey was very difficult for Bingley. We met your cousin Collins at an inn; he was travelling there as well to confront some difficulties from his past. He sensed there was a heavy weight on our shoulders, and

179

confidences were exchanged.

Each one of the four of us had fathers who were imperfect, to varying degrees. The behavior of each man has heavily influenced the lives of their children. It has formed a bond between us that cannot be shaken. While I do not have much in common with your cousin, my regard for him is just as deep as it is for Wickham and Bingley. It was never my intention to behave disdainfully in his town, and it pains me deeply. I have much to atone for, but please believe me when I tell you that I would give my life for that man.

Returning to my story, the fraudulent steward at Larkwood was also a father, a fact of which I was unaware. He had a son, who was around seventeen years of age at that time. When his father went to prison, the wife and son were forced to the streets. Had I known of their existence, I would have endeavored to help them. It is not a woman or child's fault when their father is deceitful.

The boy's mother died within a year after her husband was imprisoned. How the young man made his way, I know not. Our paths collided, however, when he made the acquaintance of my sister, Georgiana, who is more than ten years my junior.

My own excellent father died five years ago, and her guardianship was left to myself and Colonel Fitzwilliam. About a year ago, she was taken from school and an establishment was formed for her in London. We hired a companion for her, in whom we were wholly deceived. She persuaded my sister to request to spend the summer in Ramsgate, where she was introduced to the young Mr. Lowry.

The young man paid a call one evening on my sister. Mrs. Younge, who was a confederate of Mr. Lowry, left the two alone. My young sister, no more than fifteen years of age, was not a willing participant in what followed. A footman heard her screams, but the door was barred from the inside. By the time he was able to enter, the young man's revenge was complete. He attempted to escape from the window, but he did not notice a passing horse and carriage, which trampled him to his death.

Understandably, my sister was quite distraught. I took her to my uncle's home, where she would be safe and protected. I remained with her, devoting myself to her recovery, until she regained much of her cheerful nature. She strongly en-couraged me to go to Netherfield and settled herself at the home of my uncle, the earl, where Colonel Fitzwilliam took over her care.

I went to Netherfield with a conflict of deep emotions. I was eager to see my friend again, but I was loath to leave my sister. These feelings were in addition to the significant pain I experienced after being thrown from my horse. I do not make excuses for poor behavior, but I hope you will acquit me of malicious intent.

It quickly became apparent that Bingley was interested in your sister. The more I saw them in company together, the more anxious I felt. The betrayal of Bingley's father was difficult for him, as well as for his sisters. He deserves a wife who returns his affections in equal measure, and I confess I did not see any expression of particular regard. I expressed my concerns to him, but his sister Miss Bingley assured me she had the matter well in hand.

In regard to the conversation you overheard at the Netherfield ball, I mean no disrespect when I tell you that you are incorrect in your interpretation. Had you been privy to the entirety of the discourse, you would know that I was, in fact, not speaking of your sister to Bingley. Instead, I was referring to Miss Bingley and Wickham.

Over the past year, Miss Bingley has made her admiration for myself very apparent. I do not mean to flatter myself in speaking of her regard; it is a subject Bingley spoke with me about himself. I did not return her affections, and he was aware of the matter.

To my surprise, Wickham paid great attentions to Miss Bingley during our stay at Netherfield. At first, I thought he simply meant to spare me her devotion. While I admire the lady and have no wish to hurt her, I also do not wish to give her a false impression. It is difficult to know how to behave in her company.

Anyway, I digress. The night of the Netherfield ball, I was amazed to discover he had solicited her hand for the first set, as well as for a second set. I had not realized their relationship had progressed to such a degree.

My warnings that night were for Wickham, who upon confrontation expressed his desire to request her hand in marriage. Before you think ill of me for judging her for her father's actions, please know that I do not hold her accountable in any way for the horrors she has endured at his hands.

However, her experiences left her fearful for quite some time. I remember after a society event of some kind, a young man tried to steal a kiss from her. This sent her into such a terror that she was nearly catatonic for an entire week. Bingley was extremely concerned about her, as were Wickham and I.

At the risk of sounding indelicate, Wickham is a bit of a rake. He enjoys the pleasurable company of women and regularly seeks out that company in less than reputable ways. He has never abused a woman, nor seduced an innocent, but he is frequently offered favors that he willingly accepts.

My concern about a relationship between the two was for both of them. Her fear of physical intimacy, coupled with his proclivities, made me extremely uneasy about the future happiness for both. She would not be happy if he found himself unsatisfied in a marriage with her and sought relief elsewhere. I could not bear seeing such misery for either person.

I must apologize for how indelicate this letter has been. I know that much of this is not discussed in society, especially between a gentleman and a maiden, but I knew not how to otherwise correct the misconceptions that have arisen between us.

I now get to the part of the story that addresses your accusation that I have kept your sister and Bingley apart in London. Please be assured that I trusted Miss Bingley's certainty that your sister cares very much for her brother, although I cannot see it myself. Although, considering I did not see your ire towards me, and I clearly kept my own feelings too well hidden, I see how I must have been in error.

Nonetheless, the original plan was for me to remain in London. Bingley was to return to Netherfield with his sisters after matters of the engagement between Wickham and Miss Bingley were organized. To my horror, however, I returned to London to discover that my sister was with child. The man who forced himself upon her had left more than just a wounded soul behind.

My sister's melancholy returned with a fury. For days, she hid herself in her bedroom. She refused to eat, to bathe, or to even allow a maid to comb her hair. Miss Bingley visited several times, which prompted the first delay in their return to Netherfield.

One morning, I heard my sister's maid scream. I rushed upstairs to find that my sister had broken her mirror and was using the glass shards to slit her wrists and stomach. I was able to convince her to put the glass down, and a doctor was summoned.

After stitching and bandaging the cuts on her arms and stomach, the doctor determined that the baby was uninjured. He strongly recommended that my sister be removed to a country estate where she could recover until the baby was born. Miss Bingley insisted on accompanying her, and Bingley went along to provide protection.

I was forced to remain here in order to hide the truth. I make calls to the Bingley household to keep his affairs running and to make it appear as though they are in residence. As Bingley had closed the majority of his house for his stay in Netherfield, only a few servants know the truth, and they are loyal to him. He is a good master, and his generosity is respected.

On the day your sister paid her call, I was visiting an empty house. I could not share the truth with her. My sister and the Bingleys have, in fact, retired to one of my estates in Scotland. We hoped the distance and the location would be of benefit to both of them. It means, however, that any cards, letters, etc., are extremely delayed. Miss Bingley cannot send a letter postmarked from so far away.

One small blessing has come from this horrible situation: in helping my sister recover emotionally, Miss Bingley is healing some of her old wounds. The words she says to my sister help her realize the truth about her own situation. It makes me hopeful for her marriage to Wickham.

This, madam, is a faithful narrative of the events which have so concerned you, and I hope you will keep my confidence. I can only trust that your discretion and kindness towards your own sister will help you understand the situation I faced and the actions I have taken. If your feelings toward me cause you to doubt the truthfulness of this letter, you may appeal to Colonel Fitzwilliam. As co-guardian to Georgiana, he is aware of the entire situation.

I will attempt to find some way of putting this letter in your hands tomorrow before I depart for London, and afterwards, Scotland. It is almost my sister's time, and the story is that I will collect her from London and take her with me while I visit that estate.

I will only add, God bless you.
Fitzwilliam Darcy.

Chapter 17

Elizabeth could not even begin to describe the tumult of emotions she felt as she read Mr. Darcy's letter. With a strong prejudice against anything he might have to say, she initially scoffed at his opening paragraphs when no expression of apology was immediate. The tone of his letter was that of haughty insolence, and she was disgusted with his pride.

But when she read of the account of how he became acquainted with Mr. Bingley and the tragedy that occurred shortly thereafter, she could feel nothing but shock and disbelief. That someone of her acquaintance could have suffered so badly! She'd had no idea that Miss Bingley's cool demeanor was a wall she had placed to shield herself from the cruelties of her father.

Then, as she read the circumstances surrounding Miss Darcy, she began to weep. "This must be false! It cannot be true!" she cried.

When at last she had gone through the whole letter, she crumpled it and put it into her pocket, determined to never see it again. However, she did not walk more than a few steps before she removed it again and sat on a fallen log.

It was on that uncomfortable resting place where she read and reread the letter. At first, she was shocked that Mr. Darcy dared to share something so personal about Miss Bingley. However, she reasoned that her cousin William was already aware of the account, and it was possible that Darcy had permission from the lady to share her story if need be. *No, I will not judge him without foundation again*, she vowed.

Elizabeth thought back on every encounter she ever had with the man. How differently each event now appeared! Not only were the memories tinged with his feelings towards her, but she could see the raw emotion behind each of his actions.

"How despicably I have acted," she cried aloud to herself. "I, who have always prided myself on my discernment! How often have I proclaimed myself to be a great studier of character? Yet to misunderstand a gentleman so completely; what a wretched creature I am. Had I been in love, I could not have been more blind as to the truth. But vanity and pride were my weaknesses. Till this moment, I never truly knew myself."

Her thoughts were full of poor Miss Darcy. What would become of her and the child? Was she healing well? When would the baby be born? *Imagine, feeling such despair that you were willing to end your own life by violent means.* She wept thinking of the poor girl, who took the face of her youngest sister in her mind. *How would I feel if it were my Lydia to experience such a tragedy? I would never wish to dance or smile again.* The tears gained new strength at this notion.

She then thought again of Mr. Darcy. What a caring elder brother! In Meryton, she had seen families who disowned daughters fell with child without marriage. Granted, she had never heard of a young lady who had been forced into the situation. *But it's not as if the gossips would give any leeway,* she admitted. *No, they would say the girl must have done something to encourage the man.*

After wandering the lane for two hours, giving way to every type of thought, she suddenly felt conscious of her long absence. She was burdened with a heavy fatigue that she had not known before as she made her way back to the parsonage. She steeled herself to appear as cheerful as usual, repressing any reflections that would interfere with her normal conversations with Charlotte and Maria.

Upon entering the home, she was immediately informed by her friends that the two gentlemen from Rosings had called during her absence. Mr. Darcy left almost immediately, but Colonel Fitzwilliam sat for at least an hour, hoping for her return. Elizabeth vocally expressed disappointment in having missed them, but inside herself, she was secretly relieved to have avoided their attentions. She hoped she could escape their notice until their departure.

The two gentlemen left Rosings the next morning, and Mr. Stanley waited in his garden in order to make last-minute farewells. As the carriage drove by, he bowed in its direction and stayed prostrated until it was out of sight.

Elizabeth breathed a sigh of relief when she heard Mr. Stanley return to the house, loudly announcing the great honor bestowed by the gentlemen, who deigned to wave at him as they passed. She no longer thought so ill of Mr. Darcy, but she was too embarrassed to face him again.

The days following their departure seemed to be a torture, however. Every hour something would occur that would remind her of Mr. Darcy and the entire situation. She struggled to demonstrate her usually lively spirits, and she was unsuccessful in fooling Charlotte for long. Thankfully, Mrs. Stanley's suppositions were on Elizabeth being morose over the colonel's absence.

"You know it would never do," Charlotte said kindly. "He is in need of a woman with a large dowry."

"He is amiable, and I miss his lively company, but my heart remains untouched," Elizabeth assured her friend.

On the last day of her time at Hunsford, an invitation came from Rosings to dine that evening. To Elizabeth's regret, much of the evening was spent with Lady Catherine lamenting the absence of her nephews. These feelings, however, inspired in Elizabeth the first genuine bit of amusement. *How would she have acted tonight if I had been presented as her future niece?*

These musings were interrupted by the lady herself. "You are very dull this evening, Miss Bennet! I daresay it is because you will be leaving yourself. You must write to your mother and beg to stay a little longer!"

"I thank you, madam, but my father has written to hasten my return."

Lady Catherine argued against this, but it soon became clear that Elizabeth would not be swayed. The conversation then turned to the correct way to pack gowns, where to stop and change horses, and what to do if the weather proved difficult. Her ladyship monopolized the discourse for the remainder of the evening until they departed and were wished a good journey.

Elizabeth curtsied to Lady Catherine and her daughter. To her surprise, Miss de Bourgh returned the curtsey and held out her hand to Elizabeth. The frail young woman had a surprisingly strong grip, and she looked deeply in Elizabeth's eyes. "Godspeed, my dear Miss Bennet," she whispered. "I wish you every happiness."

Although it was not spoken, Elizabeth could not help but suspect that Miss de Bourgh was aware of Darcy's proposal and the contents of the letter. The young lady gave her a shy smile, which Elizabeth returned in kind before leaving with her party. They returned to the parsonage and almost immediately settled in to bed.

The following morning, Mr. and Mrs. Stanley dined with Elizabeth and Maria. Few words were necessary as Mr. Stanley waxed eloquently on the many kindnesses their guests had received from Lady Catherine's condescension. At length, a servant entered to announce the chaise had arrived. They went outside to direct its loading, and finally Charlotte determined it was ready.

Elizabeth bid her friend an affectionate farewell, complete with a warm embrace and fervent promises to write frequently. Mr. Stanley handed Elizabeth into the carriage and asked to be remembered to her cousin. She acquiesced, and then Maria entered as well. The door was closed, and the two began the journey towards London.

"Goodness!" cried Maria after several minutes of silence, "how quickly time has passed! It seems as though we were here no more than a day or two, and yet so many things have happened!"

"Yes, a great many," Elizabeth smiled kindly at the younger

woman.

"We have dined nine times at Rosings! I cannot wait until I can tell Kitty and Lydia all about it!"

Elizabeth only smiled again in response. After a few minutes, she feigned sleep until she heard Maria's soft snores across the carriage. Then she opened her eyes, staring out the carriage window without really seeing the view for the four hours it took them to arrive in London.

Upon arriving at Gracechurch Street, Elizabeth was gratified to see that her sister looked well. There was little opportunity of studying her spirits, however, as there were several engagements that evening that Mrs. Gardiner had kindly arranged for them. But Jane was to return to Longbourn, and Elizabeth would have an opportunity to observe her sister at home.

Elizabeth, Jane, and Maria arrived at the inn where Mr. Bennet's carriage was to meet them. Elizabeth was somewhat surprised to see the flowers already in bloom. She mentioned the fact to her sister, who blinked at her in surprise.

"It's the second week of May, Lizzy."

How can it be May? Elizabeth asked herself. *It feels as though time has flown.*

The carriage left Maria at her home, and—finally—Jane and Elizabeth reached Longbourn. As Elizabeth descended from the carriage, the Bennet family in its entirety came pouring out of the house.

"Jane! Lizzy!"

Lydia thrust herself to the front of the group and flung her arms around her sisters. "La, it has been so dull with you both gone!"

Kitty followed closely behind. "It is only dull because you refuse to find a suitable pastime," she retorted.

Mary was next, her waistline much larger than it was when Elizabeth had last seen her sister. As Jane had left for London much earlier, she was even more surprised at the change in her middle sister.

"I declare, Mary!" Jane exclaimed with delight. "When do you think the baby will come?"

Mary beamed as Collins put his arm around her. "Any day now!"

Elizabeth's mind went immediately to Miss Darcy and her similar situation. *Her baby may have already come*, she thought. She sent a swift prayer toward heaven, pleading for the safety of the traumatized young girl and her babe.

Mr. Bennet smiled at his eldest daughters. "I am glad you are come back, girls. The house has been uncommonly quiet with only two daughters in the house."

"Oh, my dear girls!" interrupted Mrs. Bennet, waving her handkerchief in the air and dabbing at her eyes. "I have missed you! Come inside and tell me all about the gentlemen you have met on your travels!"

Elizabeth rolled her eyes at Jane. Instead of smiling in return, Jane's eyes filled with tears.

"Mama," Elizabeth said hastily, "might we freshen up first, please? I long for a bath, and I think Jane has gotten some dust from the road in her eyes."

"Oh my, yes!" Mrs. Bennet ushered the girls into the house. "I will speak with Hill about dinner while I wait for you."

Jane rushed upstairs. Elizabeth attempted to follow but was unable to reach her sister before the door was closed. Sighing in resignation, Elizabeth turned towards her own room, where a bowl of hot water was lying in wait. She used the rag to bathe her body and changed into fresh clothing before going downstairs to see her family.

Jane joined the family as Elizabeth was telling about Rosings and all the finery inside the great estate. "Everything Mr. Stanley had to say about its grandeur is accurate," she informed them.

"And Lady Catherine? I imagine she and her daughter are quite fine indeed," Mrs. Bennet stated.

"Lady Catherine is very aware of her position," Elizabeth replied delicately. "Miss de Bourgh has poor health, but she seems to be a kind young woman from what I could tell."

"La, what I would do with that kind of fortune!" Lydia declared with laughter. "All the officers would be in love with me!"

"In love with your money, you mean," Kitty retorted.

"It is immaterial," Collins interjected, "as you are not yet out, Lydia. Even if you were as grand an heiress as Miss de Bourgh, you would still not be allowed to receive suitors."

Lydia sat back on the settee, crossing her arms with a sulk on her face. "Well, I would just elope with the most handsome one, then! Then I would not have to be out."

Her sisters gasped in horror. "You would do no such thing," Mr. Bennet said with uncharacteristic sternness. "If you were to do so, I would withhold your dowry entirely. You would be forced to live in a tent with your new husband, washing your own clothes and with no pin money."

Lydia's jaw dropped. "But surely the officers make an income? They are officers, after all!"

Jane and Elizabeth exchanged an exasperated look. "No, Lydia, they do not. Some of them are sons of gentlemen and receive an extra income from their families, but that is not guaranteed," Jane said kindly.

"If you were to elope, I would never see you again," Mrs. Bennet stated firmly.

All eyes turned towards her in surprise.

"Flirting is one thing," she continued, "but an elopement is something else altogether. A true lady would never lower herself so."

Mr. Bennet smiled approvingly at his wife. "I am glad you see the right of the matter."

Mrs. Bennet gave him a shy smile in return. "I was once in love with a redcoat myself, but my father explained what life would be like married to a soldier. I much prefer being a gentleman's wife."

Chastened, Lydia sat silently for the remainder of the day while the rest of the family shared all the events and gossip that had occurred in the months since Jane and Elizabeth went away. The conversation lasted through dinner and late into the night.

It was with merry hearts that they all retired to bed. Elizabeth had hoped to speak privately with Jane, so she waited until she was certain the others were asleep before creeping quietly down the hall and entering her sister's room.

She crawled into her sister's bed. "Lizzy?" Jane asked sleepily.

"Oh, Jane, I have so much to tell you," she exclaimed.

Elizabeth spent the next hour detailing all that had occurred in Hunsford.

"Oh, poor Mr. Darcy!" Jane breathed when Elizabeth reached the part where he said he loved her. "To have been in love with you all that time."

Her tender nature was even more distraught as she heard Elizabeth tell of her response. "Oh, Lizzy, how he must have felt! He was so sure of his success. It must have increased his disappointment greatly, especially when faced with your vehemence."

"I am very sorry for his pain," admitted Elizabeth, "but his reservations against the match will probably drive away any regard he once had for me. You do not blame me, though, Jane?"

"Blame you? Certainly not! You did not love him, and you gave the only answer you could."

Elizabeth then told her of the letter, repeating the entire contents to her sister, including those of Mr. Bingley's current location and the true reason Miss Bingley did not reply.

What a difficult stroke this was for Jane! She would have willingly gone through life ignorant of such wickedness. She could scarcely believe the entire world could hold so much evil, let alone be collected together in one man.

"I do not know when I have been more shocked!" she cried. "Poor Mr. Darcy. Poor *Miss* Darcy. And poor Miss Bingley, to have had such a father. Oh, Lizzy, I cannot bear it!"

And indeed, Jane's eyes were filled with tears, and she wept piteously for the traumatic experiences her friends had endured. Elizabeth held her sister and cried with her.

"At least this means Mr. Bingley and Miss Bingley were not false friends," Elizabeth sniffed.

"I know you are too kind to rejoice in your correctness," Jane said. "I should have listened to you. I simply did not want to raise my hopes."

"I understand, Jane," Elizabeth said tenderly. "Perhaps if you felt less, you could talk about it more."

"Exactly."

The conversation died away, soft crying taking its place once more. When at last their tears were spent, they fell into a wretched slumber. So deep was their exhaustion that they did not hear the crowing of the rooster or feel the warmth of the sun cross through the chamber window.

Chapter 18

The following days slowly turned into weeks. Almost immediately, it seemed, it was June, and it was time for Mary's lying-in.

"Stop fussing, Lizzy," Mary said as slapped her sister's hands away from a pile of bedding. "It is not as if I haven't done this before. In fact, you are more nervous now on my behalf than you were the first time I did this!"

Elizabeth bit her lip anxiously. "Yes, I know. I don't know why I am so nervous for you."

But she did know. Before, Mary having a baby was something new and exciting. It brought the joy of a tiny babe into the world. Now, however, Miss Darcy's horrible experience cast a long shadow over everything. It was almost as if knowing that such horrible things could occur made everything feel ominous.

What was Miss Darcy doing right now? Was someone helping her wash linens? Somehow Elizabeth could not picture Miss Bingley doing such menial work. Did the young woman, who was no more than a child herself, cry for her dead mother in the dark of night? Was she terrified about what was to occur? Did she even *know* what was going to happen?

Or had it already happened? Perhaps the babe had come already; Elizabeth was not certain on the timing. All she knew was the attack had happened before late October, which was when Mary suspected she was with child. But Mary would know the signs better, wouldn't she? An innocent girl like Miss Darcy may not know what missed courses meant.

Stop it, Elizabeth Bennet! she chastised herself. *Think about your own sister, not someone else's!*

Elizabeth let out a long sigh. "I'm sorry, Mary. I came to be of use to you, but it appears I am causing more stress than I am helping!"

Mary looked at her sister curiously. "You and Jane have both been acting strange since your return from travelling. Did something happen?"

Elizabeth bit her lip again, wondering what to say. "I saw Mr. Darcy at Hunsford. Apparently, his aunt is Lady Catherine!"

Mary gasped. "Mr. Stanley's patroness?"

"Yes! And he was visiting her for Easter. He apparently goes every year."

"But why would this discompose you so? Unless… did you receive news about Mr. Bingley?"

"Of a sort," Elizabeth replied. "It appears as if Mr. Bingley's business truly is legitimate. I am not at liberty to disclose all the details…"

"Certainly not!" Mary said firmly. "You know I would not wish to hear gossip in any case. But I cannot see how this news could affect you and Jane so poorly. It is good, is it not, that Mr. Bingley is not a false friend?"

"Yes," agreed Elizabeth, "but it also makes it difficult for Jane to move on. If she knew there was no hope, then she could have closure."

"That does make things feel difficult," admitted Mary. "I can see why it would leave her feeling unsettled."

"Precisely! And with Jane unsettled, I feel unsettled as well. I am sorry I let it spill over into my time with you."

"Oh nonsense," Mary said, waving a hand in the air. "I need something else to think about! I will probably go crazy over the next few days otherwise."

"When will Mama come over?"

"Most likely tomorrow. I admit I was surprised that she was so helpful when little Samuel was born."

"Would you like me to take him back to Longbourn with me?" Elizabeth offered. "He could spend time with his aunts and grandfather over the next few weeks."

"That would be very helpful," Mary said hesitantly. "Although I would miss him quite dreadfully."

"I will bring him over every day to visit," Elizabeth promised.

"Very well, then. Thank you, Lizzy."

Pleased to have a distraction, Elizabeth began to gather her nephew's belongings to take back to Longbourn with her. It took several minutes for her to locate his favorite blanket, but soon she was on her way with a babe in her arms.

She had not made it far to Longbourn when it began to rain lightly. "Come, Samuel, we must make haste!"

Covering the boy with the blanket, she began to walk more quickly. As the drops fell fast, she sped up to a run. Behind her, she thought she heard the sound of a carriage. She turned around and stepped to the side under a tree. To her surprise, the carriage stopped.

The door flew open. "Get in," cried Mr. Bingley.

Elizabeth gaped at him for a moment, but she remembered the boy in her arms and hurried inside. The door closed, and only then did she think about the propriety of being in a gentleman's carriage.

To her relief, an elderly woman occupied one of the seats. She nodded at Elizabeth, who inclined her head in return.

"Thank you, Mr. Bingley," Elizabeth said gratefully.

She took the seat next to the elderly woman and removed the blanket from Samuel's head. He looked wide-eyed around the carriage, then stuck his thumb in his mouth and curled into Lizzy's chest.

"Beautiful boy," Bingley remarked.

"Yes, he is Mary's oldest. She is going in for her lying-in this week, so I offered to take him to Longbourn. I was not expecting rainfall, or I would have waited!" Elizabeth said, brushing the boy's hair from his face.

"He's very well behaved." The elderly woman smiled kindly at the two of them.

Elizabeth returned the smile and looked questioningly at Bingley.

"My apologies! Miss Elizabeth, may I introduce Mrs. Nelson to you? She is my mother's sister, and she is to be in charge of the nanny while we are at Netherfield. I've just fetched her from London and came to open the house."

At that moment, the carriage stopped. Elizabeth looked out the window to see they had arrived at Longbourn. No longer being soothingly rocked by the motion of the carriage, Samuel began to cry.

"Here, allow me!" Bingley hopped down and quickly went to the front door. He grabbed an umbrella from the servant who opened it, then returned for Elizabeth and Samuel, who was sobbing at this point from being wet, cold, hungry, and not with his mama.

Mr. Bingley escorted Elizabeth to the front door. Mrs. Bennet was there, waiting. She immediately began to fuss over the young boy and ordered Elizabeth to her room to change into dry clothes.

Mr. Bingley was invited in, but he demurred due to Mrs. Nelson's presence in the carriage. He promised he would return to call once he had his household established, then he vanished into the rain.

Elizabeth watched him go with wide eyes. *He is bringing a nanny. That can only mean one thing: he has married Georgiana Darcy. Oh, how will I ever tell Jane?*

She pondered this question as she changed into a clean dress and sat by the fire to dry her hair. Unfortunately, she had not come up with an answer by the time Jane entered her room a few minutes later.

"Lizzy? Mama said that Mr. Bingley brought you home?" Jane's voice shook slightly as she asked the question.

"Yes, he passed us as the rain began," Elizabeth explained. "He had an aunt in the carriage with him, so all proprieties were observed."

"Did he say what brings him to Meryton?"

Elizabeth hesitated a moment. "He said that he will be setting up the house. His aunt is to oversee a nanny."

Jane went pale. "So he did marry Miss Darcy, then."

Elizabeth stared at her sister in surprise. "How on earth do you know that?"

Jane shrugged. "I thought he might, once you told me he had gone to Scotland with her and Miss Bingley. It makes sense—marrying her would save her reputation and give the baby legitimacy."

"But Jane, how can you be so calm about this?" Elizabeth asked in consternation.

"Because I did not allow myself to hope," Jane said simply. "Merely knowing that he did not abandon me did much to ease my heartache and confusion. I had not misinterpreted our moments together. I will always consider him the most amiable man of my acquaintance, but I could not bring myself to think he would return to me after all these months."

Elizabeth's eyes filled with tears. "I am so sorry, Jane," she whispered.

"I will be well, Lizzy. It will all be forgot, and I can meet him now as a common and indifferent acquaintance."

With that, Jane silently left Elizabeth's room. Elizabeth only allowed the tears to fall when she heard muffled sobs coming from her sister's room.

The days passed slowly. Mary's second child was born—another son named William Thomas Bennet. Elizabeth and Jane kept themselves occupied with helping Mary during the confinement after the baby's birth. After a month, Mary was churched, and the child was christened.

Thankfully for Jane, Mrs. Bennet was focused so much on the new baby that she entirely forgot about Mr. Bingley's return to Meryton. It was only after Mary was once again able to leave her home that Mrs. Bennet made time to visit her sister Mrs. Phillips, who broached the subject almost immediately.

Mrs. Bennet returned home from that visit all aflutter. "What do you think, girls? Mr. Bingley has returned! They say there will be a married lady and her baby, but no one knows who she is."

Elizabeth did her best to redirect the conversation. "Mama, I heard that there is to be another assembly in a fortnight."

"An assembly! May I go?" Lydia interjected eagerly. "I will be sixteen next month, and Kitty was allowed to attend assemblies when she was my age!"

Mrs. Bennet blinked at her youngest daughter, surprised. "My word, is it July already? Where has all the time gone? Of course you shall attend! We will need to begin immediately if you are to have a proper dress fitting of a young lady out in society!"

"Before you make any purchases, Mama," Lizzy said hastily, "you may want to consult with Papa on the matter."

"I suppose you are right." Mrs. Bennet sighed in resignation. "I will speak with him at once. Come along, Lydia."

Five minutes later, Elizabeth heard squeals of delight coming from her father's study. "It appears Papa has given his consent," she remarked with a wry smile.

"It will be nice to have all of us attend an assembly together," Jane said happily.

"Plus, the purchases necessary to help Lydia come out will do much to occupy Mama's attention away from Netherfield," replied Elizabeth.

Jane merely bowed her head back over her embroidery, and Elizabeth allowed the subject to drop.

The following days were filled with trips to the modiste, conversations about lace and necklines, and speculation as to who would be the first to ask Lydia for a dance once her father stood up with her for the first set.

At last, the day of the assembly arrived. It was a hot July day, and the ladies were grateful for a small breeze. Lydia boasted that the weather was in honor of her come out, and her sisters all smiled at her indulgently.

Mr. Bennet came out of his study and looked at the chaos as the girls prepared themselves. "Well now, what's all this?" he asked in surprise.

"We're getting ready for the assembly, Papa!" Lydia exclaimed as she twirled around to show off her new gown.

"The assembly? Today? Certainly not! I was sure it was tomorrow. I made plans to read my book this evening." Mr. Bennet's eyes twinkled as he winked at Elizabeth.

Lydia let out a cry of dismay. "No, Papa, it is tonight! You must come. You simply must! I cannot be the only Bennet girl to not dance with her father for her first dance!"

Tears filled the girl's eyes, and Mr. Bennet quickly sobered. He walked over to her and gave her a gentle hug. "There, now, Lydia, dry your eyes. Surely you should know your papa well enough to tell when he is making a jest."

Lydia sniffed and looked up at him. "You knew it was tonight all along?"

"Yes, my dear," he said, kissing her gently on the forehead. "I would not miss it for all the world, even if you are one of the silliest girls in all of England for falling for my little joke."

Lydia gave him a watery smile. "You know this means I will now have to tell you all about the lace we chose for my dress the entire ride to the assembly."

Mr. Bennet gave a surprised bark of laughter. "Ha! And it would serve me right!"

Everyone smiled at the exchange. Mr. Bennet leaned toward indolence, but each daughter knew she was loved in her own way.

"Now, hurry, Lydia," he said, patting her on the head. "I believe your mother is calling for you to take your turn with the maid for your hair."

Lydia's hands flew to the riotous curls that fell down her shoulders. She let out a squeal and dashed up the stairs.

Mr. Bennet turned to Elizabeth and remarked, "I had not intended her to take me so seriously. She has spoken of nothing else for two full weeks!"

"She is nervous, Papa. We were all emotional for our first dances."

"I forget, sometimes, how tender a young girl's heart can be," he sighed.

"We love you in spite of that, Papa," Elizabeth teased. "Now you had best get dressed, or else Mama will never let you hear the end of it!"

After another hour of preparations, the Bennet family was ready to leave for the assembly. They stopped at the Collins's parsonage to collect Mary and her husband, and they left behind one of their maids to help the nanny for the night.

Upon arriving at the assembly, each member of the Bennet family gravitated towards their friends. Kitty and Mary found Maria Lucas, and Mary sat with some of the other young wives in the neighborhood.

Elizabeth and Jane stood together. "It feels odd to be dancing without Charlotte here," Elizabeth said sadly.

"So much has changed in the last year," Jane added. "Who would have thought last summer that we would have passed through all of this?"

"I will be sad to leave you again in a few weeks," Elizabeth told her sister. "As eager as I am for the Peaks, I will miss your company."

"It is a shame it has had to be postponed so many times," replied Jane. "We will do well enough here. There is baby Will to keep me occupied, and Lydia will need to be chaperoned on calls. Now that she is out, I anticipate her begging to go visiting every day!"

The two girls laughed as they affectionately watched their youngest sister speaking with Maria and Kitty, using animated gestures as she laughed gaily. The musicians began to warm up their instruments, but after a few minutes, they stopped and stared towards the entrance.

The guests turned towards the doors to see what had caused the stir. Walking in through the front doors was Mr. Bingley.

Chapter 19

Jane gave a soft gasp and grabbed Elizabeth's hand. "I had not expected to see him tonight, Lizzy!"

Mr. Bingley's eyes were focused directly on Jane. Although he bowed and extended greetings to Sir William and other people who moved forward to greet him, his eyes continually went back to her.

Eventually, Mr. Bingley was able to separate himself from the crowd. He immediately made his way towards Jane. Elizabeth felt her sister's hand tighten on hers the nearer the man came.

He stopped in front of both ladies and gave a deep bow. "Miss Bennet, it has been far too long." He reached for her hand and gave it a kiss.

Jane gasped and flushed a brilliant red, snatching her hand from his. With a soft cry, she turned and rushed out of the room.

Bingley looked after her, the confusion clearly on his face. "What...?" he asked, looking at Elizabeth.

She met his eyes coldly. "I believe, Mr. Bingley, that you must excuse my sister. She has been overcome with emotion. Perhaps the atmosphere of the room is oppressive for her at the moment."

Bingley looked at her with befuddlement. "I don't understand, Miss Elizabeth. Darcy said... that is... well... I was led to believe that my return to Netherfield would be very welcome to the community here."

"It depends on the reason for your return, sir," she replied fiercely. "I am sure that many here would be eager to make the acquaintance of Mrs. Bingley, but certainly you cannot expect for the situation to remain as it was when you were here before."

"Mrs. Bingley?"

"Yes, your wife. The community is aware that you have installed your aunt to oversee the nursery at Netherfield. Presumably, when there is a baby, the mother typically accompanies it."

Bingley stared at her for a few moments, then understanding dawned across his face. He let out a short burst of laughter and covered his mouth.

"There is nothing humorous about my sister's distress, Mr. Bingley," Elizabeth said frigidly. "Now if you will excuse me, I must see to her comfort."

Elizabeth turned to walk away, but Bingley stretched out his hand and grabbed her arm. She looked pointedly down at where the offending limb touched her, then raised her eyes to glare at him. "Unhand me now," she said through clenched teeth.

Bingley dropped her arm as if he had been burned. "My apologies, Miss Elizabeth! I simply could not allow you to leave without clearing up this wretched misunderstanding."

"Misunderstanding?"

"Yes! This is all a dreadful mistake! You see, I am *not* married. There *is* no Mrs. Bingley! The baby is my niece."

Now it was Elizabeth's turn to stare in confusion. "Your niece?"

"Yes, precisely! When we left Netherfield in November, it was with the intention of returning almost immediately. However, as I am sure you are aware," he gave her a meaningful look, "my sister and Mr. Wickham had grown quite fond of each other."

"Yes," she said slowly, "I had heard something to that effect."

"Well, business in London took longer than expected, and there was a need to travel north for a while. Caroline and Wickham decided they could not wait to be married, and so upon our arrival in Scotland, they were wed immediately. The child was born only a few weeks ago, and the baby was given the name Anne Wickham. Caroline and Wickham remain at the house this evening to help their daughter settle in."

Again, Bingley gave Elizabeth a meaningful look. At once, it made complete sense to Elizabeth. *Wickham and Caroline have chosen to raise Georgiana's child as their own!*

Elizabeth let out a sigh of relief; it felt as though a weight had been lifted from her shoulders. Almost giddy, she said with a broad grin, "That is excellent news, Mr. Bingley! Most excellent! I congratulate you on the healthy birth of your niece!"

Mr. Bingley's smile matched hers, and they shook hands. "Now please excuse me, sir. I must acquaint my sister with your happy news immediately! I promise you she will be delighted to hear it!"

Elizabeth did not think it would be possible for Mr. Bingley's smile to widen further, but it did. As Elizabeth walked away, she paused for a moment. Turning back, she inquired with faux lightness, "And will Mr. Darcy be joining the party as well?"

Mr. Bingley's face fell slightly. "Not at this time, sadly. Miss Darcy's health has been fragile lately. She was travelling with her brother, and her health is still somewhat frail. Once she has regained sufficient strength, he will take her to Pemberley so he can oversee the harvest and her recovery at the same time."

Elizabeth's heart was torn in two. She was delighted to hear that Miss Darcy had not perished in childbirth—which was all too common for ladies that young—but she was sorry that she would not see Mr. Darcy anytime soon.

"With your permission, I could pass along your greetings and best wishes," Bingley looked at Elizabeth anxiously.

"Yes, please do! Tell Mr. Darcy that I will pray for his sister's recovery, and that he will be greatly missed here. There are some in the community who were hoping to see him again."

Mr. Bingley nodded in understanding. "I will inform him immediately in my next letter."

Elizabeth curtsied, then hurried from the room in search of Jane. After wandering a few corridors, Elizabeth found her sister standing on a balcony. As she approached, she heard Jane's muffled sobs.

Jane spun around at the approaching footsteps, wiping frantically at her eyes. Her shoulders sagged in relief as she recognized Elizabeth.

"Oh, Lizzy, what am I to do?" Jane fell into her sister's arms and wept.

"Jane, don't cry! I have the most wonderful news!"

Jane lifted her head and looked at her sister, blinking away tears. "How can anything be wonderful when the man I love has married another? And when it is obvious that he returns my affections?"

"Because he isn't married!" Elizabeth exclaimed.

"Not... married?" Jane repeated stupidly.

"No! It appears his sister Miss Bingley married Mr. Wickham quite suddenly after leaving Netherfield last year, and *they* are the baby's parents. They will be staying with Mr. Bingley until things are situated. *Miss* Darcy," she emphasized, "is at Pemberley with her brother."

Jane began to laugh. Not the quiet, demure laugh of a lady, but the hysterical laugh that only comes when you are deliriously happy and cannot keep it in for another moment.

She laughed so hard she began to cry again. Elizabeth embraced her sister, and both laughed and cried for several minutes. Eventually, Jane pulled away and wiped at her face. "I should probably return to the assembly, but I must look a mess. Everyone will talk."

"Shall I make your excuses and send you home?"

"No, I would not like to miss Lydia's first time being out."

"If we hurry, we may be able to see the end of her dance with Papa," suggested Elizabeth.

The two girls straightened their hair, arranged their dresses, and dried their eyes. Fortunately, they arrived as the second dance of the first set was beginning. Lydia's face beamed with delight as she moved down the line with her father. Her joy was infectious, and Mr. Bennet soon sported a smile that had not been so wide in years.

When the dance concluded, he brought his daughter back to her mother and sisters. "Oh, Mama!" exclaimed Lydia. "I have never had a more wonderful time!"

Mrs. Bennet scarcely had time to answer before several young men surrounded her daughters, begging for sets. To Lydia's delight, her card was soon filled. Kitty's card followed closely behind, and both girls gleefully went to the floor with their partners for the next set.

Jane's card was empty for the next set, which she was grateful for. She had not fully recovered her composure after encountering Mr. Bingley. Looking around, she saw him walk towards her hesitantly. Remembering Miss Bingley's words all those months ago about him deserving a wife who truly loved him, she gave him a gentle smile of encouragement. That was all he needed to quicken his pace and arrive at her side.

"My dear Miss Bennet," he said, bowing over her hand and placing a kiss on it. This time, she did not pull away.

"I am very glad to see you again, Mr. Bingley," she said softly.

Elizabeth looked at the couple and felt as if her heart were going to burst from her chest.

"Would you care to dance with me?" he asked Jane.

She murmured an agreement, and the two took a spot on the floor with the other couples. Elizabeth watched as the two danced, their eyes on one another, oblivious to the rest of the room.

A sudden wave of tears hit Elizabeth's eyes. In that moment, she realized she wanted nothing more than to be in Darcy's arms, dancing with him. She gave her head a little shake. *Where did that come from?*

Her opinion of Mr. Darcy had improved significantly over the months. She did not feel as though she loved him the way he professed to love her; rather, her knowing him better improved her opinion of him.

He had gone from being the last man whom she could ever marry to being one of the best men of her acquaintance. The way that he cared for his sister in spite of her situation demonstrated his goodness and gentleness. He was not perfect—their first meeting could testify to that—but his willingness to humble himself and apologize showed how much he cared for her good opinion.

Her musings were interrupted when a young man from a neighboring estate approached and asked her to dance for the following set. She resolved to set aside her preoccupations for the duration of the assembly. It was difficult to do, but she was able to shove all thoughts of Mr. Darcy to the back of her mind until the dancing was complete.

Once home, however, sleep was long in coming. The words he spoke when first proposed echoed repeatedly in her ears: "You must allow me to tell you how much I ardently admire and love you."

Finally, sleep came. It was not restful, nor was it disturbing. Instead, she dreamt she was at a ball at Netherfield. She was waltzing with a young man. At first, she was scandalized to be even considering such a thing. Where had she learned to waltz?

Her shock was quickly overcome by a different sensation. She could feel his thighs brushing against her legs, his hand firmly around her waist, his chest pressed tight against her. As they twirled around the room, the intensity increased until she was practically breathless.

She lifted her eyes to the young man's face to ask for a respite, only to discover she was in the arms of Mr. Darcy. His dark eyes stared down into hers, burning through to her very soul. Her mouth went dry, and she licked her lips. His face lowered towards hers, and then—

"Lizzy!"

Elizabeth gasped and sat straight up in bed. "What? What is it? What's wrong?" she exclaimed, looking wildly around the room.

Jane was sitting on the end of her bed. "Are you unwell, Lizzy? You look flushed, and you were breathing strangely as you slept. I almost couldn't wake you!"

"No, I am... I am fine, Jane. I must have been having an odd dream or something, that is all. What time is it?"

"It is not quite breakfast, yet," Jane answered. "The rest of the family is still asleep. I woke up with the sun, but no matter how hard I tried, I was unable to sleep again."

"Thoughts of Mr. Bingley keeping you awake, perhaps?" teased Elizabeth in an attempt to cover her own embarrassment.

Jane blushed deeply. "Oh, Lizzy, I never dreamed I could be so happy! He has asked to call upon me today."

Elizabeth's face broke into a wide smile. "Do you think he means to propose, then?"

"Perhaps. He may simply wish to ask for a courtship."

"What do you intend to answer?"

Jane gave her sister a mockingly severe look. "Yes, of course! What other answer could there be? Do I need to word it differently, do you think?

"As long as you don't tell him he is the last man in the world whom you could ever marry, I think you are safe," Lizzy smiled wryly.

Jane threw a pillow at her sister, who responded in kind. The girls giggled for a few moments, then Elizabeth said sadly, "I shall miss you when you are married."

"Oh, Lizzy, I am not going anywhere soon. Besides, I will not be very far. As you know very well, Netherfield is only three miles from here."

Elizabeth gave her a small smile. "Until you tire of Mama's constant presence in your home and beg Mr. Bingley to purchase an estate far away."

"Perhaps Derbyshire?" Jane asked slyly. "You could come stay with us! Perhaps you might encounter a certain gentleman."

"More likely I will be an old maid and teach your ten children how to play piano very poorly!"

"Lizzy, do be serious," Jane admonished, fighting a smile. "Do you wish to see Mr. Darcy again?"

"I expect I shall," Elizabeth replied lightly. "After all, you are my dearest sister, and you shall hopefully marry his dearest friend. We are bound to come into one another's company in the future. I shall treat him with every courtesy."

With that, Elizabeth rose from the bed and declared her intention to dress for the day. "After all, we cannot have Lydia eating all the best breakfast options!"

Jane gave her sister a frown but acquiesced, and the conversation was placed on hold while they dressed and went belowstairs to eat their breakfast.

Upon finishing the meal, the family adjourned to the drawing room. Shortly after settling in, a knock was heard at the door, and Mr. Bingley was admitted.

"Good day, ladies," he said, executing a deep bow. "I trust I find you all well after the assembly?"

"Oh, Mr. Bingley!" exclaimed Mrs. Bennet. "We are so delighted that you have returned to Netherfield! And with your sister and her daughter, too! I always suspected Mr. Wickham had a partiality towards Miss Bingley. I said so frequently, did I not, girls? I flatter myself to say that no one can recognize attachment better than I can."

Mrs. Bennet continued her prattling as Mr. Bingley stole increasingly agitated glances at Jane. Finally, when Mrs. Bennet paused for breath, Elizabeth interjected, "Mama, I believe Mr. Bingley must be quite eager to take a walk after travelling so far to return. Perhaps Jane and I could show him the new blooms in the garden?"

"What a wonderful idea!" cried Mr. Bingley, gratitude shining in his eyes. "I would love to see the area."

Kitty began to ask if she could see the new blooms as well, but she was quickly hushed by her mother. "No, child! I have something particular I wish to discuss with you. Elizabeth will go with them, and you and Lydia shall remain here."

Jane and Elizabeth fetched their cloaks and bonnets, then joined Mr. Bingley at the front door. Once outside, Elizabeth slowly began to separate herself from the couple, who seemed oblivious to her machinations and were conversing in quiet voices. Elizabeth continued to drift away from them until their words were no more than low murmurs.

Suddenly, the murmurs stopped, and Jane gasped. Elizabeth looked up sharply to see Mr. Bingley down on one knee in front of the eldest Bennet daughter.

"Jane Bennet," he said in a loud, strong voice. "These months apart have only confirmed to me what I suspected back in November. I love you, and I cannot bear to ever be apart from you again. Please do me the honor of accepting my hand in marriage."

Jane nodded, tears streaming down her face. Mr. Bingley stood up, and she threw her arms around his neck. "Yes, I will marry you!" she sobbed. He placed his arms around her waist and lifted her into the air. He spun her, laughing for joy, then gently set her down again. He leaned in and kissed her gently on the lips.

Elizabeth watched the scene, her own lips tingling as she remembered her dream from the night before. Forcing the image and her jealousy aside, she moved forward towards the happy couple.

"I will go to your father at once!" Mr. Bingley exclaimed. He turned to go into the house, then turned back around to face Elizabeth. "Thank you for your help last night. Your sister has made me the happiest of men!"

"I am delighted to have you as a brother," Elizabeth beamed at him.

Mr. Bingley bowed, then set off towards Longbourn with long strides that could almost be called running—if gentlemen did indeed run.

Jane turned to Elizabeth, her face alight with joy. "He loves me, Lizzy!"

"Of course he does, you goose!"

"He said he always loved me, that he missed me desperately while away. He loves me! Oh, why cannot everyone be as happy as I am?"

Elizabeth smiled at her sister. "Because they do not have your goodness."

"I must go to Mama and tell her." Jane began to walk away, then turned back. "If only we could find such a man for you, Lizzy."

An image of Mr. Darcy flashed in Elizabeth's mind, but she pushed the thought away. "Perhaps if I am very fortunate, Mr. Stanley will have a brother."

Jane looked surprised, then let out a peal of laughter. She turned back to the house and went inside.

Elizabeth sat on the bench, fighting the urge to cry. She was happy for Jane, she really was. But she was also a little jealous of her sister's joy. She winced slightly as her mother's voice echoed through the open window of the drawing room.

Taking one last fortifying breath, Elizabeth braced herself and pinned a smile on her face before following Jane into the house.

Chapter 20

Mrs. Bennet immediately settled down into planning the wedding. At first, she demanded the couple wait for six months in order for her to plan the perfect day. Bingley, however, was adamant that he not spend another minute apart from his beloved. His future mother, fearful that he might cry off, petulantly agreed to a wedding immediately after the three weeks of banns were called.

Bingley had arrived in Meryton with the settlement papers all drawn up so there would be no need for him to return to London for business. The first banns were called that Sunday, and Elizabeth could not tell whose smile was the widest: Mr. Bingley's or Mrs. Bennet's.

With the help of Mr. Phillips, Mr. Bennet signed the settlement papers. Collins insisted on being present, as well as their giving a copy of the papers to Jane herself. She was somewhat overwhelmed with the amount of pin money being given to her, but Bingley assured her that it was quite appropriate. "It is very fitting for your station. Caroline assures me that you will need every penny."

Provisions were also made to increase the three unmarried sisters' dowries. Mr. Bennet and Collins protested that it was all too much, but Bingley remained unusually stubborn on the matter. "I will provide for my new sisters in the same way that I provided for my own."

After everything was finally agreed upon, the house fell into a furor of wedding plans. Mrs. Wickham—the former Miss Bingley—was not able to pay a call on her future sister until the week before the wedding, as she was helping her new daughter settle into the nursery.

When at last she came to visit Longbourn, Elizabeth was amazed at the change in the formerly reserved woman. Her smile was softer, and her eyes were calm and warm, whereas before they seemed a bit cold.

"My dear Miss Bennet," Mrs. Wickham said, extending her hands and giving Jane a kiss on the cheek. "I am so delighted to welcome you to the family!"

"Thank you, Mrs. Wickham," replied Jane with a soft smile.

"None of that! We are to be family!" exclaimed the lady. "Please call me Caroline."

"And I am Jane."

"And I am Elizabeth, or Lizzy if you prefer," Elizabeth added. "I hope you do not mind if I consider you as another sister."

Caroline's eyes softened even further. "I would be honored. Your family is everything that is kind and welcoming," she added wistfully.

"I must congratulate you on your new daughter," Elizabeth said. "Babies are a wonderful joy."

Caroline's eyes lit up, and she began to chatter about everything her new baby was doing. Every smile, each gurgle, was described in minute detail. Far from being bored, however, Elizabeth was enthralled. She had seen Mary undergo a similar transformation, but that was about a child she had given birth to herself. It was incredible to watch this previously cool woman thaw under motherhood, especially when the child was not of her womb.

After several minutes, Jane was called away by her mother to give her opinion about a dish for the wedding breakfast. Elizabeth scooted closer to Caroline and said softly, "It is a wonderful thing you have done, becoming a mother."

Caroline responded with a fixed gaze. "I understand from Mr. Darcy that you are aware of the entire situation."

"Yes, I am," Elizabeth admitted, watching Caroline anxiously. "I hope it is not too much of an imposition that Mr. Darcy confided in me. There were some... misunderstandings about the situation on my part, and he was seeking to alleviate my sister's pain."

"It is, in fact, a bit of a relief to have another woman entirely aware of my past and present circumstances," Caroline said with feeling. "Until now, it has been a secret burden shared only by my siblings and the Darcys. I have spoken of it with Louisa on occasion, but it brings her such pain as well. And dear Georgiana has her own trauma to deal with. Helping her through it has helped me, but knowing that someone wholly unconnected with me is aware of it and has not passed judgment has lifted a weight I did not know existed."

"I believe my only thoughts have been those of sorrow, not condemnation," Elizabeth assured her. "My cousin Collins had a very difficult childhood, and no one thought to blame him for the sins of his father. Why should your situation be any different?"

A look of relief passed over Caroline's face. "Thank you, Elizabeth. You cannot know how much that means to me."

"Please know that you can speak with me at any time should you feel the need. I know I often feel comfort when I can share my burdens and concerns with a sister or friend."

Tears filled Caroline's eyes, but she blinked them away and gave a smile. "I will remember that."

The two women sat in silence a moment before they, too, were drawn into the conversation about wedding plans.

"And who will be standing up for you, Mr. Bingley?" Mrs. Bennet asked the groom.

"I had hoped Darcy would be able to come, but his sister is still too delicate in health to be able to travel. I have asked Collins to stand up with me in his place."

"What an honor!" cried Mrs. Bennet, clapping with glee. "I could not have wished for a better son than William. And now I shall have two, and they shall be friends as well as brothers! For William has always been more a brother than a cousin to my girls, even before he married Mary."

Turning to Caroline, she added, "And I would be pleased to consider you another daughter. I know your own parents have passed, and you must feel the loss of your mother keenly during this time with your baby. I have raised six children; you may come to me with anything you need."

Caroline looked at Mrs. Bennet, startled. "Why, thank you, ma'am. That is very kind of you."

Mrs. Bennet beamed at her and said, "There is always room in my family for more."

Once again, Caroline's eyes filled with tears. Elizabeth reached out and squeezed her new sister's hand. "You are no longer alone. You have a husband, a daughter, and new sisters, if you wish them."

Caroline looked around the room, her heart in her eyes. "Thank you, Mother Bennet," she said at last. "I am truly grateful to be here."

Mrs. Bennet beamed again, then turned the conversation back to the wedding clothes. "Oh, there is so much to be done! If only you had been willing to wait another month or two. But I supposed with Jane being so beautiful, you would not want to wait. We will just have to do the best we can. Perhaps you can go to London for clothes after the wedding."

"That is the plan," Mr. Bingley informed her. "I would like to take Jane to London for some shopping before we go on our wedding trip."

"Where will you be going?" Elizabeth asked him curiously.

"Originally, I had thought to invite you, Lizzy, to accompany us on a tour of the north country. I know you had planned to go there with the Gardiners this summer, though," Mr. Bingley responded.

"Yes, but unfortunately, the plans have changed again. With your wedding, Mr. Gardiner is unable to get time from work to be here and make a tour of the north before bad weather makes travel impossible," Elizabeth said sadly. "They assure me we will try again next year."

"In that case, perhaps you would like to accompany Jane and me? I would like to take Jane to see Staffordshire, as I still have some family living there whom I wish her to meet. Then Darcy has kindly offered to let us stay at Pemberley while we tour some of the great houses in Derbyshire."

Elizabeth's heart leaped to her throat. She fought to keep her voice calm as she said, "I would not wish to intrude on the Darcys."

"Not at all," Bingley hastened to assure her. "In fact, Darcy specifically said in his letter of invitation that any of the Bennet and Bingley households would always be welcome at Pemberley at any time."

"Why, I declare!" Mrs. Bennet exclaimed. "I had not expected such gentlemanly behavior from him. That is very good of him indeed. Perhaps we should all—"

"I'm afraid, Mother Bennet, that Miss Darcy is somewhat ill," Bingley said quickly. "Another time, he would invite us all. For my wedding trip, however..." Bingley trailed off, blushing.

Jane also turned a bright red, and Mrs. Bennet smirked. "Ah, yes, I had quite forgotten. I know what it is to be newly married. Don't worry, Mr. Bingley, I will not intrude on your trip."

"But she may take over your home when you return," Elizabeth whispered to Caroline.

Caroline giggled quietly behind her hand in a charmingly girlish way. Raising her voice, she said, "Mother Bennet, I would greatly appreciate your company while my brother is away. My dear Wickham and I are only recently married, and neither of us is accustomed to babies."

The entire room could see the wheels turning in Mrs. Bennet's head. "The babe was born in July, was she not? Then that would mean..." Her voice trailed off. Then she said, "Well, no matter, you are married now, and that is what's important. I would be happy to come give advice at any time, my dear."

"Thank you," Bingley mouthed to his sister from across the room. She returned it with a small wink.

"That was very well done," Elizabeth whispered approvingly. "I think you will be just fine with Mama."

"With Louisa and Hurst at his estate for her confinement, I'm afraid I am feeling quite lonesome. Wickham spends time with me, but he is very occupied managing Darcy's affairs by letter until Darcy can find a new steward."

"Will Mr. Wickham no longer fill that position?" Elizabeth asked with some surprise.

"Mr. Darcy has gifted us a small estate in Derbyshire as a wedding present," Caroline confided quietly.

Elizabeth's eyebrows rose high into her hairline. "That is *extremely* generous of him!"

"He says it is no more than Wickham's due for all his years of friendship and loyalty. Darcy said Wickham is more of a brother to him than any brother by blood could ever be. In fact," Caroline lowered her voice to whisper, "there is a very small chance that they may be half-brothers."

Elizabeth gasped, then looked around to make sure that nobody had heard. Thankfully, the remainder of the room was engaged in conversation with Mrs. Bennet about wedding plans. "How is that possible?"

"Apparently Darcy's father was drunk one night just after Darcy was born, and a maid claims he took advantage of her. She fell pregnant shortly after, but the man did not remember anything and was very fond of his wife. Wickham's father offered to marry the girl, as he had fancied her from afar. But the maid had shared her favors with others before and after Wickham's birth, so there is no way to really know."

"How terrible for all the parties," Elizabeth said with horror. "I cannot imagine anyone being so willingly deceitful."

Caroline pressed her lips together. "Much of the evil in the world is perpetrated by men, but there are some women who are just as wicked. Let us be grateful that my father, Collins's father, and Wickham's mother never came in contact with one another."

"And that their children have had the diligence to rise above their parents' evils," agreed Elizabeth.

The conversation was interrupted when Mrs. Bennet turned her attention towards the new gowns her daughters would require. Elizabeth was summoned to her mother's side to discuss lace.

Elizabeth laughed and pulled Caroline along with her. "If you are truly to be my sister, that requires you to suffer Mama's attentions to your gowns as well!"

Caroline allowed herself to be pulled across the room. Mrs. Bennet included the young woman in the conversation as if she had always been part of the family, and Caroline's heart continued to heal.

That afternoon set the tone for the following days until the wedding. Once the fabric and lace were chosen, there were fittings for the dresses, as well as matching bonnets, shoes, jewelry, handkerchiefs, and other fripperies that Mrs. Bennet deemed necessary.

Mr. Bennet and Collins insisted that no expense be spared. Mr. Bennet leaned towards indolence in running his estate until young William came to live with them. When Mr. Bennet saw the marks on the boy's body, he vowed to be the type of father that the late Mr. Collins never was. That included being deliberate in moderating his wife's income and providing for the future, even though exerting himself went against his nature.

As a result, the coffers at Longbourn were quite full. Although Collins focused heavily on his ordination and responsibilities as a rector, he also made certain he was a diligent landlord and master. Over the years, Longbourn's income had increased, and some of the excess was set aside for the Bennet daughters.

Mrs. Bennet's joy at having a daughter so well settled knew no bounds. With the freedom to spend at her leisure—when normally such desires were curtailed by a budget—she was in her element. Jane's gentle and unassuming nature made her the perfect subject for her mother's planning, as the girl was quite content with anything so long as Bingley was the groom.

Happy was the day that Mrs. Bennet got rid of her eldest daughter in marriage. Although, she would always insist that she was gaining a son, not losing a daughter. The sun arose on Jane's wedding day with warmth and cheer, as if nature itself was blessing the happy couple.

The morning was spent getting Jane and her sisters into their gowns, pinning up hair into elaborate styles, and making sure everything was perfect in their appearance. Mrs. Bennet fluttered between bedrooms until her daughters laughingly insisted the woman get herself ready.

The Gardiners had arrived the day before the wedding. Mrs. Bennet and Mrs. Gardiner had stayed up with Jane the night before, discussing everything that would occur on her wedding night.

After the conversation, Elizabeth slipped into Jane's room to share one last night together as sisters before Jane became a married woman. The poor girl was completely mortified from the conversation, and Elizabeth laughed at how red her sister's face had become.

Elizabeth pressed her sister several times to share the details of the conversation, but Jane simply pressed her lips together and shook her head, refusing to say a word about the subject. At length, Elizabeth allowed her sister the privacy desired and changed the subject.

Now the moment had arrived. Elizabeth placed the finishing touches on Jane's hair and stepped back to admire her sister. "Oh, Jane, you have never looked so beautiful."

Jane blushed and looked in the mirror. "I hope Charles thinks so as well."

"He will, and then he will say it again tonight!" teased Elizabeth.

Jane threw a scrap of lace at her sister. "Behave, Lizzy, or I will not allow you to come on the wedding trip!"

"Who would you take instead? Lydia?" retorted Elizabeth.

Jane made a face, and the two girls laughed. Just then, Mrs. Bennet rushed into the room. "Make haste, girls! It is time to leave! You do not want to be late, or Mr. Bingley might decide to change his mind!"

Elizabeth laughed at the look of alarm on Jane's face. "I think if Mr. Bingley was willing to wait all these months for Jane, he would be willing to stand at the church for an extra minute or two."

"I would not wish to keep him waiting any longer, though," Jane said firmly.

The Bennet family made their way to the church. Mr. Bennet helped Elizabeth, then Jane, descend from the carriage. He extended his arms and put his hands on Jane's shoulders. "My dear Jane," he said in a hoarse voice, "I am so proud of the beautiful woman you have become."

Jane's eyes filled with tears, and she gave her father a warm embrace. He then offered his arm to his two eldest girls, and they entered the church.

Elizabeth walked down the aisle first, escorted by Collins, who was standing up for Bingley. The two took their places next to Bingley's side, and then Jane came into view. Elizabeth heard Bingley's sharp intake of breath, and her eyes teared up as she noticed the mist in his.

Bingley continued to blink furiously, with his eyes locked onto his bride. He had always considered her to be an angel, but today she was more than that. She was an ethereal goddess. The love and adoration flowing from his face made Elizabeth's heart tug.

As Bingley and Jane recited their vows, Elizabeth could not help but think of Mr. Darcy. The couple in front of her blurred, and suddenly she could see herself standing in Jane's place. Mr. Darcy was in front of her, placing the ring on her hand and promising to worship her with his body. She could feel his hand holding hers, and in that moment, she knew—she loved him.

Elizabeth blinked, and she was back in the present. Jane and Bingley had turned to face the crowd and were beginning to walk to the register. Elizabeth hastily took Collins's extended arm and followed behind her newly married sister to sign as a witness.

The wedding breakfast was perfect. Elizabeth could not tell if

Bingley or Jane had the larger smile. Mrs. Bennet was in her element, accepting the congratulations of her friends and neighbors on the fortunate alliance her daughter had made.

Elizabeth watched with a touch of envy as Bingley leaned over and whispered intimately into Jane's ear. The bride blushed and nodded, and Bingley helped her rise from the table.

Everyone bid farewell to the couple, who were only journeying as far as Netherfield for the wedding night. Caroline and Wickham promised to make themselves absent for the evening to give the new couple their privacy. The next morning, the Bingleys would travel to the London townhouse, where they would remain for a week. The Gardiners would bring Elizabeth with them until it was time for the wedding trip.

As the carriage pulled away, Elizabeth felt as though the days until she could go north would last for an eternity. She only prayed that nothing would delay their plans. She had to see Darcy again.

Chapter 21

Elizabeth eagerly looked out the window of the carriage. Jane and Bingley sat on the seat opposite hers, oblivious to her anxiety as they held hands and gave one another secret glances.

The August sun burned brightly, but Elizabeth scarcely noticed the heat. They had been travelling on the Bingley's wedding trip for two weeks, and they were finally making their way to Pemberley.

Elizabeth had been dismayed to discover on the first day of their journey that Bingley intended to end the trip with a stay at Pemberley. At first, she almost demanded they return her to Longbourn. She was certain that he would hate her.

After a few days, however, she came to the conclusion that she would never be happy in life knowing he was somewhere in the world thinking ill of her. Meeting in person and apologizing would bring her closure, even if he had no desire to see her again.

This newfound determination to speak with Darcy made the beginning of the trip pass slowly. While she enjoyed seeing the countryside, touring many of the great houses, and meeting some of Bingley's family, her true desire was to see Mr. Darcy again.

A giggle interrupted Elizabeth's contemplation, and she turned to see Jane and Bingley staring at her with amusement. "We are almost there, Lizzy," her new brother said with a smile. "In fact, I believe… yes, this is it."

Bingley rapped on the carriage roof, and the horses came to a stop. Elizabeth looked out her window, but she only saw trees. "Have we arrived?" she asked in confusion.

"In order to see Pemberley properly for the first time, you must stop here and exit the carriage," he informed her.

Bingley helped his wife down, then turned to offer his hand to Elizabeth. She stepped down from the carriage, and he led both women around to the other side.

"There," he said, pointing.

Elizabeth gasped in delight. Down the hill, across a park, sat a majestic home. It was a large, beautiful stone building that stood on a swell of earth. Behind it was a ridge of high, woody hills that extended as far as she could see. In front of the home was a stream that gradually grew larger, but it looked natural as opposed to being falsely adorned.

"I have never seen a more beautiful place," she whispered to herself. "Just think: of all this, I might have been mistress."

Even Jane, who was no great lover of the outdoors, was taken aback by the splendor of the estate. After several minutes of studying the grounds, they boarded the carriage again and went down the hill to the front of the manor.

Those few minutes seemed to stretch into an eternity. The previous months of anticipation all led to this moment. Elizabeth could scarcely breathe or sit still. It took every bit of self-control she possessed to not bounce on the seat or jump out of the carriage and run the remainder of the distance.

At long last, the carriage came to a stop. Elizabeth gripped her hands tightly together as she waited impatiently for Bingley to help Jane out of the carriage. When it was her turn, she practically leapt down. Upon gaining her footing, she looked up towards the door.

He wasn't there.

Elizabeth looked around, confused. She was certain Mr. Darcy would have at least followed propriety and been there to greet his friends. Even if he no longer had feelings for her—and she did not dare to hope he still loved her after her callous rejection—surely he would not have abandoned the newlyweds?

Bingley, too, looked bewildered. He strode up to the door and knocked. A footman answered, and Bingley presented his card. The servant's eyes widened, and he turned to speak to someone behind him before beckoning them into the front hall.

The housekeeper came rushing up to them. "Mr. Bingley, sir!" she said, flustered. "We were not expecting your arrival until the eighteenth!"

Bingley's face wrinkled in confusion. "I'm sorry, Mrs. Reynolds, but I wrote to Darcy and informed him we would arrive on the thirteenth."

Everyone paused and looked at one another. "Allow me to fetch Mr. Hughes," the butler suggested.

"Who is he?" Bingley asked.

"The acting steward while Mr. Wickham is away."

Bingley agreed, and a footman dashed away at top speed. There were several moments of awkward silence; no one quite knew where to look. A small sigh of relief sounded in the corridor as two sets of footsteps were heard coming quickly down the hall.

A thin, young man with disheveled hair and glasses walked swiftly towards them, carrying a piece of paper. Introductions were performed, and Mr. Hughes showed Bingley the letter Mr. Darcy had received. Jane read the note over her husband's shoulder.

"Blast!" Bingley groaned, earning him a sharp look from his wife. He looked around ruefully and said, "My apologies. It appears an ink blot turned my three into an eight."

"I'm afraid, sir, that Mr. and Miss Darcy are not in residence. They went to Matlock for a few days and plan to return the day after tomorrow," Mr. Hughes explained.

Bingley looked around in consternation. "Well, then, we shall just have to get some rooms at the inn at Lambton!" He rubbed his hands together. "Just think of it as an adventure, my dear."

"Certainly not," Mrs. Reynolds said in offended tones. "I would lose my place if Mr. Darcy heard that you were not given rooms here at Pemberley!"

Without waiting for a response, Mrs. Reynolds turned and began issuing sharp orders at passing maids and footmen. Within minutes, the Bingleys and Elizabeth were ushered upstairs into their rooms, with their trunks close behind them.

The door closed behind Elizabeth, and she looked around the room in awe. She knew Mr. Darcy was wealthy, and the grand appearance of Pemberley should have prepared her, but she was unable to comprehend just how fine her rooms were.

The floor was covered in thick, rich carpets. Fine draperies and wallpaper adorned the room, and a large bed with thick pillows and a soft mattress sat in the center. There were a few settees and over-stuffed chairs placed comfortably near the windows and fireplace, and some small bookshelves sat along the walls.

I think the entire guest wing of Longbourn could fit into this room, she thought in dismay. *No wonder Mr. Darcy thought so highly of himself in comparison to us.*

Elizabeth began to remove her bonnet and pelisse, when a soft knock was heard at the door. A young maid entered and bobbed a curtsey. "Beggin' your pardon for the intrusion, miss, but Mrs. Reynolds has asked me to tend to you during your stay here."

Elizabeth looked at the girl in surprise. "I had planned on sharing my sister's maid. I would not wish to take you from your regular duties."

To her surprise, the girl's face crumpled slightly. "It would be no trouble at all, miss. It would be an honor to act as a lady's maid. There are so few opportunities, you see. Miss Darcy is not out yet, so there are few guests."

Elizabeth gave the girl a reassuring smile. "In that case, I would be most grateful for your assistance. What is your name?"

The girl's face lit up, and she curtseyed again. "Sally, miss. Thank you!"

Sally bustled over to where Elizabeth's trunks had been placed near a door. After opening the door, the maid began to unpack. Curiously, Elizabeth moved forward and gasped. Through the door was one of the largest dressing rooms she had ever seen.

"I do not think my clothes will fill up even a quarter of the closet," she laughed nervously.

"Oh, never mind that, miss," the maid assured her. "Even Miss Darcy does not take up all of her closet, and she gets a full new wardrobe every season."

Elizabeth's eyes raised slightly at this. "What else can you tell me about Pemberley?" she asked curiously.

The maid began to chatter all about the house, the tenants, and the Darcys. "My mother was so excited when I was hired on here," she informed Elizabeth. "Everyone knows the Darcys are fair to their servants, and they take care of you like you were their own kin. Why, just last month when Lucy fell in the kitchen and burned her arm something fierce, Mr. Darcy paid for the doctor and even paid her wages all this time, though she still can't move it the same way she used to, poor thing…"

Elizabeth listened in wonder as the maid continued to rattle on. "My goodness," she said when Sally paused to breathe, "it seems as if Pemberley is almost too good to be true!"

"It truly is, miss," Sally said firmly. "I cannot think of a single person who would have something bad to say about it. Sure, sometimes the tenants get out of sorts, but they know Mr. Darcy will always treat them fairly, even if they don't like a decision he might make. And some of the neighborhood ladies might be perturbed that he hasn't chosen one of their daughters yet, but my ma says that he's good enough for the daughter of an earl or a duke…"

Sally's prattling faded as a roaring filled Elizabeth's ears. Initially, Sally's words caused Elizabeth to yearn for Mr. Darcy's presence even more. The longer the girl spoke, however, the more Elizabeth's anticipation turned to insecurity and dread.

I shouldn't be here, she thought fretfully. *The last time we spoke, I was wrong about so many things. How could his love have survived such a brutal assault?*

Elizabeth sat heavily on the bed, her head aching and her heart pounding.

"Miss, are you ill?"

Sally looked up from the trunk in alarm and crossed over to Elizabeth. She placed her hand on Elizabeth's forehead, then crossed the room and pulled on the bell. Elizabeth scarcely noticed Mrs. Reynolds's entrance nor Jane's a few minutes later. It was only when the stays on her dress were loosened that her mind was recalled to the present.

"Not to worry, Lizzy," soothed Jane. "We are going to help you into your nightgown and let you sleep. You don't have a fever, but all the travel must have tired even you!"

Voices swirled around her, but Elizabeth took no notice as darkness fell over her.

Elizabeth awoke with a start. She sat up in bed and looked around the darkened room. *Where am I?*

Moonlight filtered in through the drapes, and she saw the shadows of several large chairs. At once, the events of the evening came flooding back to her. *I am in Mr. Darcy's house, and he is not here to greet me.*

The faint light from the window fell over a clock near the fireplace, which showed that it was about one o'clock in the morning. She felt a little chill, in spite of it being summer, and she stood to search for her dressing gown.

Finding it draped at the end of the bed, she wrapped herself in it. Her stomach growled loudly, and she looked around. *Didn't Jane say something about a tray being sent up?*

Unable to find a tray, she went to the door and looked out. She did not wish to wake Sally, so she thought she might try to find the kitchens herself—or at least a footman who was on duty for the night.

She walked aimlessly down the hall, looking around for someone who could help her. *Surely in a manor this size, there would be a footman or two on duty throughout the night?*

Just as she was prepared to give up and return to her room, she turned down another corridor and spied a well-lit room with an open door. *Maybe the acting steward can give me some direction.*

Elizabeth walked into the room and stopped, her mouth dropping open slightly in amazement. She had entered the most incredible library she had ever seen. It was even larger than the bookstores she had visited in London near Gracechurch Street!

Bookcases covered the walls from floor to ceiling for two entire floors. At one end of the room, large windows were framed by elaborate curtains. Spiral staircases went up each side of the windows to the second floor, where a balcony went around the entire room, providing access to the upper level of shelves.

"Do you like it?"

Elizabeth gasped in shock and spun around to face the voice. Over in the shadows, sitting unnoticed on a chair near the fireplace, was Mr. Darcy!

"It's the most beautiful room I have ever seen," she told him sincerely.

"It has been the work of many generations," he said, standing up and walking towards her. The flames from the fireplace reflected in his dark eyes, which stared, piercing into her own.

"I had not thought you were here," she said, suddenly very aware of her lack of dress.

"Mr. Hughes sent a note to Matlock upon your early arrival. I came as quickly as I could."

"I believe we were right on time, sir. It is you who were late," she teased.

"Am I too late, Elizabeth?"

Darcy stood in front of her, so close she could feel the heat radiating from his body. If she were to move just the slightest amount, she would be pressed up against him.

His question pierced her soul. "Never," she whispered.

Suddenly his arms were around her waist, his lips pressed against hers. She moaned slightly and stood on her tiptoes to give him easier access. The slight movement caused him to shudder, and he pulled her firmly against his body. He deepened the kiss, and she returned his passion with every pent-up feeling in her heart.

He tore his mouth away from hers, his breath coming in ragged gasps. "We must stop," he panted.

His words penetrated the fog in her mind. She realized her fingers were entwined in his hair, her breasts against his chest. Heat rushed to her face, and she dropped her hands. Taking a step back, she wrapped her arms around her cold body.

"What must you think of me?" she whispered, tears filling her eyes.

Darcy took a step towards her and pulled her into his arms again. "I think you are the most incredible woman I have ever met."

"But I behaved like…"

"Like I had always dreamed and never dared to hope for."

Gently taking her chin in his hand, he lifted her face until her eyes met his. "It is I who should apologize to you. I should not be taking advantage of you in my home in the middle of the night."

Elizabeth looked around the room, blinking. She had entirely forgotten the lateness of the hour or the complete inappropriateness of their situation. She turned her gaze back to him. "I should probably return to my room."

Her stomach made a noise of protest, and she blushed. "I did not wish to disturb a maid, but I am afraid I missed dinner."

Darcy smiled and gestured towards a table with some biscuits. "Please, help yourself. I missed dinner as well."

She crossed the room and began to eat. Darcy joined her, and the two ate in silence for several minutes. When her hunger was sated, she reluctantly stood to return to her room.

"Wait," he said, standing as well. "I cannot let you leave without knowing… that is, I had planned to wait, but… will you marry me?"

Elizabeth looked at him in astonishment. Darcy flushed slightly and said, "I had planned to wait until I had time to court you properly. I dared not hope that your feelings had changed. I thought you might still hate me. But I could not stop loving you, and I wanted to have the opportunity to show you that I have changed. After tonight, though, I cannot—"

"Yes."

Darcy blinked at her, stupefied. "Yes?" he repeated.

"Yes, I will marry you," she said, a smile forming on her lips.

Darcy's face split into a wide grin. In two steps, he was at her side, pulling her into his arms again. He held her tightly, lifted her off the ground, and spun her around. She giggled with delight. He set her down and pressed a firm kiss on her lips.

"You have made me the happiest of men, Elizabeth!" he said with delight. "I promise I will do everything I can to make you happy."

She smiled softly at him. "You already do," she responded, laying her hand on his cheek.

The moment was interrupted by a noise in the hallway. Both jumped slightly, looking towards the door.

"As much as I hate to put an end to this moment, I think it best if you returned to your room," Darcy said.

Elizabeth nodded and made her way to the door. Before leaving, she turned and looked at him one more time. "I love you," she said, then disappeared into the shadows.

Chapter 22

By the time Elizabeth returned to her bedroom, she was convinced she would never fall asleep. The next thing she knew, however, Sally had entered her bedroom and was quietly lighting the fire.

A smile crept across Elizabeth's face as the memories from the night before flashed in front of her. She burrowed farther into the warm covers on the soft mattress, not wanting to lose the comforting feeling of his arms around her.

She must have fallen asleep again, because she blinked, and the sun was much higher in the sky. She sat up and looked around.

"Good morning, miss," Sally's cheerful voice came from the dressing room.

"Yes, it is a good morning!" exclaimed Elizabeth.

Eager to see Darcy again, she got out of bed and quickly dressed with Sally's help. Once she had completed her toilette, she went downstairs in search of the breakfast room. Thankfully, this time there were several footmen on hand to point her the right direction.

When she entered, Darcy immediately stood.

"Good morning," she said with a smile and a blush.

"To you as well," he replied.

Darcy moved to her side and escorted her to the seat next to his. He pulled the chair out from the table. As she sat, he leaned down and gave her a quick kiss on the neck. She gasped slightly, and he retreated. As he filled her plate from the sideboard, she looked around the otherwise empty room. She began to ask him where the Bingleys were but became distracted by the contents of her plate.

"You chose all my favorites!" she exclaimed with surprise.

Darcy flushed slightly. "I may have been paying closer attention than I thought when you were staying at Netherfield."

She gave him a warm smile. "And here I thought you were only looking to find fault."

Darcy choked slightly on his coffee. "Quite the opposite, I assure you."

She lowered her eyes under his intense gaze. Reaching for her fork, she asked, "Have Bingley and Jane come down?"

Darcy cleared his throat. "It is my understanding that Bingley requested their breakfast trays be sent to his room."

"Ah, I see," she said, slightly embarrassed.

There was a moment of awkward silence, then they both began to speak at the same time.

"About last night…"

"You must allow me…"

Laughing slightly, Darcy gestured at her with his fork. "Ladies first."

Elizabeth shook her head. "I defer to the gentleman in this case."

"Very well," Darcy acknowledged. He sat forward slightly in his chair and gave her a piercing look. "I wanted to ensure that you do not have any regrets this morning. I know that sometimes we may make decisions in the heat of the moment that, in the light of day, we may have cause to regret."

Elizabeth sucked in a quick breath. "Do you have any regrets?" She held her breath, waiting for his answer.

"None," he said firmly, "but I will not hold you to a commitment if you were regretting the answer you gave. My wishes remain unchanged, but one word from you will silence me on the subject forever."

"I do not have any regrets," she said softly. "In fact, I was going to tell you how much I enjoyed our time together yesterday evening."

Darcy's face split into a wide grin. "I am pleased to hear it. I hope to spend many more evenings with you thus engaged."

Elizabeth blushed again, but she met his gaze determinedly. "And I as well." There was a moment of silence, then Elizabeth said, "I do want to apologize, however, for the horrible things I said in Hunsford."

"What did you say that I did not deserve? I cannot think about my words that night without abhorrence. I regretted everything the moment I left the parsonage, but I could not return. A letter was the only way I could explain without making things worse by my own stupidity."

"I was so ashamed of myself when I read your letter. I could not have misunderstood more thoroughly than had I willfully chosen to."

"Did you think better of me, then?" he asked.

"Yes, of course. I only wish society would have allowed me to respond to your letter."

Darcy chuckled. "It would have resolved things sooner, certainly."

"We might be married now instead of merely engaged." She laughed.

There was a moment of silence, then Darcy said, "I suppose I should make plans to speak with your father."

Elizabeth shook her head. "My mother entreated my father to give Bingley charge over me. She was afraid that if I encountered one of his wealthy friends and somehow managed to induce them to propose, they would change their mind on their journey to Longbourn."

Darcy let out a bark of laughter. "Be that as it may, I believe I still wish to speak with your father and receive his blessing."

Elizabeth's heart warmed at this evidence of his thoughtfulness. "Perhaps you could journey back with us when we leave here and return for home?"

He shook his head. "As much as I would not wish to be parted from you, I will need to remain here for the harvest. With Wickham gone and Hughes in his place, I will need to be more involved than usual this year."

She nodded in understanding. "What would be most convenient for you?"

Darcy hesitated briefly. "My sister will be arriving today from Matlock. With your permission, I can introduce her to you today and ride to Longbourn tomorrow."

"So soon?" she asked, disappointment clouding her voice.

"I can, of course, delay things if you wish," he replied coolly.

Elizabeth looked at him blankly. "I had thought to this fortnight together without the... distractions in Meryton. Your journey to and from Longbourn would use up half that time."

Darcy's shoulders relaxed. "I thought perhaps you wished to delay for other reasons."

"Oh, no, not in the least!" she exclaimed, putting a hand on his arm. "As eager as I am for my father to give his blessing, I did not wish to be separated from you so soon into our engagement."

Darcy covered her hand with his own. "I do not wish to be apart from you, either."

Elizabeth bit her lip. "I wish there was a way to communicate immediately over long distances."

He smiled at her. "Perhaps in the future there will be."

They sat for several moments in quiet contemplation. "Perhaps there is a way to keep us together," he ventured.

"Yes?"

"Instead of remaining here for a fortnight, we could leave tomorrow together. I could get a special license in London, and then we could go to Longbourn and be married immediately. This would allow me to return here in time for the harvest with you, but your family would all still be in attendance."

Elizabeth hesitated a moment. "I would hate to disturb Jane and Bingley's wedding trip. They still have two weeks before returning to the world and society."

"It is somewhat selfish of me, I confess," he allowed. "But let us put the question to them. If they do not mind doing so, would you be willing to marry me in two weeks?"

"I would marry you tomorrow if I could," she said fervently.

The fire in her eyes caused him to lean over and kiss her with an intensity that took her by surprise. She let out a low moan and returned the kiss with equal passion. Darcy tilted her head to deepen the kiss.

"What is going on here?" a loud voice demanded.

Elizabeth pulled quickly away from Darcy. Both stared at the intruder in shock. Lady Catherine de Bourgh stood in the doorway to the breakfast room, face purple with rage. Behind her, a butler hurried forward.

"My apologies, Mr. Darcy," the man gasped. "She was not willing to wait in a drawing room."

Darcy nodded in understanding. "Quite all right. It is not easy to gainsay my aunt."

"I certainly am not!" she declared. "And I insist on being satisfied! Darcy, I cannot believe you have allowed this… this… chit to take you in with her wiles!"

Elizabeth gasped, and Darcy's face went rigid. "I will thank you to not use such language when speaking of my fiancée," he said coldly.

Lady Catherine's eyes bulged. "Then it is true! Reports of an alarming nature have reached me at Rosings. I heard from Mrs. Stanley how Miss Bennet's sister was recently wed to my own nephew's closest friend. I saw how she flirted with both of my nephews while at Rosings. When I discovered that she would be residing at Pemberley as part of the wedding tour, I knew the danger of you forgetting what is owed to your family! I immediately set out to put a stop to this travesty."

She took a deep breath and sighed. "But as you are not married, there is still time. I do not know how she brought you so far astray from your duty, but it is of little importance. I am certain she will accept a fair settlement, and we can stop any gossip by announcing your engagement to Anne immediately."

Elizabeth's eyebrows raised far into her head. She looked at Darcy, but his surprise was so evident that he could not speak. She stepped forward. "I am sorry to disappoint you, Lady Catherine, but I have accepted Mr. Darcy's offer of marriage, and no amount of money would convince me to go back on my word."

"Nonsense, girl," Lady Catherine retorted. "I'm sure that ten thousand pounds would be sufficient for you. It is, after all, much more than you could expect to receive from your father."

"Indeed, you are mistaken," Elizabeth replied coolly. "I love Mr. Darcy, and that is worth more than the entirety of your fortune."

"Miss Bennet," replied her ladyship in an angry tone, "I am not to be trifled with! However insincere you may choose to be, you will not find me so. I am well known for my frankness of character, and I will not act otherwise now. Your alliance would be a disgrace. You will be slighted and hated by all of society, and your name would never be mentioned by any of us."

"These would be heavy misfortunes indeed," Elizabeth countered, "if I cared for such things. But as the wife of Mr. Darcy, I would have such extraordinary sources of happiness that I would have no cause to repine."

"Obstinate, headstrong girl! If you were sensible of your own good, you would not wish to quit the sphere in which you were raised. Oh, to see the shades of Pemberley thus polluted! My poor sister would be rolling in her grave to see her son married to such a harlot! Mark my words, girl, once I tell everyone about you and your wickedness, you will not be allowed anywhere again!"

Elizabeth gasped in outrage. She opened her mouth to retort, but Darcy had finally found his voice. "Silence!" he bellowed.

Lady Catherine gaped at him. When he was satisfied that she would not continue, he said in a deadly calm voice, "You have said quite enough, Lady Catherine. You can have nothing further to say, and I must insist that you leave Pemberley at once."

He stepped forward, took her arm, and forcefully escorted her from the room. Elizabeth could hear the woman's tirades up until the carriage door was slammed behind her.

Darcy returned to the breakfast room where Elizabeth sat, calmly eating her cold breakfast. "I cannot begin to apologize for my aunt," Darcy began.

He broke off when Elizabeth laughed. "I dare say that was not quite the reaction I expected from the first person we told of our engagement."

Her continued giggles finally brought a smile to his face. He sat at the table. "I'm afraid, my dear, that our plans will need to change. I must ride to Matlock immediately, as my aunt is going to her brother, the earl. Georgiana is there, and I wish to arrive before she does. If I go by horseback, I can take a shorter path."

Elizabeth nodded in understanding. "I would offer to accompany you, but I am afraid I am not much of a horsewoman. Besides that, the servants might think we had decided to elope!"

Darcy's eyes widened at first, then he sniffed and stuck his nose in the air. "A Darcy servant would *never* dare to gossip against their master."

Elizabeth eyed him nervously before she saw the slight tugging at the corner of his lips. "Well, then," she replied with mocking tones that mirrored his own, "I shall be quite content to remain here at my leisure with every servant at my beck and call."

The two exchanged a smile, then Darcy arose to take his leave. She stood with him and found herself quickly wrapped in his arms. He pressed a gentle kiss to the top of her head, then left the room, calling for his horse to be prepared.

Elizabeth sat at the table. The levity she had shown Darcy gave way to exhaustion. Not only had she slept little the night before, but the effort she put into not allowing Darcy to see how truly shaken she was by the encounter had stolen all of her energy.

She contemplated for several minutes. Would Darcy give way to the pressure of his family? Lady Catherine was clearly against the marriage, but what would the earl say? Being Lady Catherine's brother, he quite likely shared many of her characteristics. *Then again, Jane, Mary, and I are all sisters,* she thought with a smile. *No need to borrow trouble by speculating.*

She determined that it was time to speak with Jane and Bingley. She rang for a servant and asked someone to deliver a message to her sister that it was important she speak with both of them as soon as possible.

As she waited for them, Elizabeth thought through all the different possibilities. By the time they arrived, she determined that whether or not Darcy was still willing to marry her, she would need to leave Pemberley as soon as possible.

At first, the Bingleys were delighted with Elizabeth's news of Darcy's proposal. As she continued her tale, however, the mood in the room swiftly changed. Jane was appropriately horrified when she heard of Lady Catherine's behavior towards Elizabeth. Bingley appeared uncharacteristically stern, but he did smile when Elizabeth told them about her responses to her ladyship's haranguing.

Elizabeth concluded by saying, "Either Mr. Darcy will return from his uncle's estate having changed his mind about marrying me or he will have stood his ground. Either way, I think it best if I prepare to leave for Longbourn. I would wish to stay here, but I am afraid that even if he continues with our engagement, the gossip will not treat us kindly if I remain in his household."

"Surely no one would believe Lady Catherine, especially with Charles and myself here as chaperones!" protested Jane.

Elizabeth laughed softly at her sister. "Jane, you are too good! But I am afraid you are incorrect. I would not wish to begin my marriage with such a scandal hanging over our heads."

Jane made to protest again, but Charles took her hand and said fondly, "My dear, I am afraid your sister has the right of it. We should make plans to leave as soon as Darcy returns."

"Oh no!" cried Elizabeth. "Please do not interrupt your wedding trip for me! I will be quite fine travelling by post if Mr. Darcy will spare a manservant to accompany me."

"Certainly not!" responded Bingley severely. "Your brother would murder me if I allowed you to travel by yourself. It is no trouble at all for Jane or myself to accompany you. There will be many other opportunities to visit Pemberley in the future."

When it was clear that Bingley would brook no further argument, Elizabeth thanked him and privately resolved to do all in her power to make amends for ruining their honeymoon.

As the majority of their things had yet to be unpacked from the day before, it was quite simple for them to pack again to leave Pemberley. Once their preparations were completed, there was nothing left to do but wait for Darcy to return so they could discuss the situation together.

Elizabeth returned to the library to await him. She chose a book at random and sat on a comfortable chaise to attempt to occupy her mind. Instead of reading the words on the page, however, she closed her eyes and thought back over her entire relationship with Darcy.

Things had changed so drastically since that first night at the Meryton assembly when he proclaimed her not handsome enough to tempt him. She had gone from loathing to loving in months. She tried to pinpoint exactly when she had fallen in love with him, but it seemed as if she were in the middle of it before she had even begun.

Even though she couldn't stand the sight of him when she stayed at Netherfield for the duration of Jane's illness, she couldn't deny the attraction she felt towards him. From the first moment she laid eyes on him, she felt him to be one of the handsomest men she had ever seen. That attraction made his comments about her appearance that much more painful, and she had lashed out in kind.

Prior to receiving his letter at Rosings, she had seen qualities in him that went against her preconceived notions of his pomposity. His kindness towards others and the occasional jest contrasted with the arrogance and superiority she had credited him with. When he proposed to her, all the puzzle pieces fell into place. Everything about his character that seemed to be a contradiction suddenly made sense.

Elizabeth had spent many hours over the previous months reading and rereading his letter. That window into his soul brought her onto a level of intimacy with a man that she had not experienced outside of her father and her cousin. Knowing the hurt and pain that drove him, how could she not come to respect him? From that respect, admiration grew and blossomed into love.

Now, as she sat waiting for him to arrive and determine her fate, she knew that if he chose to end their twelve-hour courtship, she would never be able to love again.

Please, she pleaded towards heaven, *let him choose me.*

Chapter 23

Darcy leaned forward on the carriage seat and placed his head in his hands, massaging his temples. Sitting across from him, Georgiana looked on with concern. "Are you all right, brother?" she asked.

He gave her a wan smile. "It has been a difficult day."

The interview with his uncle had gone better than he expected. Lord Matlock, while a cold and austere man, was also very logical. He recognized that Darcy could not marry Anne and sire an heir. He would have preferred to see Darcy marry high in society, but he also knew he had little say over Darcy's choice.

The difficulty began when Lady Catherine arrived at Matlock. Her shock at seeing Darcy caused her to fall silent, but only for a moment. She opened her mouth and let loose a stream of vitriol that caused even the earl to gasp in dismay.

"Quiet, Catherine!" the earl thundered when he found his voice. "I have already given Darcy my blessing. As I am the head of this family, that will be enough from you!"

"Should my aunt choose to continue her hatred towards my fiancée," Darcy interjected coolly, "I will have no choice but to cease all contact with her until an apology has been issued."

"Quite right," the earl responded tartly, to Lady Catherine's horror. "I also think it is time to remove Anne from her mother's influence, seeing as how the woman is clearly incapable of reason and self-control."

At this point, Darcy excused himself to collect his sister and return to Pemberley as soon as possible. He was dismayed to discover during

Lady Catherine's diatribe that she had been to Longbourn to find Elizabeth. He could only imagine the gossip that had resulted from her encounter with the Bennet family.

His thoughts were pulled back to the present when Georgiana said, "I look forward to meeting Miss Elizabeth. I hope she will like me."

Darcy gave his sister a comforting smile. "She will love you, Georgiana."

"She wouldn't if she knew the truth about me," she said softly.

He winced slightly. "Dearest," he began, "she knows all."

Georgiana gasped in dismay, and tears filled her eyes. "Why would you tell her of my shame?" she whispered in panic.

Darcy took one of his sister's small hands in his own large one. "Because she thought Caroline and Bingley to be false friends when they did not respond to her sister's letters while in Scotland."

She let out a small whimper, and he continued, "Elizabeth Bennet is one of the kindest, most genuine people that I know. She has been nothing but kind to Caroline in spite of her father's actions. She does not hold her accountable for the man's perversities, and I know she feels the same about you."

Georgiana took several slow breaths and nodded. Her relaxation was short-lived, however. She became tense once again when they arrived at Pemberley. He knew the only way to relieve her anxiety was to allow her to meet Elizabeth, so he quickly escorted her into the house.

"Where is Miss Bennet?" he asked the footman taking his hat.

"I believe she is in the library, sir," the man responded.

Darcy held his sister firmly by the arm and urged her towards the room. She resisted slightly but allowed herself to be tugged along. Her face was pale, and he kept hold of her arm to prevent her from darting away.

Elizabeth looked up from her book when she heard the door open. "Darcy!" she cried with delight. She ran to him and threw her arms around him.

He let go of his sister to return the embrace, then leaned down and kissed her firmly on the lips.

"I take it this means you have not decided to withdraw your offer?" she asked him with a smile, but the tremor in her voice revealed her nervousness.

"Never!" he cried in alarm.

She gave him a full smile, which she then turned on his sister. "This must be Miss Darcy," she said warmly.

"It is a pleasure to meet you, Miss Bennet," whispered Georgiana, giving a pretty curtsy. Her face was still pale.

"Oh, please, do call me Elizabeth! Or even Lizzy, if you'd rather. For we are to be sisters, and I would love above all else if we could be friends, as well."

Georgiana's shoulders sagged in relief, tears once again filling her eyes. "I was so afraid," she choked out.

"Oh, my poor dear girl," Elizabeth cried, pulling Georgiana in for a tight hug. Elizabeth held the young woman as she sobbed into her soon-to-be sister's shoulder. "There, there, it is all right. You are safe, and you are loved," Elizabeth soothed, stroking the younger girl's hair.

Darcy's heart filled with warmth as he watched the two women he loved most in the world find solace and comfort in one another's arms.

After several long moments, Georgiana pulled back. Wiping her eyes, she whispered, "Thank you."

Elizabeth smiled at her gently. "Of course, my dear. I look forward to spending time with you after the wedding."

"You will allow me to stay, then? You do not wish for me to set up my own establishment?"

Elizabeth looked shocked. "Certainly not! I depend upon you to not only help me with running Pemberley and meeting tenants but also to be my friend and sister! I am coming from a large household, you see. I would not know what to do if I only had your brother for company!"

"Are you certain you would not prefer one of your own sisters?" Georgiana asked cautiously.

"You will be one of my own sisters," Elizabeth said firmly. "My Bennet sisters may visit or stay here as they so desire, but Pemberley will always be your home, Georgiana, should you wish it. I would love to have you here for as long as you desire."

Georgiana dissolved into tears again and threw herself into Elizabeth's arms. Elizabeth patted the girl on the back and looked up at Darcy with a slightly bewildered expression.

"I told you Elizabeth would love you," Darcy said to his sister.

Georgiana pulled back once more. "I have never been happier," she said fiercely. "Now, I believe you two have much to discuss. I will be in my rooms, unpacking from Matlock."

The girl gave a brief curtsy and dashed from the room. Elizabeth turned to Darcy and said, "I hope everything went well?"

Darcy related everything that occurred at Matlock. Elizabeth was relieved to hear that the earl did not object to their marriage. While she was now confident that Darcy would not renege on his offer, she knew it would smooth the way to have Lord Matlock's acceptance.

Once he had finished, Elizabeth told him about the Bingleys' response. She concluded by saying, "Given the fact that Lady Catherine has been at my home, I think it best if the Bingleys and I leave for Longbourn this afternoon."

"I agree," Darcy said immediately. "I will need a day to arrange things here, but I will follow you tomorrow. I plan to bring Georgiana with me, and I will stop in London to purchase a special license and have my solicitor draw up wedding papers for your father." He took her hands in his and looked into her eyes with a serious expression. "I know a quick wedding is not necessarily what you would wish for, but I think it important to get ahead of the gossip mill."

Elizabeth gripped his hands tightly in response. "All I wish for is to marry you. I am happy it will be from Longbourn, as I wish to bid farewell to my family and neighbors. But I do not need to have a long engagement."

Darcy gently cupped her cheek with his hand, then leaned down to kiss her. All thoughts fled away as his lips touched hers. He intended for it to be a soft kiss, but passion quickly flared between them.

"Ahem."

The couple broke apart and saw Bingley standing at the door, eyebrow raised and arms crossed in mock disapproval.

Darcy grinned sheepishly at Bingley and said, "I simply cannot help myself."

Bingley returned the grin with one of his own. "I understand the feeling, my friend. Am I to congratulate you, then?

Darcy quickly rehearsed everything that had occurred at Matlock, along with the decision to follow the Bingleys to Longbourn.

When he finished, Bingley nodded in approval. "Excellent. I will send an express to Caroline so she can prepare for our arrival as well as yours."

"I am sorry for interrupting your wedding trip," apologized Darcy.

"Nonsense, old man! Jane is delighted for her sister, and to be honest, we are looking forward to returning to our own home," Bingley replied. "I am glad you are following us; I was not anticipating explaining to Mr. Bennet about your engagement."

Darcy looked at his friend in surprise. "You do not think he would deny his permission?"

Elizabeth looked at him uneasily. "It's only that he is unaware of my change in opinion about your character."

"I see," Darcy replied. He was quiet for a moment, then said, "I will have to endeavor to rectify his opinion of me."

"And I will not be silent about how much I love you," Elizabeth assured.

Bingley nodded. "I will vouch for your character. I planned on doing so, but it will be easier if you are present!"

"Then Georgiana and I will make my way to Longbourn with all haste," Darcy replied.

Elizabeth bit her lip. "I meant to ask you about that," she said thoughtfully. "Will Georgiana be all right living in the same house with Miss Wickham?"

Darcy looked hesitant. "I am uncertain. I know she would wish to be at my wedding, but I worry that seeing the baby will undo all the good that has been accomplished."

"Perhaps you should discuss the matter with her," Elizabeth suggested. "If she chooses to come and it becomes too much, I know my parents would welcome her at Longbourn for the duration of her stay."

Darcy nodded. With that resolved, Elizabeth and Bingley left the library in order to make final arrangements for their trip to Meryton.

When it came time for them to depart, Darcy and Georgiana joined them at the carriage to bid them farewell. Darcy and Elizabeth clasped hands tightly, which is all they were allowed by propriety in such a public setting. When everything was settled, Darcy handed her inside.

As the carriage drove away, Elizabeth turned and looked back at Darcy and Pemberley for as long as she was able. Only when they finally faded from view did she turn her attention towards her companions. She hoped it would not be the last time she would see Darcy or his home.

The journey to Longbourn passed slowly for Elizabeth. Jane and Bingley did their best to distract her, but Elizabeth simply could not be entertained. She laughed and smiled when engaged but was prone to silence and distraction. Much of her journey was spent looking absently out a window or staring blankly at a book, all the while tapping her feet rapidly.

When at last the carriage left her at Longbourn and continued on to Netherfield, she was greeted by her very concerned family.

"Why have you returned so quickly?" Mrs. Bennet demanded. "We did not expect you for another two weeks! Did that awful Lady Catherine force Mr. Darcy to banish you from his home?"

"Now, Mother Bennet, I am certain that Darcy did no such thing," said Collins soothingly.

Collins and Mary had been taking tea at Longbourn when the carriage arrived. Everyone gathered into the drawing room to discover why Elizabeth had returned so early. Even Mr. Bennet had left his study to understand why his daughter had arrived so early.

"No, Mama, Mr. Darcy was every bit the gentleman," she said. "Lady Catherine did arrive at Pemberley."

"She thought you were going to marry Mr. Darcy!" laughed Kitty. "Can you imagine being wed to such a boorish man?"

Elizabeth flushed slightly, and Mr. Bennet narrowed his eyes at his daughter. "Lizzy, has Mr. Darcy made you an offer of marriage?"

Squaring her shoulders, Elizabeth said simply, "Yes, he has."

The entire room erupted into chaos. Each member of the family expressed their surprise in manners most befitting their personality. After several seconds, Mr. Bennet raised his voice and shouted, "Quiet!"

The chatter immediately ceased, and all eyes turned back towards Elizabeth. "Well?" demanded Mrs. Bennet.

"Well, what?" Elizabeth obstinately retorted.

"Oh, for heaven's sake, Lizzy! Are you or are you not engaged to Mr. Darcy?" cried her mother.

"I am."

The room once more erupted into astonishment but quickly quieted when Collins raised his hand for silence. "Lizzy, are you certain this is what you wish? Because last I understood, you did not even like him. Do you really want to marry such a man?" he asked her with a piercing stare.

"It is!" she stated emphatically. "I do like him. I love him. I did not always love him, but after coming to know him better, I love him now more than I have ever loved anyone."

"I would like to speak with Mr. Darcy myself before this goes any further," Mr. Bennet declared. "I absolutely forbid anyone to speak of this outside of this household until I have given my explicit permission." Mrs. Bennet opened her mouth to object, but he gave her a sharp look. "Anyone who speaks of this arrangement will lose their pin money for an entire quarter."

Subdued, everyone agreed. Mr. Bennet then turned back to his daughter and said, "Elizabeth, I will see you in my book room in five minutes. William, I would appreciate your attendance as well."

Elizabeth nodded, then used the opportunity to dash up the stairs and take a few calming breaths. Once she had changed into a fresh dress, she went to join her father and Collins in the study.

When she entered her father's book room, both Mr. Bennet and Collins looked at her with serious faces.

"Elizabeth, I did not wish to make these inquiries in front of your mother and sisters," Mr. Bennet began, "but are you out of your senses to be accepting this man?"

She opened her mouth to respond, but her father did not give her the opportunity before he continued. "We all know him to be a proud and arrogant man. Lizzy, you must answer me truthfully: are you being forced into this marriage?"

Elizabeth's eyes widened. "No, Papa! No, I have not been compromised in the slightest."

Mr. Bennet closed his eyes and let out a sigh of relief. "Then what other possible reason could there be for you to attach yourself to a man so dour? I beg of you, my girl, to not allow yourself to enter into an arrangement where you cannot respect your partner."

"You must understand, Lizzy," interjected Collins, "that when I last spoke with Darcy, he made it quite clear that although he was attracted to you, he could not bring himself to lower himself by offering for someone of your station."

Elizabeth winced. "Yes, I know he had some objections to our family's status. But that is all in the past now."

"I know you will have many more fine carriages than Jane—" began Mr. Bennet.

"It's not like that at all!" Elizabeth cried desperately. "Had I wished for that, I would have accepted his offer in Hunsford!"

Mr. Bennet and Collins stared at Elizabeth in shock. "Am I to understand that he made you an offer when you were staying with the Stanleys?" Collins asked incredulously.

Elizabeth spent several minutes explaining her encounters with Darcy at Rosings, including his disastrous proposal. Mr. Bennet's face darkened in anger at hearing the words Darcy had used.

"What could possibly tempt you to accept this man, then?" he demanded.

Elizabeth hastily went on to explain how Mr. Darcy had cleared up all of her misunderstandings in a letter, which caused Collins to frown in disapproval.

"It was very wrong of him to put you in such a position," he lectured. "You should not have accepted his letter when you had no understanding with him!"

Elizabeth groaned in frustration. She looked at Collins and said, "William, Darcy told me everything. Everything about his past, the Bingleys' past, and all that has occurred since with his sister."

Collins's eyes widened in astonishment. "I see," he said slowly.

"Well, I do not see," snapped Mr. Bennet.

Elizabeth bit her lip, then looked at Collins beseechingly. "I cannot betray his confidence."

Collins nodded and said, "Father Bennet, I am aware of what Darcy must have shared with Elizabeth. It truly is not her place to share it. However, I am fully aware of what he would have shared with her. I cannot say more, but I will tell you that the Darcys and the Bingleys have had experiences with fathers who were similar in character to my own."

Understanding blossomed across Mr. Bennet's face as Elizabeth nodded vigorously. "When he explained his experiences and reasons behind his actions," she said, "it helped me to see him in a better light. It does not mean that he changed in essentials, but rather, my knowing him better helped me see what a truly good and honorable man he is."

Mr. Bennet let out a sigh. "I can see how this came about," he said. "However, I will withhold my permission and my blessing until the man arrives here to speak with me himself."

"He was to leave the day after us," Elizabeth assured her father. "He is stopping in London to fetch a license, as well as the settlement papers."

She hesitated, then said, "I'm afraid Lady Catherine's rantings were heard by servants both here and in Derbyshire. There may be some gossip."

Mr. Bennet's face grew very serious. "So this engagement is the result of a compromise, albeit unintentional?"

"No, no!" Elizabeth said hastily. "I had already accepted Darcy's proposal when Lady Catherine arrived."

"Very well, then," said Mr. Bennet, his expression lightening slightly. "I shall speak to Mr. Darcy when he arrives. In the meantime, we will speak of this to no one."

With a heavy heart, Elizabeth braced herself for some of the longest days of her life until Darcy was once again with her.

Chapter 24

The following days moved slowly for Elizabeth. Although Darcy had left a day behind her, she knew it would take at least an extra day or two in London for him to purchase the license and finalize the settlement papers.

During those days, Jane and Bingley frequently invited Elizabeth to Netherfield as a way for her to escape her mother's effusions. While Mr. Bennet did much to quell his wife's excitement at her daughter's fortunate alliance, the lady could be found frequently muttering phrases such as "ten thousand pounds a year" and "he's as good as a lord."

Since Longbourn remained somewhat insulated during those few days, Elizabeth had no real knowledge of any gossip that may have spread. She knew Hill was not one for spreading the household's business, but she had a little less faith in the discretion of some of the younger maids. In any case, Lady Catherine's ire would have been such that Charlotte would have written something to her mother about the situation. Elizabeth anticipated a visit from Lady Lucas the very day she received her next letter from her daughter.

On the fourth day of her return, Elizabeth received a note from Netherfield. Bingley had received an express from town, informing him that Darcy and his sister would arrive that afternoon. Jane invited Elizabeth to Netherfield so she could greet her betrothed without the interference of family members at Longbourn.

Elizabeth was extremely grateful for this consideration. She casually mentioned her intention to walk to Netherfield at breakfast.

When nobody objected to her plans—after all, they were quite in line with her activities on the prior days—she left shortly after finishing her meal.

Eagerness to see Darcy caused Elizabeth to quicken her pace. Several times, she had to consciously remind herself that it was not very ladylike to run. She also laughed slightly at her foolishness, as her own arrival time would not affect how quickly the Darcys would travel.

Upon her arrival at Netherfield, Elizabeth was informed that the Bingleys were still in their chambers. Mr. Wickham was working in the study, the butler said, but Mrs. Wickham was with the baby in the nursery. Elizabeth decided to join them there as opposed to waiting alone in the drawing room.

When she reached the nursery, she heard faint singing. She gently opened the door to find Caroline sitting in a rocking chair, soothing the baby with a lullaby. One hand dangled a rattle just in front of the child's eyes, who watched the toy with intense interest. Elizabeth had never seen Caroline so content.

Caroline heard the creak of the door and looked up. She smiled at Elizabeth. "Please come in and join us."

"I hope I do not intrude," Elizabeth replied, closing the door behind her.

"We are just enjoying some time together," Caroline said. "I have been wishing to speak with you privately, in any case."

"Oh?"

"We never did get to finish our conversation at Longbourn. I know Darcy shared my history with you, as well as his reasoning for being against my marriage to Wickham."

Elizabeth blushed slightly at this reference to things that a maiden typically did not discuss. Caroline laughed and said, "Come, now, Elizabeth! In a few weeks, you will be a married woman yourself. What difference does it make if you hear about such things now or then?"

Smiling somewhat sheepishly at her friend, Elizabeth said, "I admit

I am quite uninformed about what occurs in the marriage bed. I am a country girl, so I imagine it is somewhat the same."

Caroline nodded. "It is. Depending on the type of match—love, arranged, practical, or otherwise—the marriage bed varies in how enjoyable it is for both parties."

Elizabeth nodded slowly. "My mother's friends regularly discuss excuses they use to avoid their duties. My mother does not participate in those conversations, however."

"Your father seems to care for your mother," Caroline remarked.

"Yes, for all her silliness, he is fond of her. However, I do not enjoy thinking about what happens behind closed doors," Elizabeth said with an embarrassed laugh.

Caroline laughed, too, but a sorrowful expression crossed her face. "Unfortunately, that was not an option I had when my father was alive."

Elizabeth was mortified. "Oh, I apologize! I had not meant to—"

Caroline waved a hand of dismissal. "It is no matter. I am somewhat used to others' comments and am somewhat immune to them. I only mention it because it is related to what I wished to speak about with you."

Elizabeth furrowed her brow. "How so?"

"I wanted to relieve your mind about my relationship with Wickham. I know Darcy told you of my fear of physical intimacy."

Elizabeth could only nod, her face turning a brilliant red. Caroline chuckled at the sight.

"I will not give you specific details. All I will say is that I am perfectly happy with the patience and tenderness my husband showed during our first several months of marriage. Since I was supposedly with child, it would have been very bad if I had gotten pregnant before Anne was born. Wickham used that time to help me become accustomed to gestures of affection, such as hugs or gentle kisses."

Feeling as though she had intruded on something private, Elizabeth could only listen in silence. She did not have the words to reply to her friend, but Caroline did not seem to need any response.

"I simply wanted to assure you that I am now completely, utterly content with all aspects of my marriage. I did not want you to worry for me or Wickham," Caroline finished.

"I... thank you for letting me know. I admit to being somewhat concerned for your happiness when I heard of the decision you had made." Elizabeth had finally found her voice.

"I knew you would," Caroline said with a warm smile. "You are the kind of person who thinks of others and genuinely hopes for the best for them. I did not want you to always be wondering or worrying."

The two women shared a smile. Caroline looked at her baby and murmured, "It appears as if this dear little one has fallen asleep. Come, I will lay her down, and we can take tea in the drawing room while we wait for the Darcys."

Elizabeth watched Caroline lay the baby in the crib, then knock on the door to the nanny's room. Caroline gave some brief direction, then motioned for Elizabeth to follow her out the door.

Once the two women were downstairs and settled in the drawing room, Caroline rang for tea. After everything had been brought, the maid exited the room and closed the door behind her, leaving the two ladies alone once more.

Elizabeth stirred her tea absentmindedly while surreptitiously eyeing Caroline. Biting her lip, Elizabeth took a deep breath and said, "Caroline, do you mind if I ask a personal question?"

"I think we've gotten past the point of needing to ask first," replied Caroline with amusement.

"I understand Darcy will be bringing his sister. How do you feel about her presence here with Anne? Do you know how she feels? Will she be quite well, do you think? Or will the baby's proximity bring back her trauma?"

"Your concerns do you great credit," Caroline said. She paused to take a sip of tea, then said, "Had you asked me even three months ago, I would have told you that it was not a good idea to have Georgiana here. First, let me assure you that I love Anne; she is my daughter, no matter what the circumstances of her birth are. Georgiana's presence will only disturb me if she herself is distraught or overwhelmed. I am not jealous of that relationship."

Elizabeth nodded in understanding as Caroline continued speaking. "However, Georgiana went through something quite traumatic. Not only was her situation created with violence, but her body also went through many changes and difficulties that one so young should never have to endure. The physical toll made quite an impression on her mind, as you are well aware."

"I wonder, then, if it is wise that she should be allowed to come," Elizabeth said cautiously.

"After Anne was born, the darkness that enveloped Georgiana seemed to lift significantly. It was almost as if by removing the baby, her emotions were able to right themselves once more. Oh, yes, she still will have difficulties, but she no longer feels the despair and hopelessness that she felt when the babe was inside of her."

"I think I understand," Elizabeth said slowly. "We had a tenant woman who became severely depressed every time she was with child. Once the babe was born, she was her customarily cheerful self."

"From what Louisa tells me about what she hears from other women, it's not uncommon for some women to become depressed when they are with child. Other women, however, experience the reverse. They are delighted whilst pregnant, but after the baby is born, they sink into a gloom for the first year or so."

"I wonder why that is," Elizabeth mused.

"I haven't the faintest idea, I'm afraid," Caroline replied. "I think that some women must go through changes in their mind as well as their bodies when they are with child. However, there is so little even a doctor knows about the human body that we may never truly know."

"You think this happened with Miss Darcy, then?"

Caroline nodded. "Yes, I do. After Anne was born, it was as if someone had lit a candle in Georgiana's eyes. She spoke of the future with hope and seemed somewhat more at peace."

"I certainly hope that it continues whilst she is here," Elizabeth said.

"I do as well."

Elizabeth hesitated, then said, "I told Darcy, but if Miss Darcy becomes overwhelmed at any point during her stay at Netherfield, she is more than welcome to remove to Longbourn."

"That is very good of you," Caroline replied with a smile. "I am certain both Darcy and Georgiana will be greatly benefitted by having such a kind addition to their party. Pemberley will be a cheerful place. I will enjoy visiting you there."

"Is your estate nearby?" Elizabeth inquired.

"No more than twenty miles, I believe."

"I will be very glad to have such a good friend as a neighbor."

The conversation was interrupted by a knock at the door. A maid entered, and said, "A rider just came to say that the Darcys will be arriving shortly."

Caroline put down her teacup. "Well, then, Elizabeth," she said, standing and smoothing her dress. "Shall we go outside to greet your fiancé?"

Elizabeth stood as well. Caroline gave the maid instructions to have the Bingleys informed, then both ladies prepared themselves to meet the new arrivals. Jane and Bingley joined them within a few minutes, and Wickham came a few minutes after that.

Looking in the mirror along the wall, Elizabeth smoothed a curl back from her face. To her astonishment, she saw that her hands were trembling slightly. She gave her head a little shake. *Pull yourself together, Lizzy!* she told herself sternly.

After an agonizingly long wait, Elizabeth heard horse hooves and carriage wheels in the distance. The group made their way outside to greet the Darcys, with Elizabeth walking behind.

A smart chaise and four pulled into the drive, and Elizabeth's heart began to beat faster. She felt as though it were going to leap from her chest and into the carriage. Her foot tapped impatiently as the door was opened.

Darcy emerged from the carriage, and Elizabeth's breath caught in her throat. Her thundering heart seemed to stop when he looked around and made eye contact with her. She couldn't stop the full smile from spreading across her face. The look he gave her in return caused butterflies in her stomach.

"Brother?"

Darcy's eyes shifted from Elizabeth to his sister behind him. He flushed slightly as he realized she was waiting for his assistance to come down. Her amusement was obvious as he cleared his throat and extended his hand.

Once Georgiana was safely on the ground, Darcy turned to greet the Netherfield party. While he shook hands and bowed with people, his eyes remained focused on Elizabeth with a piercing stare. None were offended by his lack of civility. Rather, they viewed it as evidence of his love.

The remainder of the party returned to the house, but they went unnoticed. Darcy took two steps towards Elizabeth and pulled her into his arms.

"At last," he murmured, pressing a kiss into her hair.

Elizabeth inhaled and the scent of sandalwood filled her senses. She burrowed her face into his chest as his large hands stroked her back.

"I missed you," she said simply, pulling back to look into his eyes.

"Not more than I missed you," he returned with a soft smile.

He leaned down and kissed her. It began as a gentle brush of his lips against hers, but she moaned and leaned into him. That small noise caused him to groan and pull her tight against him. The kiss deepened as his hands wandered lower. She let out a small gasp, and he took advantage of her open mouth to sweep his tongue across hers.

"Darcy!"

The moment was interrupted by Bingley's amused-yet-exasperated voice calling for his friend. Darcy stepped back from Elizabeth, breathing heavily. Her face was flushed, her lips swollen. Darcy cleared his throat and fought to clear the haze in his mind.

"Yes, Bingley?" He winced at the breathless sound of his voice.

"I think it best you both come inside and join the rest of us in the drawing room."

Darcy nodded, unwilling to speak again and embarrass himself further. He looked at Elizabeth and was unsurprised to find her face a brilliant shade of red. What he did not like, however, was the look of guilt on her face or the way she looked at the ground, wringing her hands.

He reached over and took one of those small hands in his own large ones. "I love you, Elizabeth," he said huskily.

She looked up at him, and he was heartened to see her square her shoulders and lift her chin. "I love you, too."

The two walked hand in hand to the door where Bingley awaited them. Darcy gave his friend a sharp look, which prompted a short burst of laughter.

"Not to worry, my friend," said Bingley, clapping Darcy on the shoulder. "I'll not say anything of your improper display just now."

Darcy sighed slightly, but his relief was short-lived when Bingley added, "After all, you'll need all your strength to ask Mr. Bennet for permission to marry his favorite daughter."

Bingley laughed again at the look of horror on Darcy's face.

What if he says no?

Chapter 25

Darcy tugged nervously at his cravat. He and Bingley were riding to Longbourn alongside the carriage that held Elizabeth, Georgiana, and Jane. The Darcys had spent an hour refreshing themselves in their rooms before joining the others in the drawing room. The company agreed that the Bingleys, the Darcys, and Elizabeth would go to Longbourn for afternoon tea.

Darcy had not truly considered having to ask Mr. Bennet for permission to marry Elizabeth. While he knew, of course, that he would have to discuss the matter with her father, he had not taken the time to contemplate exactly what that conversation would look like. Based on Bingley's humor at his expense, Darcy's nerves were becoming increasingly uneasy the closer they came.

Good Lord, I sound like Mrs. Bennet, he groaned to himself. *Next thing you know, I will be fanning myself and calling for smelling salts.*

This private jest lifted his spirits, until Longbourn itself came into view. At that point, his cravat decided to choke its master once again.

Elizabeth led the way into her home and led her guests into the parlor, where Kitty, Lydia, Mrs. Bennet, and the Collins family sat. Introductions were made with respect to Miss Darcy, who was immediately pulled away by the youngest Bennet girls into a discussion about the latest fashion magazine.

Darcy watched his sister with concern for the first several minutes. It wasn't until he saw her giggle at some joke Lydia made that he began to relax. He turned his attention back to Elizabeth, only to find her watching him with an understanding smile.

"Do not worry," she assured him. "She is quite safe with Kitty and Lydia. I told them that Miss Darcy was shy and sensitive, like the youngest Miss Long. They will know how to make her feel at ease."

Darcy smiled his thanks at her. Mrs. Bennet, upon noticing that Mr. Darcy had joined in conversation, exclaimed, "Mr. Darcy, we are ever so glad to have you come to our home! It has been several months since we have last seen you here! Is there something particular that has brought you back to Meryton?" she asked with faux innocence.

"Mama!" cried Elizabeth in embarrassment.

"I believe what Mother Bennet means to say, Darcy, is that it is quite a surprise for all of us to have you return," Collins interjected smoothly.

"Yes, I know I left suddenly last autumn. I found as the months passed that I missed Hertfordshire more than I anticipated. I am somewhat ashamed that my behavior when I was here before reflected my concern over leaving my young sister behind. We are the only two left of our family, you see, and we do not separate very often. I am afraid my behavior was a reflection of the inner turmoil I felt, and for that I most heartily apologize."

Mrs. Bennet's face turned sympathetic, and she gave him a kind smile. "How long has it been just the two of you?"

"Many years, madam," he replied.

"I daresay you have become more of a father than a brother to your sister, then. Your anxiety at leaving her is understandable. I am never at ease when one of my girls is away from home, no matter what age they are."

This genuine display of empathy and camaraderie from Mrs. Bennet caused Darcy so much surprise that all he could do was blink at her for several seconds. Unexpected tears clouded his vision, and a lump formed in his throat. "Thank you for your kindness, Mrs. Bennet," he finally said in a choked voice.

Warm affection filled his chest as Mrs. Bennet smiled at him gently. "Now, I understand you may wish to speak with Mr. Bennet?"

she asked, changing the subject.

Darcy felt the blood drain from his face. "Yes, if it is convenient," he said somewhat shakily.

Elizabeth, seeing his pale face, said, "Mama, I will take Mr. Darcy to Papa."

Mrs. Bennet winked at her daughter and said, "Of course, my dear!"

Elizabeth led Darcy out of the room and down a small corridor. Once they were out of sight of the room, Elizabeth turned to face him. She gave him a quick kiss on the cheek and said, "It will all be well. Papa does not bite very hard."

Darcy let out a surprised bark of laughter, and Elizabeth grinned at him slyly. She walked a few more steps and knocked on a closed door.

"Enter," came a voice from the other side.

Elizabeth reached out her hand and gave Darcy's a gentle squeeze before opening the door. "Mr. Darcy is here to speak with you, Papa."

Darcy stepped through the door, and to his dismay, Elizabeth closed the door without following him through.

"Mr. Darcy," said a stern voice, "please take a seat."

Darcy swallowed nervously, then sat on the chair in front of him. Across a cluttered desk sat Mr. Bennet, whose eyes were sharp and cold.

"I understand you have something you wish to discuss with me?" the elder gentleman said coolly.

"Yes, sir. I have come to ask permission to marry your daughter."

"Excellent. I will let her mother know. You may leave."

Darcy stared at the man in disbelief. "You mean, that's it?"

"Certainly. Were you expecting anything else?"

"Well, I... that is..." Darcy faltered.

"I think you and Kitty will do very well together. Granted, she is a little young to be marrying, but perhaps you are simply looking for a friend for your sister."

Darcy's mouth fell open in horror. "No!"

"No? You have changed your mind?"

"Yes, sir. I mean, no, sir." Darcy took a deep calming breath. "What I mean to say, sir, is that I wish to marry your daughter Elizabeth."

Mr. Bennet looked at Darcy seriously. "Well, now that does change things a bit. Why should I allow you to marry her when we all know how much you disdain her?"

Darcy flinched. "I do not! I love her."

"You certainly have an interesting way of showing your love: calling her merely tolerable, telling her brother that her family is not of your station, and exposing her to the vitriol of your family."

Darcy's head hung in shame. "You are right. I have done all of those things. I do not deserve her. I have done everything I can to apologize and make amends for each of those grievances. She has graciously chosen to forgive me, and she accepted my hand in marriage."

Mr. Bennet frowned. "I am loath to part with my daughter to someone so unworthy of her. Unfortunately, with your aunt's vocal crusade, I am afraid I have no choice in the matter. In spite of your actions, however, Lizzy assures me that you are worthy and that she loves you in return. But time will tell."

"Upon my honor, sir, I will do everything I can to be a good husband. I will take care of her."

Mr. Bennet's frown deepened. "See that you do, or you will have her brother and myself to answer to."

Darcy nodded vehemently.

"Now leave!" barked Mr. Bennet. "The wedding will be at the end of this week. God help us all."

Darcy shot to his feet and dashed out of the room. Out in the hall, he almost crashed into Elizabeth, who was listening at the door. Smiling with pity, she said, "I am sorry Papa was so hard on you. Don't worry; he'll see in time the good man that you are."

"But what did he say that I did not deserve, Elizabeth?"

"All you can do is move forward, my love. We cannot change the past, but we can alter the future with our daily actions."

Darcy grabbed her hands in his and held them up to his lips. "I swear, Elizabeth, I will never give you any reason to regret marrying me."

Mrs. Bennet was dismayed at the short amount of time Mr. Bennet had given for the wedding. Any pleas she made in an attempt to change his mind fell on deaf ears. Loath as he was to part with his next eldest daughter, Mr. Bennet was fully aware of the ramifications should news about the engagement and Lady Catherine's visit have time to grow. A quick wedding was in the best interest of all parties involved.

Darcy immediately sent an express to Matlock, who wrote that his eldest son, the Viscount, would attend on his family's behalf. Lady Catherine sent a letter of disapproval, which was immediately burned.

The week leading up to the wedding was extremely busy, and the happy couple spent all their time with Mrs. Bennet, making decisions about food, decorations, and clothing.

Fortunately, Georgiana had recovered sufficiently to handle staying at Netherfield. With Darcy and Bingley about to become brothers, the child was indirectly considered Georgiana's niece. Therefore, no one thought twice of the young girl who was technically not yet out spending time in the nursery with the baby. Georgiana was able to witness firsthand the love the Wickhams had for baby Anne, which did much to soothe her wounded soul.

At last, the day of the wedding arrived. Mrs. Bennet was able to browbeat the seamstress in Meryton into finishing a dress for Elizabeth so she could be married in something new. Darcy promised his future mother-in-law that he would take Elizabeth to the best modistes in town to purchase her trousseau after the wedding.

As Elizabeth dressed in the finest gown she ever owned, she looked in the mirror at herself. Her stomach was full of butterflies, and she felt as if she could not draw breath. She sat on the bed, just staring at the face looking back.

This is it. The next time you come into this house, you will no longer be a member of the household.

Tears filled Elizabeth's eyes as memory after memory flooded through her mind. Playing with dolls in the nursery with Mary. Sitting next to William as he sounded out words in Papa's large family Bible. Whispering secrets with Jane late into the night. Playing chess with Papa in his study. Sitting with Mama and choosing ribbons for Elizabeth's come-out ball.

As she looked back on her life, she thanked Providence for all the blessings she had enjoyed. The last year had taught her much about the evils of the world, but she also witnessed firsthand the perseverance and determination of strong men and women who refused to allow others' actions to hold them back.

A gentle knock on the door interrupted her musings. "Come in," she called, wiping at her eyes.

Jane came into the room with a gentle smile. "I am here to fix your hair, if you'd like."

Elizabeth smiled ruefully at her sister. "You always did manage my curls the best of all of us."

Jane sat behind Elizabeth and began brushing out her waist-length locks. The two enjoyed the silence for several moments.

"Are you nervous about tonight?" Jane asked.

"A little," Elizabeth admitted. "While I have some idea of what is to happen, and Caroline spoke most reassuringly to me the other day, I admit to being a bit fearful of the unknown."

Jane nodded. "A bit of apprehension is understandable, even when you are marrying for love. But I believe that Mr. Darcy will be very kind. After what his sister has experienced and what he knows about Mrs. Wickham, I don't think he could be anything but gentle."

Elizabeth opened her mouth to say more, but Mrs. Bennet bustled in. "Oh, there you are, girls!" she exclaimed. "Why is your hair not finished, Lizzy? Make haste! It is almost time to leave!"

Jane began pulling Elizabeth's hair up into an elegant twist, with several of the curls arranged artfully to frame her face. Once the coiffure was secured with pins, Jane added several flowers to enhance the look.

"Oh, Lizzy," Mrs. Bennet breathed. "You look beautiful."

Elizabeth stood from the bed to look at her full profile in the mirror. She had to agree with her mother; she had never looked so well before. Her eyes shone, and her cheeks flushed with the joy and excitement of the day.

The moment was interrupted by Mr. Bennet calling up the stairs that the carriage was ready to take them to the church. The three ladies hurried down to join the rest of the family. Mr. Bennet looked at his family with pride as they made their way out the door.

Once at the church, everyone took their places inside while Mr. Bennet and Elizabeth waited for their turn to go down the aisle. He put a hand on each of her shoulders and gently kissed her forehead. "Are you certain you wish to do this, my dear?"

Elizabeth nodded. "Yes, Papa, I am. I did not always love him, but I love him now so very dearly."

"Then, shall we?"

Mr. Bennet extended his arm, and Elizabeth rested hers on top of it. The two entered the church, and all eyes turned towards her.

It was all Darcy could do to keep his knees from buckling when she walked through the door.

"Breathe, man," he heard Charles whisper, but his mind couldn't process the words.

All of his senses were completely focused on the beautiful woman in front of him. As she drew closer, all the things he loved about her came into focus. Her bright eyes. Her smiling lips. The curve of her neck that followed down to the curves of her body.

He drank it all in. It seemed as though a million years passed in the blink of an eye in the time it took for her to reach him. Suddenly, she was at his side, and her father was handing her off to him.

Darcy finally inhaled, took her arm, and turned to face Collins. Elizabeth's cousin-turned-brother smiled at Darcy in understanding, then began the words of the ceremony.

As with most weddings of the day, the ceremony itself was quite short. Words were read from *The Book of Common Prayer* and vows were exchanged. Darcy's hands shook slightly as he took the ring from Bingley and placed it on her delicate hands.

"I now present Mr. and Mrs. Darcy."

Darcy and Elizabeth turned away from Collins and faced their loved ones in the crowd. Elizabeth's cheeks hurt from smiling, and she could not wait to leave the building so she could finally let out the happy laughter that had welled up inside of her.

Elizabeth leaned down and signed her surname of Bennet in the register for the last time. As she stood up, her eyes met Darcy's. The intensity in his gaze made her catch her breath. He leaned in and gave her a swift kiss on the lips, causing a few gasps to echo in the reverent chapel. He winked at her roguishly, and she hid a smile.

As they left the church, several of the Meryton residents and Longbourn tenants stood waiting. Darcy lifted Elizabeth into the open carriage and withdrew a pouch of coins. After pouring some into his hand, he tossed them into the air for the children to scramble and grab. Their cheers sounded in his ears, and he looked at Elizabeth with a full grin.

"Shall we go, Mrs. Darcy?"

"Yes, husband."

The two drove off towards the wedding breakfast, certain in their future happiness.

Epilogue

Elizabeth looked across the drawing room at her husband of twenty years and gave him a smile. Darcy sat with their youngest child, a five-year-old named William. He was attempting to put together a simple puzzle, and Darcy was patiently helping the boy fit pieces next to one another.

Next to Elizabeth sat Jane Marie, their ten-year-old daughter. Jane Marie was learning how to do needlework from her mother, but it was not going very well. After sticking herself with the needle for the third time, Jane Marie threw the sampler onto the settee and sat back in a huff.

"I will never be able to do this well!" she whined with all the drama of a child about to enter puberty.

Elizabeth stifled a laugh. "You will never become truly proficient at something unless you practice, my love."

Darcy let out a burst of laughter from across the room. "Now you sound like Lady Catherine."

Elizabeth smirked back at her husband. Over the years, Lady Catherine had slightly thawed in her attitude towards Mrs. Darcy, but she was still as eager to correct as she ever was. Anne had passed away without marrying or siring an heir, leaving Rosings to revert to the de Bourgh line. Lady Catherine maintained residence in the dower house, where her influence was significantly decreased. The tenants and residents of Hunsford were relieved to discover the new master of Rosings was a firm but fair man.

A maid entered the room with a letter and handed it to Darcy. He looked at it, then passed it over to Elizabeth. "The boys have written to us," he remarked.

"Finally!" she exclaimed. "Bennet and George returned to school weeks ago!"

The eldest of the Darcy children were fifteen-year-old twins. After five years of marriage, Elizabeth feared she would never be able to have children. To her great surprise, when she finally became with child, she delivered both an heir and a spare! Mrs. Bennet's raptures at the time were best left unmentioned.

Elizabeth delicately opened the letter and skimmed through its contents. "It appears as though George came down with a cold he caught from young Charles, which is what delayed their writing."

Young Charles was the fond nickname given to the Bingley's second child and oldest son, who was sixteen years of age. His elder sister, Penelope, was nineteen years old and had come out to society the year before.

"I knew young Charles should not have spent the summer at Longbourn," Darcy said smugly. "Samuel always takes him out of doors in the rain."

"He doesn't know it is going to rain," protested Elizabeth.

"But yet it always does," replied Darcy.

Elizabeth rolled her eyes at her husband but was forced to admit that Samuel Collins, age twenty-two, had the unfortunate luck of getting rained on quite frequently. Thankfully, he had robust health and rarely fell ill.

Samuel had recently graduated from Oxford and had taken orders. He planned to follow in his father's footsteps as pastor in Meryton. Mr. Collins had taken over the management of Longbourn about five years ago.

The door opened, and Mr. Bennet came into the room. "I understand you heard from the boys?"

Elizabeth nodded and handed her father the letter she had skimmed. Mr. Bennet took his spectacles out and began to read it aloud. He had come to live at Pemberley when Mrs. Bennet passed away suddenly of a heart attack five years prior. The shock of losing his wife seemed to age Mr. Bennet ten years. He turned Longbourn over to Collins and moved in with Elizabeth.

Although it took several years, Mr. Bennet had finally come to respect and appreciate Darcy. As promised, Darcy did all in his power to make Elizabeth happy. This included convincing Bingley to sell Netherfield to the Wickhams and purchase Wickham's estate in Derbyshire so Jane and Elizabeth could be near one another.

Caroline and Wickham had one more daughter, in addition to Anne. This daughter was born ten years after her sister. Society considered it wise on Mrs. Wickham's part to avoid being frequently with child, which was not the case. Little did they know that Caroline longed for more children and was happy sharing a room with her husband.

Mr. Bennet set the letter down and said, "I bet Mary is beside herself with Samuel having caused another one of his cousins to get caught in the rain."

Darcy laughed. "I doubt that. Mary is one of the most practical women I know. She would not bother over a trifling little cold. She has too many children to worry about instead."

Mary Collins, née Bennet, had a total of eight children: three boys and five girls. Providentially, Mary was one of the fortunate women who was able to tolerate pregnancy and childbirth with remarkable ease. She often expressed the wish to have more children, but it was not to be.

"Will they be joining us for Christmas?" Jane Marie asked eagerly.

One of Mary's children was the exact age as Jane Marie. The two cousins were born only weeks apart, and they were as close as sisters could be. One could almost always be found scribbling a letter for the other. Darcy often jested that it would be cheaper to hire a dedicated rider to go between the houses of the Bennet sisters rather than pay for postage between the two cousins.

Elizabeth smiled at her daughter. "Yes, they are planning on it."

Jane Marie clapped her hands eagerly, and her elder brother followed suit. Elizabeth met Darcy's eyes over their daughter's head and smiled at him. This prompted him to leave his son at the puzzle, and Mr. Bennet immediately took the open seat. Darcy walked over and playfully nudged his daughter over, eliciting a giggle from the girl as Darcy settled between them.

"You seem somewhat pensive this evening," he said quietly to her.

She smiled at him and said, "I was just thinking about how happy I am. So much has happened in our twenty years of marriage."

"Any regrets?"

She wrinkled her nose at him and scoffed. "Of course not, you silly man. Even the most difficult times have been worth it, because we were together."

Indeed, there had been some difficult times. A year after their marriage, Kitty contracted a bad cough that quickly turned into pneumonia. The girl had passed away before the express had even reached Derbyshire. Elizabeth had wept for months at not having been there for her sister since she had married a man so far away.

Kitty's death changed Lydia significantly. She was her same, lively self, but she developed a maturity her parents had feared she would never develop. This maturity became extremely appealing to Colonel Fitzwilliam, who was now General Fitzwilliam. He had seen much of war, and when it came time to marry, he found he could not abide the empty-headed chits of the *Ton*. Lydia's liveliness, tempered with compassion and deep feeling, led them to have a strong, supportive marriage. Their only daughter was named Catherine, and she was currently eight years old.

Some of the other difficult times included pregnancy losses, crop failure, and Georgiana's marriage prospects. After her horrifying experience, she completely refused to consider coming out to society. Determined to become an old maid, she did not marry until she was past the age of thirty. A local baron's wife passed away in childbirth, leaving three young children motherless. Georgiana had befriended the woman several years prior. When the baron approached her with a proposition of a marriage of convenience, she accepted willingly.

Elizabeth jumped slightly when Darcy began rubbing her back. "A penny for your thoughts?" he asked quietly.

"I was just thinking about our wonderful life together. It's difficult to believe that we just passed twenty years of marriage. Some days I feel ancient, but other times it feels as if our wedding day was yesterday."

"I'm pretty sure we recreated our wedding night just last night," Darcy said, waggling his eyebrows at her.

"Oh, stop it!" she said, blushing slightly and looking around the room.

Darcy leaned over and put his lips to her ear. "We could go recreate it again if you are having difficulties remembering."

Elizabeth bit her lip as the familiar butterflies came alive in her stomach. She looked around Darcy's head at their daughter, who was oblivious to the world as she focused intently on her stitching. "Follow me in ten minutes," she whispered.

She stood and walked calmly towards the door, fighting to keep the anticipation at bay until she was out of the room. As she left, she turned back and looked at her family. Warmth filled her heart, and she said a prayer of gratitude that the sins of the fathers would not carry on to their children's children. They had overcome, and the new generation would be one of happiness and strength.

THANK YOU

Thank you for reading THE SINS OF THEIR FATHERS, a Pride & Prejudice variation by Tiffany Thomas.
You may also enjoy Tiffany's other Jane Austen variations, found on Amazon.

Please leave a review on Amazon! A five star review means you think others would enjoy this book, too.

Join Tiffany's mailing list to learn about upcoming releases, free and discounted books, and more.

www.authortiffanythomas.com

ABOUT THE AUTHOR

Tiffany Thomas is a chocoholic former math teacher and home-schooling mom with Crohn's Disease. She loves Jane Austen and can often be found in bed with ice cream and her the latest JAFF. She and her husband (who is an engineer) have three kids and live in Texas. They enjoy spending time with their family, geeking out over sci-fi together, and working on their blog Saving Talents.

www.ingramcontent.com/pod-product-compliance
Lightning Source LLC
Chambersburg PA
CBHW060902250626
47159CB00008B/2837